Petra's Ghost

Petra's Ghost

C.S. O'CINNEIDE

DUNDURN
TORONTO

Cover image: Ricardo Frantz (road); Jean-Pierre Pellisier (texture)
Printer: Webcom, a division of Marquis Book Printing Inc.

Library and Archives Canada Cataloguing in Publication

O'Cinneide, C. S., 1965-, author
    Petra's ghost / C.S. O'Cinneide.

Issued in print and electronic formats.
ISBN 978-1-4597-4468-4 (softcover).--ISBN 978-1-4597-4469-1 (PDF).--
ISBN 978-1-4597-4470-7 (EPUB)

    I. Title.

PS8629.C56P48 2019   C813'.6   C2018-906395-5
                                   C2018-906396-3

1 2 3 4 5   23 22 21 20 19

  Conseil des Arts du Canada   Canada Council for the Arts   Canadä   ONTARIO ARTS COUNCIL CONSEIL DES ARTS DE L'ONTARIO an Ontario government agency un organisme du gouvernement de l'Ontario

We acknowledge the support of the **Canada Council for the Arts**, which last year invested $153 million to bring the arts to Canadians throughout the country, and the **Ontario Arts Council** for our publishing program. We also acknowledge the financial support of the **Government of Ontario**, through the **Ontario Book Publishing Tax Credit** and **Ontario Creates**, and the **Government of Canada**.

Nous remercions le **Conseil des arts du Canada** de son soutien. L'an dernier, le Conseil a investi 153 millions de dollars pour mettre de l'art dans la vie des Canadiennes et des Canadiens de tout le pays.

Printed and bound in Canada.

VISIT US AT

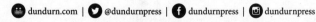

  dundurn.com | @dundurnpress | dundurnpress | dundurnpress

Dundurn
3 Church Street, Suite 500
Toronto, Ontario, Canada
M5E 1M2

For my Camino brothers, Rob and Michael

And for my husband, Marcus, who makes all journeys possible

Quatuor viae sunt quae ad sanctum Jacobum tendentes, in unum, ad Pontem Regine, in oris Hispanise coadunantur.

Four roads meet at Puente la Reina in Spain and become one route to Santiago.

— Codex Calixtinus, twelfth century

Los Angeles Daily News
STILL NO TRACE OF AMERICAN
TOURIST ON SPAIN'S CAMINO
DE SANTIAGO

MADRID — Beatrice McConaughey, 32, of Laguna Beach, was last seen August 20 at Villar de Mazarife, in the northwestern Spanish province of León. McConaughey disappeared while walking the Camino Francés, one of the most popular of the pilgrimage routes to Santiago de Compostela, an ancient path that attracts thousands each year. More than six weeks after her disappearance, Spanish police say the investigation remains open.

CHAPTER I
Alto del Perdón

THE SEA IS MISSING.

Daniel stands tall in the early morning on the soaring ridge of *Alto del Perdón,* searching for a phantom ocean. All he can make out are a patchwork of farmers' fields. They hover in and out like a mirage beneath the thinning mist settled in the valley below. His navy nylon jacket snaps and billows in the stiff breeze of the exposed hillside. Half a dozen towering wind turbines emit low moans as their massive metal blades turn steadily behind him. At the base of one is a boldly coloured framed backpack, lying open where Daniel has left it at the side of the trail. In his hands he holds a small burlap bag, with Petra inside.

A long line of rusty cut-out men and women are positioned sentinel-like on the ridge, a flat metal monument to all those who, over the centuries, have walked the *Camino de Santiago,* the five-hundred-mile pilgrimage they call "the Way." Daniel watches as the silhouettes of the heavy sculpture shudder with the force of the wind. He takes a deep breath of the fresh mountain air. The scent is all wrong to him. Unnatural, without a taste of seawater in it.

The rocky outcrops and high altitude, the mist below, they all trick him into thinking he is back in Ireland on the coast of Kerry, where he spent summers as a child by the sea. He and his sister had explored the rugged cliffs above the shoreline for hours, standing far out on the ledges, daring each other.

"Stop being *eejits*," his father would bellow from the safety of a lawn chair under the awning of their parked caravan. And Daniel and Angela would trudge back from the sweet seduction of certain death, utterly defeated. Their two older brothers would have deserted them earlier, having the sense to commit their risk taking out of sight of a parent. Maybe he and Angela were idiots after all.

Ever since his first day walking the Camino, climbing through the pass of the French Pyrenees to the Spanish border, Daniel has expected to look down and see the swell of whitecaps, to drink in the tang of brine. The Pyrenees were almost fifty miles ago now, but he still feels the want of salt in the air. He switches the rough brown bag containing Petra to one hand and pulls a stash of sodium-laden beef jerky from his pocket. As if to compensate, he takes a furious bite.

He is less than a week into his pilgrimage through northern Spain, hiking from Saint-Jean-Pied-de-Port at the border in France to the cathedral in Santiago that houses the shrine of Saint James. The full journey will take him over a month to complete. He travels alongside other pilgrims of varying nationalities and spiritual intent, mostly keeping to himself. Each night after a full day of walking, he checks in at a local *albergue*. These are modest pilgrim hostels, where five to fifteen euros will get you anything from the top bunk at a large modern municipal, to a hard stone floor of a thirteenth-century monastery. The austerity appeals to his sense of simplicity, or maybe he's just cheap.

"Sure, no one really believes the bones of Saint James are buried there at Santiago," his sister, Angela, had told him before he left. "Not even the Catholic Church."

"Perhaps," he said, as he looked down at the map of Spain on the coffee table of his living room. The laptop perched next to it on a stack of books as he Skyped his sister from his home in the States. Even so, he had traced one finger along the lonely red dotted line of the Camino, wondering what he might find at the end of it.

One of the turbines groans more loudly, hitting some temporary mechanical resistance. The laboured breath of the sound makes him uneasy. He stuffs the beef jerky back in his pocket.

"Fifty percent of Spain's energy comes from the wind," he reminds himself. He'd read it in the guidebook. This is the kind of interesting but ultimately useless fact that seems to always lodge in his brain. Like a piece of popcorn caught in the teeth, and at times just as annoying. Mostly for other people.

"Guess what the longest street in the world is," he had once asked his eldest brother as he sat with him on the tractor. Daniel had still been far too young to drive it.

"The one where I have to listen to your mouth yappin' all day."

The rough burlap bag has a drawstring at the top. Daniel rubs the little braided ropes with his thumb. There is a crinkle inside the coarse material. Plastic. He hadn't wanted the ashes to get wet if it rained. His backpack was supposed to be waterproof, but he needed to be sure. Petra would have laughed at his practicality. "Always the engineer, planning for contingencies," she would say. He cannot believe he has put his wife in a zip-lock bag, as if she were a ham sandwich or a dime of weed.

He glances over at the two-dimensional metal figures bent over with their walking staffs and donkeys, medieval pilgrims without the benefit of ergonomically correct back-packs and Thermolite hiking boots from the Outdoor Store. Daniel had bought an old-style pilgrim staff at one of the tourist shops back in France, before he started on the Camino. It had a carved wooden handle and made him look like a prat. He abandoned it in a coffee shop in Zubiri, deciding he could make it to the cathedral of Saint James in Santiago without something to lean on.

The heavy sculpture shudders again. The vibration makes a howling sound, and Daniel feels a tremor echo in his own body. If his granny were here, she'd say a goose just walked over his grave. The old woman had many say-ings. Some were old Irish; some she just made up. "These are the words of your ancestors, Daniel," she would intone, trying to make him pay mind. The land he grew up on had been farmed by Kennedys for almost five hundred years. He couldn't have escaped his ancestors if he tried.

Trying to shake off the feeling, he shifts from one leg to the other. His new hiking boots feel strange without the steel toe that he normally wears at home when inspecting a job, the familiar density reassuring his foot. Not that he's been on a job site in a while. As their construction business in New Jersey grew, Daniel and his partner, Gerald, found themselves tied more and more to the office. But of course, he's all set to sell his half of the firm — or just about. They'd had an offer from a group in New York that would be hard to turn down. There are still papers to sign that Gerald keeps worrying him about. Once that's done, Daniel's expected to come back home to Ireland and take over the farm. His father is ready to retire to his lawn chair permanently.

Nothing is keeping Daniel in New Jersey anymore, now that Petra is gone. He'd gone to the States for her and never regretted it, even though he had always felt the pull of the land he grew up on. Those bloody ancestors again. Petra, a child of the North American melting pot, did not have the same ties. Her folks had died in a car crash during her senior year at college. She had no siblings. But her roots were in America just the same, and he had made a life with her there.

Daniel has come to the Camino to spread Petra's ashes. This is what he needs to do before he can go back to Ireland. This is what he has told his sister, his parents. This is what he has told himself. So he can "move on," as everyone keeps telling him he must do. He and Petra had always planned to walk the Camino together. Ever since they saw the golden scallop shells and arrows pointing toward the Spanish pilgrimage from France on their honeymoon. He feels that bringing her ashes here serves to keep a promise. Although so many promises remain unfulfilled when someone leaves before you're ready, like a dinner guest who gets up and walks out during the main course. He could spend a lifetime trying to finish the meal that should have been a future shared with his wife, and the food would rot on the dishes anyway. Somehow, he just can't bring himself to take away her plate. It's been over a year now since Petra died and he hasn't even put their house in Paterson on the market yet.

"When are you comin' home, Daniel?" his sister, Angela, had asked during one of her weekly phone calls from her apartment in Dublin. His parents were still on the farm at Carn N'Athair in Kilmeedy, but she made the drive out every other weekend to check on them. They were all getting anxious. If Daniel didn't come home, his father would have to sell out. All those ancestors to be owned by somebody else. His granny would reach out and cuff him from the grave at the sheer shame of it.

"I've got some things to do," he said. He always had reasons. First it was the winding up of the business with his partner. Then it was critical home renovations he needed to make before he could sell. As those jobs dried up he created new ones, increasingly more futile.

"I'm after putting a bidet in the guest bathroom," he told Angela.

"Correct me if I'm wrong, but how many people when they come over for a cup o' tea are looking to wash their genitals?" Of course, she had a point. He had ignored it though.

The Camino is his latest effort at procrastination, having run out of rooms to renovate in the house where he and Petra had lived since they were married over ten years ago. Happy years for the most part, until the cancer twisted her into someone he could barely recognize. As gnarled and rake thin as the carved wooden staff he had left behind in the coffee shop. Petra wouldn't have liked that comparison. She hadn't been a vain woman, but she'd had her pride. She said the worst part of cancer was turning into something alien, like the dwarfed extraterrestrial in the movie *E.T.* All she needed to do was hide in a closet full of pinch-faced stuffed animals, she teased the doctors, and they would never find her. Daniel had brought Reese's Pieces for her the next day in the hospital to continue the joke. She had coughed — her version of laughing in those final weeks.

He should do it here. It makes sense to let the ashes float from the cradle of his hands down into the disappointingly landlocked valley below. An offering to everything he can't accept. Like having an ultrasound diagnose uterine cancer instead of the baby he and Petra had hoped for. A ruthless surprise that had spread through her body like hot gossip. He'd be angry at God, but he has enough Irish Catholic superstition to believe it might land him in hell or on the receiving end of a lightning bolt. He looks with distrust at the metal pilgrims beside him then scans the sky for storm clouds, on the off chance.

"What do I need with a uterus?" Petra had said. "It's not a vital organ. Nothing will change."

But the things that became vital after that changed them both.

Daniel continues to stand looking out on the valley, almost as motionless as the rusty pilgrims on the ridge. The burlap bag remains closed in his hands, its contents secure. Daniel's right thumb draws the string a little tighter. When he hears the voice from behind him, he jumps as if he has just stuck a wet finger into a light socket.

"I'd stand upwind if I were you."

He whips around, holding the burlap bag protectively behind his back, looking ridiculous. Like a kid trying to hide a porn magazine from his mother.

A stunted copse of trees grows on the west side of the wind turbines. Someone — a woman, judging by shape — sits alone on a rock there, partly obscured by branches and morning mist. Beside her is one of those cairns you see on the Way, built from small stones the pilgrims leave behind called "intentions," small rock embodiments of their prayers and purposes. The cairns make Daniel twitch. In Ireland they're used to mark a place of death, like a car accident, and he can't help but cross himself every time he sees one. The woman sits there with her face turned away, not acknowledging him.

"Pardon me?" he says, annoyed now that she rattled him so. He starts walking toward her, the bag still in his hands.

She remains turned in profile. Her features seem to morph with the mist and then solidify as he approaches. He stops, confused by the phenomenon. The clearer she becomes, the more everything around them starts to fade. He no longer hears the wind or the turbines. No longer feels the roughness of the burlap bag in his hand. All he can process is the one sense, the sight of her. All he can see is the rich hair tumbling down her back in long waves, natural and free, worn just the way he had always liked. He reaches toward her involuntarily. His fingertips still remember the feel of those rich strands slipping gently through his hands.

"Petra?" He takes a few tentative steps closer. His other senses have returned. He can smell her coconut shampoo now.

The woman doesn't move. He still can't see her face, but in her lap her hands are clasped together, a shadowy tube slithering out from the back of her right one. The ever-present IV.

"Petra, is that you?" he whispers, not believing.

The woman doesn't answer. Her long hair trembles in the wind.

Daniel begins running toward her. She turns her head at the sound of his heavy footfalls then jumps up from the rock and knocks over the cairn. She stumbles and falls on her ass as the intentions spill out all over the ground.

"What the hell?" she yells at him.

He looks at the woman sprawled in the dirt. Her hair is no longer running free down her back in waves, but tied in a high ponytail beneath a pink ball cap. The white stitching on it reads, "Kiss me, I'm smart." She juts out her lower lip and blows a piece of hair out of her eyes, the result of overgrown bangs.

"What the fuck is wrong with you?" the woman says as she gets up and brushes gravel off the seat of her hiking pants. "You scared the shit out of me."

He sees the tube now. It hangs not from the back of her hand, but from the hydration bladder in her backpack. Her hair is honey brown, not pale blond like Petra's. Her face doesn't even remotely resemble Petra's. Though her body is toned and fit as Petra's had been — before she got sick. How could he have mistaken her for Petra? He needs to get a grip. Start wearing his hat more often in the full sun.

"If you plan to attack me, I suggest you get it over with," she tells him as she zips up the front of her jacket. She reaches for her backpack, which he notices is the smaller-framed duplicate of his own, right down to the colour, bright turquoise. He had wanted black, but the girl at the Outdoor Store had ordered the wrong one, and it had been too late to make an exchange. He had tried to roll it in the mud a few times to make it look manlier, then felt like a git for doing so. His sister had told him he should be too evolved to feel emasculated by a colour.

"What? I mean no." Daniel watches her pull the hip belt of the pack tight around her middle, adjust the load lifters on both sides. "I thought," he pauses, "I thought you were after saying something." He's not sure of anything now. Maybe she hadn't said anything. Maybe he had just run at a woman alone in a secluded spot for no reason. The Camino was usually safe, but there had been incidents lately. No wonder she'd shouted at him.

"I said, 'I'd stand upwind if I were you,'" she says, looking down as she snaps the sternum strap across her chest into place. He wasn't completely mad then. He had heard her speak after all.

"And why might that be?" Daniel asks. She has managed to annoy him again, despite the fact he's still shaking.

"So the ashes don't blow back on you in the wind," she says, coming toward him, her thumbs hooked in her shoulder straps, standing impossibly close. He can see the faded sprinkle of freckles along the bridge of her nose, smell the dried overripe fruit of a power bar on her breath. "I saw it happen to a guy earlier. He ended up with his son all over his rain pants."

And with that, she walks away from him, making her way down the ridge, her backpack with the attached white scallop shell bouncing with the sway of her hips. It was an enduring symbol of the Way, that shell, representing one of Saint James's many miracles. Daniel hadn't attached one to his own pack, though most did. He had never been good with outward symbols, preferring to play his cards and his purposes close.

He watches the woman slowly sink out of sight, hiking down the other side of the peak. The wind blows his curly black hair into his face when he turns back to look at the valley. She was right about the risk of getting Petra caught in an updraft. This isn't the right place for her.

Daniel goes back to get his pack, placing the burlap bag carefully inside. He buries it deep at the bottom beneath his guidebook and passport. Then he pulls out the broad-brimmed hat he wouldn't be caught wearing anywhere else and pulls it down over his unruly windblown hair.

When he stands, he lifts the pack onto his shoulders and feels the weight settle into the strength of his back. But he still carries the heavy doubt of the sea in his mind. Just as he carries what's left of his wife, unable to accept what happened to her any more than the scent in the air. He wonders whether five hundred miles will be enough to finally lay her to rest, when he was the one who killed her.

The towering wind turbines turn, stoic against a harsh sky, as he follows the path where he has just watched the woman who is not Petra disappear.

✳

The stones on the way down from *Alto del Perdón* are slippery with the rain from yesterday. Daniel takes his time picking his way along the trail. He can't afford to twist an ankle, not when he still has weeks of walking to go. Banked on either side of him are stunted grass and low brush. The occasional huge boulder sits marooned at the side of the trail, as if washed up on the shore of his imagined sea. Gravity rams his toes into the front of his boots. Maybe it is a good thing there is no steel in them.

He is surprised when he comes around a bend and finds her waiting for him, a curious look on her face. Somewhere between amusement and wariness.

"You're different," she says, leaning against one of the boulders. It is a statement with a hint of a question.

"How?" Daniel asks her. He stops, braces himself sideways on the hill.

"Just different."

"The accent," he says, guessing. Daniel's accustomed to being outed by the sound of his voice. Most people know as soon as he opens his mouth where he's from; although, there was a lanky American a few days ago that had thought he was English. That and the fact that the guy never shut up made him want to punch him in his skinny gut.

"Maybe," she says. Her accent betrays her as well. She is also American. "I thought maybe you were from around here, at first."

Daniel's granny had always said he had "the look of the Spaniard," an Irish pronouncement reserved for those with dark and not-to-be-trusted attractiveness. "The Spanish Armada did some marauding in my country a few hundred years ago," he tells her. "Left a fair amount of their gene pool about."

She waits awhile before answering as if weighing the pros and cons of marauding gene pools. "Mind if I walk with you?" she says, apparently deciding in favour of his DNA.

"Free country," Daniel replies. He's still a little pissed about how she caught him off guard before. But then again, she did save him from wearing Petra on his jacket.

"My name's Virginia," she says, holding out one gloved hand. "People call me Ginny."

"I'm Daniel," he says, stepping toward her to return the handshake. He can feel the coldness of her fingers through the thin wool. He forces a smile. Then not knowing quite what to do next, he starts back down the hill.

"Who you got in the bag, Daniel?" she asks, falling in behind him.

"None of your feckin' business, that's who I got in the bag."

"That's a bit harsh."

Realizing it probably was, he tries a peace offering.

"Beef jerky?" he asks, holding out the red-and-black cellophane bag.

"No, thanks."

He puts the hard cured meat back in his pocket. When he pulls out his hand again he rubs it together with the other one, blowing on them. He's got gloves in his backpack, but he doesn't bother with them despite the warmth of the autumn sun not yet reaching this side of the valley. He started early this morning while everyone else was still asleep at the *albergue*, not being a fan of crowds. A result of a rural upbringing with an abundance of space. Also, he's a bit of an ass before his first cup of coffee. For that reason, it is probably a good thing they don't talk all the way down. He walks silently, knowing she is behind him. He can hear her ponytail swishing back and forth on the nylon shoulders of her jacket. He remembers the hair he thought he saw flowing down her back up on the ridge, pale and almost to her waist. Wishful thinking is a powerful hallucinogen, he decides.

Soon the topography begins to change, becoming more and more level, fewer rocks, more gravel. The mist is receding with the day. When they round a final bend, the Camino lies in front of them like a length of grey ribbon undulating through plucked orchards and farm fields burnt brown from a summer of hot Spanish sun. They stop for a moment and take in the new scenery, but not for long. There are still eight miles to go to the next *albergue*, where Daniel plans to spend the night. He's in good shape but that doesn't mean walking six hours a day doesn't make him feel like an old man by evening.

He is nervous at first as they switch to walk beside one another. There is something more personal in this than travelling single file. In time, however, he relaxes into the hypnotic beat of the trail, uninterrupted by speech. Their steps strike a hollow rhythm on the tightly packed earth. Gravel kicked up by their hiking boots the only variation in tempo.

He builds up the courage to steal a glimpse of her. Just a few seconds. He takes in the determined set of her jaw in contrast to the full lips. The little divot on the outside of one slender nostril, betraying the small wildness of a former piercing thought better of. All contrasted with the serious deep-set hazel eyes she had fixed him with back up on the ridge when she had chastised him for frightening her. Ginny said he was different, but he senses she is, too. A woman of contradictions. When she catches him staring, he turns away, embarrassed. Great. Now she'll think he's a pervert.

"I'm sorry for asking you about the ashes," she says.

"No mind," Daniel tells her. "I reckon I'm just a bit sensitive about it."

"Just a bit." She pauses. "Is that why you came on the Camino?"

"I suppose so."

"Everyone has a story," she says with a look of understanding. She's right. Everyone Daniel has met on the Camino seemed to come with a history. He had met a German guy whose daughter had committed suicide. He carried ashes as well. Then there was the middle-aged woman he'd walked with for an afternoon whose husband had left her after thirty years of marriage. She had financed her trip by selling off his favourite football card on eBay.

"Why did you come?" he asks, getting the nerve up to turn and look at her again.

"To pick up guys," she says. She bursts out laughing when his face starts to redden. He turns away again and keeps walking. *Great*, he thinks. *I'm walking the Camino with a feckin' comedian.*

When they enter the first small village, the two still haven't spoken again. It's not due to any ill will, more because each has sensed the other needed some quiet time. There are two vital things a pilgrim needs to learn on the Camino. One is how to prevent blisters and the other is when to shut up. But when they pass a noisy bar full of pilgrims eating breakfast, Daniel breaks the silence to tell her he needs to get a coffee. She waits outside for him.

When he comes back outside with his steaming Styrofoam cup, the street is empty. He looks up and down the road but can't find her. Then she speaks from behind him and scares the shite out of him for a second time. *Where the hell did she come from?*

"You notice they are all bars here," she says.

Daniel wipes his hand where he spilled a bit of the hot liquid on it when she startled him. "The canteens, you mean?" He takes a deep sip of the *café con leche*, steadying himself. Feckin' heaven. "I have. Saw two fellas yesterday knocking back shots at seven in the morning with their tea and croissant."

"I've seen the same thing. They're always so serious though. Like alcoholism is a job they had to show up for when they'd rather stay in bed."

"You got to admire their work ethic," he says, taking another sip. This time when she laughs, he smiles instead of blushing.

The two follow the yellow arrows and scallop shells that take them through the small village and keep them on the Camino. Some of the signs and symbols are painted roughly on the walls of old stone buildings. Some are built into the pavement beneath their feet. They meander through village streets and alleyways on a route used by pilgrims for over a millennium. It leads not just to the cathedral in Santiago, but past most of the churches within walking distance.

Daniel can see the belfry of one coming up on the right. When he looks up, he can make out a huge nest perched precariously on the top. Every church in Spain seemed to have at least one resident stork. Daniel watches to see if the bird is roosting as he walks by, but the nest is abandoned. If there are any eggs, they have been left unattended.

"Why do you think they brought babies?"

"Huh?" His response to her question is inelegant but authentic. Babies are the last thing on his mind, despite his concern for the eggs.

"Why do you think they always said that the storks brought the babies?" she explains, pointing at the nest.

"They were there," he says, musing. "It's always easiest to put the blame on whatever's close at hand."

Her eyes flash approval. "I suppose it is. Although not necessarily fair."

"Life isn't fair," Daniel says, and then regrets it. What a downer he is. He tries to recover from looking like a depressing git, even though for the last year he has probably been one. "Did your parents blame the storks?"

"My mother gave me a detailed explanation at the age of four, complete with a discussion of the missionary position and a picture book with fallopian tubes."

"Impressive," Daniel says, and he means it.

"I forgot it all by the time I was six and had to have it explained again."

"Did you remember it after that?" he asks her.

"I can still sketch a vas deferens from memory," she tells him, smiling.

God, that smile. Playful but challenging. It could set a man off his balance.

"What did your parents tell you about where babies came from?" she asks.

"Nothing," Daniel tells her, fiddling with the straps of his pack.

"How could your parents tell you nothing?" she asks, pressing him.

"I asked my mother that once," he says, remembering the conversation. He was a grown man by then. "She told me, 'You grew up on a farm, Daniel, with the bull let loose on the poor cows in the field each spring. You'd think a clever chiseler like yourself might figure a thing or two out.'" He plays up his mother's Irish accent. She was from the town and had a different dialect than the rest of them.

"And did you figure it out?" Ginny asks him, completely deadpan.

"I suppose," he says. "But from my experience, I'd say women are a fair bit different from cows."

She stares at him now, and he wonders if he has gone too far comparing women to livestock and mimicking his mother with an exaggerated accent like a stock Irish moron. He really needs to get out more.

She continues to fix him with those penetrating grey-green eyes. For a moment, the pupils seem to widen, swallowing up each iris entirely. The wide black circles make him take a step back. Then she's smiling again, and the healthy hazel returns, the earlier absence of colour a trick of the light.

"Are you interested in a side trip, Daniel?" she says with a raised brow above a perfectly normal eye.

He nods dumbly. Then recovers. "Where to?"

"The site of a massacre," she says. "It'll be more interesting than cows."

CHAPTER 2
Uterga to Obanos

THE SIDE TRAIL AT Muruzábal only adds a couple of miles to Daniel's planned route. It is not every day you get to see a building associated with the Knights Templar. The Church of *Santa Maria de Eunate* is twelfth-century Romanesque and octagon shaped, a miniature of the Holy Sepulchre in Jerusalem it was modelled on. The ruins of its external cloister surround the small chapel with crumbling columns and archways. According to the guidebook, the name translates to "Saint Mary of a Hundred Doors." Daniel counts thirty-three as he approaches. Being Irish, he's not too offended by the exaggeration. He wants to tell Ginny all this but doesn't want to bore her with his need to spew facts. Instead he keeps the knowledge to himself. This effort requires a force of will that almost brings the coffee back up his throat.

Although there is a large parking lot in front for tourists, the place looks empty. This is the off-season, and the building looks gloomy and abandoned. It rests at the base of a series of rolling foothills.

"So, where's the massacre?" he asks Ginny as they cross the main road to the parking lot.

"You know Friday the thirteenth?" she says, not bothering to look both ways as they cross the highway.

"The date or the horror movie?" he asks her.

"The date," she says. "It was the day the Knights Templar were wiped out by the Catholic Church in a bloody mass execution."

"Is that why it's considered unlucky?"

"Sure was unlucky for the knights," she says. It is not lost on him that she appears to share his enthusiasm for random facts. He wonders if she knows what the longest street in the world is.

"They were the financial arm of the Church, of course."

"Yes," she says, nodding, pleased. "Their castles and churches used to be all along the Camino. A place of refuge for the medieval pilgrims, starving half the time and sick. Or injured from attacks by roving bands of thieves." She does a sweep of the parking lot with her eyes, as if roving thieves may still be an issue, then pushes a stray hair from her ponytail behind one ear. "But the money the Templars held made them too powerful. The pope had to get rid of them."

"Is that who is buried in the cemetery there, the massacred knights?" Daniel points at the small graveyard on the west side of the church just now coming into view.

"No," she says.

"Who'd be buried there, then?" he asks.

"The pilgrims who didn't make it."

As they approach, they see the site is not entirely deserted. Sitting on a low stone wall between the graveyard and the church is a lone pilgrim. He is dressed much like they are, convertible hiking pants, warm fleece and jacket, and a painter's cap to keep off the sun. He sports a beard as most men do on the Camino, shaving being one of the first daily grooming habits to go. This man's red-brown beard is better kept than Daniel's. He probably had it before he came. The man lifts his arm and waves at them in greeting. His lengthy legs jut out in front of him, one well-worn hiking boot crossed over the other.

"*Hola. Buen Camino!*" he calls out as they get closer.

"*Buen Camino*," both Ginny and Daniel respond, but it is Ginny who continues.

"*Está abierto?*" she asks him.

"*No hablo español*," the man tells her. "*Soy holandés.*"

"Dutch," she tells Daniel and then addresses the pilgrim again. "Do you speak English?"

"Yes," he says, and smiles at her. "Although not as well as German. But much better than Spanish." He has a Swiss Army knife open, slicing up a red apple. The sharp blade moves deftly in his large hands. On the stone wall he has laid out a checkered linen napkin with a large hunk of dark-skinned cheese and a crusty loaf of bread.

"The church will not open for another quarter hour. We must wait," he tells them. Daniel eyes the white juicy flesh of the apple. They hadn't stopped for breakfast, and it's nearly lunchtime. He tries not to visibly drool.

The Dutchman gestures with an open hand to the food. "Please join me," he says with a gentleman's flair. This is something Daniel has noticed about the Dutch, their graceful thoughtfulness. It is a stereotype that becomes the Netherlands, much like tulips.

"Thanks, but we wouldn't want to be disturbing your meal," Daniel says, now eying the fresh rind of the cheese as well as the apple. He doesn't want to take the man's lunch although he probably shouldn't have answered on Ginny's behalf. She doesn't appear to have noticed, though, as she sits down and tears a good-sized piece of bread from the loaf and pops it into her mouth.

"This is great," she tells the Dutchman, taking off her gloves. "Very civilized."

The Dutchman spears a piece of apple with the knife and tips it toward her. She leans in and takes it between her teeth, the shiny blade dangerously close to her lips. Her eyes close in satisfaction. He skewers another piece and offers it to Daniel.

"Please, you are hungry," he says.

Daniel hesitates for a second more and then takes the fruit from the knife point carefully with his fingers, popping it in his mouth. The tart juice wakes up his tongue, reminding him how thirsty as well as hungry he is. It is time for a break. Slipping off his backpack, he sits down alongside the other two pilgrims.

"Thank you," he says as the Dutchman cuts off a generous piece of cheese and hands it to him. Its creaminess clings to the sides of Daniel's mouth. He washes it down with a good swig from his water bottle.

The Dutchman puts down the Swiss Army knife and wipes his right hand on his pants before he extends it. "I am Rob," he says, before adding theatrically, "the most handsome and intelligent man in the Netherlands." His wry smile is infectious. Daniel shakes his hand.

"I am Daniel from New Jersey," he tells him through a mouthful of bread. Rob nods at him without any question in his eyes. People whose first language is not English don't usually detect the accent. Daniel enjoys the chance to be culturally ambiguous.

"And you?" the Dutchman asks, turning to his other lunch guest.

"I'm Ginny," she says. "From California."

"Is this where you learned your Spanish?" Rob asks her.

"Sort of," she says, cutting off a piece of cheese. "I took a course before I left. Plus, you pick things up after awhile."

Daniel wishes he had taken a course in Spanish before he left. Two days ago, he tried to order wine in a restaurant. *Vino del año* meant "young wine," he was told, the fresh kind they served for drinking early in the year. But he had pronounced it incorrectly, and the insulted waitress told him in English that he had asked for "wine of my butthole."

"Where did you learn your English?" she asks the Dutchman.

"Oh, from English speakers at my work. I owned once a moving business, but I had to sell and change to a new job. My heart," he says as he pounds on his chest for emphasis, "was not strong enough for the stress. I had, I am not sure in English...." The Dutchman pauses for a healthy burp and to search for words. "A go around for my passes," he says.

"A heart bypass?" Ginny suggests.

"Yes, that is right. A heart bypass. My wife says no more stressful work after this. I listen to my wife."

"What do you do now?" Daniel asks him.

"I am a miller," Rob tells him as he pulls another apple from his pack. "We grind wheat for bread in the old way, with a windmill."

"Wow, that is so Dutch," says Ginny.

Rob laughs, curling his fist and holding it to his mouth so he doesn't choke on a bite of apple. "It is," he admits, as he coughs. When he clears his throat, he reaches into his backpack and pulls out a short fat link of chorizo. He cuts off a slice of the spicy sausage and offers it to Ginny.

"No, thanks," Ginny says, chewing on a piece of bread before closing her mouth self-consciously.

"The chorizo is very good, Ginny, you should try it," Rob says, cutting a wedge for Daniel with his knife.

"That's okay," she says quietly.

"Are you a vegetarian?" Rob asks her, a bit more perceptive than Daniel. She had refused his beef jerky twice since *Alto del Perdón* and he hadn't caught on.

"You're not a vegan, are you?" Daniel says when she doesn't respond. "Those people are mad!" He had dated a vegan girl in college once. She had lived off fennel seeds and wheat grass. The only good thing he can remember about her is that she was biodegradable.

"No, I'm not vegan. Just nothing with a face." Ginny takes a sip from a water bottle she carries. She must have it as a backup for the hydration bladder in her pack. "I eat fish though," she adds.

"Sure, but fish have faces," Daniel says.

"Yeah, but they're ugly faces."

"This is a shame," Rob breaks in, looking serious. "There are too many things to enjoy in life to only eat the ugly faces."

Daniel takes another bite of chorizo, grinning. None of them hear the studded church doors open until a rough voice calls out from them.

"*Abierto!*" A shrunken elderly Spanish woman pokes her head out as she makes the announcement and then abruptly retreats, like a turtle pulling back into its shell.

Daniel turns to the others after grabbing a last piece of apple. "Ready to go in?"

"Sure," says Ginny, standing and brushing crumbs from her lap. She doesn't put her gloves back on. It has warmed up now with the midday. Daniel takes off his hat and stuffs it in his bag.

"I will finish eating," Rob says, pulling another crust of bread from his backpack, picking up the last piece of cheese. "I have seen it before anyway."

"You saw it before?" Daniel asks. "But it was closed."

"I am not good with my English. I mean I have seen inside churches like this before. They are all the same."

*

Ginny and Daniel walk under the main arch of the external cloister and enter through the open doors of the stone chapel. It can't be more than thirty feet across inside. At the front is a simple raised semicircular sanctuary, where a small table is laid out with a white linen cloth and the tools of the Eucharist. The silver trays of Communion are each adorned with a cross. Daniel looks up to see that the ceiling is ribbed and curved like a stone basket turned upside down. Canned Gregorian chants float up from a speaker on a folding table in the corner, where the elderly Spanish woman sits guarding a stamp pad.

All pilgrims have a "pilgrim passport" that they need to get stamped at intervals along the Way to prove they are walking. Otherwise, they can't stay in the *albergues*, which are meant only for people who are undertaking the pilgrimage to the cathedral in Santiago. You can have your passport updated at any of the major stops or attractions. Ginny lays out her passport for the woman but is ignored. The old lady has become distracted by the speaker, trying to adjust a short in the wire that causes the chanting to cut in and out like medieval club music. She flicks a fly from her ancient sun-spotted nose as she fiddles with the connection. Ginny gives up and moves on. Daniel doesn't even bother. He only gets the obligatory stamps each night at the *albergue* he stays in.

They both light candles at the front. There are real candles here. Not the usual false electric flames in a Plexiglas-lidded box that you activate with a couple of coins dropped in a metal slot. Daniel sits in one pew, Ginny in another. The Gregorian chants have been fixed and now echo again off the curved stone walls. Daniel makes the sign of the cross and lowers his head to pray. It seems appropriate; although, he doesn't make use of the kneeler, which makes him wonder at his own seriousness. *Our Father can't hear you if your knees aren't screaming* — another of his granny's sayings. That woman was a peach.

He tries hard for a few minutes, but the prayer won't come. He can't even seem to speak to Petra, as he often does at moments like these. He feels cut off from her. He's not sure whether it is because he is walking with the cute girl across the pew, or because he almost threw Petra off a cliff a few hours ago. He knows he needs a touch of the divine, but his prayers remain empty.

His eyes are still closed when he feels Ginny's cool breath in his ear. She speaks with a hush.

"Let's get out of here. This chanting is giving me the creeps." A smile comes easily to his lips in response, despite the sombre mood of the church and his thoughts.

"Not a fan of the Gregorian monk hit parade?" he asks Ginny, opening his eyes.

"I feel like I'm in *The Exorcist.*"

"Do you, now?" Daniel says, almost laughing. Talk about inappropriate.

"I do. I'm just waiting for that old lady's head to spin around."

This time he does laugh, releasing himself from more tension than he realized he held. He crosses himself again, genuflects quickly toward the altar, and turns to go with her. They are both still smirking a little as they walk up the narrow aisle. The old woman at her table watches them with a furrowed brow of disapproval. As they pass the table, she leans with her fossil-like frame toward them, then flicks another fly in the air.

"*Lo estan siguiendo,*" she says, and crosses herself. Daniel stops and looks at her. But she folds her arms atop her chest and turns her face away from him as if in protest. He waits a little to see if she will say anything more, but she doesn't. He doesn't know what to say to her. His Spanish is so pathetic. Ginny has already gone outside and is not there to translate.

"I'm sorry?" Daniel says to the woman. No reaction. Is she deaf? Or can she not hear him over the chanting. He tries once more with his limited knowledge of the local language. "*No entiendo,*" he says. I don't understand.

She turns and looks at him again, repeating what she said before, but more slowly, punctuating each Spanish word with one bent and frighteningly hairy finger in the air. "*Lo estan siguiendo.*"

Daniel doesn't understand any more than he did the first time. His confused look earns nothing more from her but a hand gesture, her index and pinky fingers held up like horns. It is a sign Daniel associates more with 80s heavy metal rock than with the Catholic Church. He assumes she is using it for its original purpose, to ward off the evil eye, rather than to profess her undying love of Iron Maiden. When she turns away again with a huff, he gives up and walks out the door.

Outside, he is surprised to see Ginny about to overtake the top of the first large hill that leads back to the main trail. She has gone on without him. In fact, she must have taken off at quite a clip to get so far in such a short time. Run even. He glances over and sees the low stone wall is unoccupied. The Dutchman has left as well. Nothing remains of his little picnic except a tattered piece of the checkered cloth caught on one of the rougher stones. It flutters in the breeze.

This is grand, Daniel thinks, *first I have a hairy old elf woman giving out to me and now I've been ditched*. He looks back up the hill, shielding his eyes from the high sun with his right hand to check whether Ginny has stopped to wait for him. He can just make out the last of her ponytail disappearing as she makes it hurriedly over the top of the hill. He can't help but feel offended. Was it the bit about the cows?

Daniel grabs his hat roughly and puts it back on. "Who cares," he says to himself. She was a bit of flake anyway. Besides, he likes to walk by himself. He is here for a purpose after all, not to go socializing.

He bends over to pick up his backpack. When he stands up again, he sees it: a dark shape moving out from a small grouping of trees at the crest of the hill. It advances slowly but purposefully from that hiding place and then out onto the path. Daniel is too far away to distinguish its features, but it is not the Dutchman, not tall enough. The figure disappears over the hill. It moves like one of those *Spy vs. Spy* characters he used to watch in cartoons as a kid.

It could be anyone, Daniel thinks. Perhaps another pilgrim that went to take a slash behind a tree. There aren't any public restrooms on the Camino. The world was their toilet.

He doesn't really believe that, though. The person seemed to be lurking in the trees; waiting until Ginny walked past. He keeps his eye on the rise as he tightens his backpack but sees nothing more. Just false intuition, he decides, brought on by the ridiculous chanting and talk of *The Exorcist.* He had always hated that shite movie. Only Hollywood could make a franchise out of a girl vomiting on a priest. Daniel is bent over retying one of his boot laces when he hears the scream. Alarmed, he looks up and hears it again.

"Jesus!" He abandons the boot and races through the archway with the lace still trailing. Overworked leg muscles pump as he runs up the steep incline, trying not to trip. The backpack bangs back and forth behind him, the weight of it slamming with each stride into the small of his back. His lungs fill to capacity with air. His side births a searing pain. He shouldn't have eaten so much face-filled chorizo.

"Ginny!" he shouts as he runs. Even at full speed, it takes some time to reach the peak of the incline. When he does, his heavy hiking boots slam down the other side of the hill, sending shock waves up the lower half of his body. He rounds the corner at the bottom and bends over, hands braced on his knees, panting. There is no one there. Just the trail stretching out ahead of him into the distance, hill after rolling hill obscuring his view. She could be anywhere. He is ready to start running again when a hand grabs his arm from behind. He whirls around, ready for attack.

"Relax. It is me." The Dutchman gives him a tentative look.

"Did you see Ginny?" Daniel asks, still gasping for breath.

"Yes," Rob says. "She has just left. She says she wishes to walk alone."

"You didn't hear a scream?" Daniel asks him.

"No," the Dutchman says, drawing the word out, the way people do when they are not too sure about you.

"You weren't seeing anyone else?"

"No, only her. Are you okay, Daniel from New Jersey?" His concern is real. Even Daniel can see that. There is no reason not to believe him. Everything is quiet, except for the far-off sound of a tractor, the chirping of birds.

"She said she wanted to walk alone?" he asks Rob again. His breath is returning, his voice less strained. The chorizo settles back down in his stomach.

"Yes," he says, waiting patiently for Daniel to calm himself. "Pretty girl," he adds as an aside.

"I suppose," Daniel admits, his panic moving toward embarrassment. This is the second time he has behaved like a lunatic today, running toward the same woman. His mother would be proud. He looks over at the long dirt trail ahead until it disappears into foothills and spent fields.

"Everyone has a story," Rob says, following his gaze.

"Sure," Daniel says, bending over again to tie up his boot lace, still trying to catch his breath. "I believe I may have heard that before."

Only later, when he parts ways with the Dutchman and is signing in at the *albergue* in Obanos, does Daniel remember what the old lady said, asking the *hospitaleiro* for a translation. Daniel's tongue hacks at the language like a crowbar. Eventually the Spanish innkeeper picks up the pieces and understands him.

"Followed," he says in English, stamping Daniel's pilgrim passport, then returning it to him with his identification and change for ten euros.

"It means 'You are followed.'"

Daniel walks upstairs feeling uneasy, but he is too tired to care. He finds his bunk bed and collapses on it, patting the bottom of his backpack protectively.

"Everyone has a story, Petra," he says as he closes his eyes wearily. The woman in the next bunk bed discreetly moves herself and her gear to another room, mindful of lunatics and perverts. He is too exhausted to notice.

✳

That night Daniel dreams in the sparse bunk bed of the *albergue* at Obanos. What he saw then. What he sees now. It all comes together into an impossible tangle in his subconscious. Like the waxy-leafed trees that line the path in his mind, choking out the light as he loses his way on the road to Santiago. In the dream, he has just spread Petra's ashes, but they blow up against him as he walks, clinging to his hiking pants along with the greasy wet leaves that have fallen on the trail.

Petra appears behind him, then on either side. A ghost in triplicate, each version a beast with a different type of claws. One as she was, one as she became, and one as he last saw her, dark with death.

The three versions of his wife rise up in front of him like mountains, then become one, blocking his way. He falls to his knees on the sharp gravel of the path and begs for her forgiveness. In answer, she turns to stone. He will never get past her now.

The sun sets on the slab of her face, as he sobs into his hands. She knows his story, and she will never let him forget it.

CHAPTER 3
Obanos to Azqueta

THE NEXT MORNING, DANIEL sits at a patio table in front of the *albergue* where he can connect to the Wi-Fi. He is nursing a coffee with gloved hands while he Skypes his sister on his smartphone. Angela's at the farm with their parents, visiting for the weekend. He can hear his father shouting in the background. His mother telling him to "cop himself on," the Irish version of "get your shit together." These are the reassuring sounds of home.

"How are you?" Angela asks with a bit of hesitation. She worries about him. He has to call regularly to assure her he is not dead or wallowing in self-pity. She takes her big-sister role seriously, even though their birthdays are only ten months apart. "Irish twins," as people call them. That is, all the people who aren't actually Irish.

"I'm better," Daniel says, and realizes he is. Despite having had a rough night, he feels more relaxed this morning. More in tune with his surroundings. Still, the nightmare from last night lingers, made worse by jumping out of bed and falling flat on his face in his twisted mummy sleeping bag. The two Spanish guys he bunked with laugh and point at him every time they walk by.

"You'd like this place where I'm staying," he tells her. "Obanos. The church has a human skull in a box on the wall. You could test it for DNA."

Angela is a nurse but also an addict of forensic crime shows. He has never understood how after spending all day knee-deep in bodily fluids, she could be so interested in the angle of blood splatter and autopsies.

"I read online about that skull," she says. She'd been experiencing his journey on the Camino vicariously, reading up on the sights and scenery as her brother passed them. She had wanted to come with him but couldn't get the time off work. "Was it Saint William it belonged to?" she asks.

"It was," he says, proud of her for knowing. "He murdered his sister for going to Santiago instead of getting married. Then felt such the maggot, he became a devout hermit and died destitute in a cave." He had learned all this from the Spanish guys, who spoke good English when they weren't laughing at him. "Every year they take his skull out and parade it down the street on a stick for the annual passion play."

"Let that be a warning to you, Danny boy."

They both laugh. God, he loves his sister. She's the only person who can call him Danny boy without getting a pop in the jaw. Daniel is fairly close to his two older brothers, both now living in England, but it's just not the same as with Angela.

Still smiling, he looks over at another table and sees a woman from last night's *albergue* putting her hair in a ponytail. It reminds him.

"I walked with someone yesterday," he confesses. At least, it feels like a confession.

"Really?" Angela says, drawing the two syllables out with interest. "Did the someone have a name by any chance?"

"Virginia," Daniel says. "Ginny." He's not sure why he's telling Angela about her. "She's from California."

"Where is she now, then?"

Daniel thinks about the figure he thought he saw come out of the trees, his frantic run up the hill believing he'd heard Ginny scream.

"She ditched me," he says.

"Well, then she cannot be a woman of any appreciable taste," Angela pronounces. "Or perhaps you told her that bit about the skull on the stick. Not all women like a good tale of saint decapitation. You could scare a girl away with that sort of shite."

Daniel should laugh, but he goes quiet instead. He doesn't like this talk of scaring Ginny away. It sounds too much like he was trying to attract her in the first place. He's not ready for that.

"Are you sure you're all right, Daniel?" Angela asks him.

"I am," he says. He's not about to tell his sister about what happened at the Templar church, or how he mistook Ginny for Petra on the *Alto del Perdón*. She'd be calling the Spanish *guardia* to have him committed.

"Have you been taking the pills the doctor gave you, for your nerves?"

Daniel flinches at the question. He doesn't like to think of himself as a man with nerves. Plus, he has the eerie feeling she was able to see into his thoughts just now.

"I have," he says, quickly recovering. "Every day with my coffee." He raises up his coffee cup so she can see it on the Skype feed. "I reckon it balances out with the stimulant effect of the caffeine."

Daniel had been having a tough time just before he left for the Camino. Nightmares like the one he had last night. Awakening to screams like he thought he heard yesterday. He'd search the house for Petra, convinced it was her calling for him. After he checked every room, he'd collapse on their bed, remembering that all that was left of her was settled in the bottom of the ostentatious urn on the top shelf of his closet. He hated the look of that urn. Once he had even taken the ugly little ceramic down from its hiding place and thrown it against the wall. He'd been drinking. It hadn't broken, but the incident frightened him enough to go see a doctor. Thus, the pills his sister was on about. Daniel doesn't like pills. A friend had given him some Ambien when he suffered from insomnia during Petra's first hospital stay. At two in the morning, he awoke to find himself in his elderly neighbour's backyard wearing nothing but a barbecue apron. Ever since, the old girl had been regularly baking him muffins and leaving them on the front stoop.

"Have you spread Petra's ashes yet?" Angela asks, getting to the point. Damn it, this is a subject he wants to avoid even more than Mrs. Boddis's muffins.

"I think we have a bad connection," he shouts at the phone, as you do when you can't hear the other person properly. Angela's eyes narrow on the video display. She knows when she's being played. He grabs the sugar dispenser off the table and starts pouring the white granules out above the screen like snow. "Sure, you're breaking up, Angela. I think I'm going to have to sign off."

"Just spread the feckin' ashes, Daniel. It's been long enough."

"Talk to you soon." He smiles back broadly, ignoring her, then presses the disconnect icon.

They may be close, but Angela doesn't understand about Petra. He needs just the right moment to let go of her. For Christ's sake, he'd written that woman a poem every day they were apart during their long-distance courtship. He'd found them after she was gone, tied up with a red ribbon in a shoebox under the bed. You just don't spread the ashes of a woman like that lightly. Even if it has been long enough and your dad is waiting for you to come take over the farm of your ancestors. There is a time for everything, and Daniel will not be pushed.

He picks up the phone from where it was propped on the table and slips it into the side pocket of his backpack. Right next to the pill bottle with the prescription he had dutifully filled before he left home but has never touched.

It is only the second time in his life he has ever lied to his sister. He finishes the last gulp of coffee and gets ready to walk.

The first time, of course, was the day Petra died.

*

Daniel bumps into the Dutchman just outside of Puente la Reina, a fairly built-up town with a cathedral and lots of bars and restaurants. All of them were closed when he had walked through, unfortunately. Too early in the day, particularly for Spain. The urban centre has now given way to vineyards and olive trees, all barren and asleep until next spring.

"Hellooo, Daniel," Rob calls to him from where he has stopped ahead on the path to take a picture of a grotto. People have left stones and pieces of paper, along with ribbons and medallions. All this spiritual flotsam surrounds a ceramic blue-and-white figurine of the Virgin Mary, giving the unfortunate appearance that the saint stands atop a garbage dump.

Daniel waves. The Dutchman waits for him and they fall in walking together.

"Did you enjoy your *albergue* in Obanos, Daniel?" Rob asks him.

"I did," Daniel says, then corrects himself. "Not really, no." He notices dark circles under the Dutchman's eyes. "How was your night?"

"I stayed in Puente la Reina in a large *albergue* with many sleeping places," Rob tells him. "I am very tired this morning."

By "sleeping places," Rob means beds. Pilgrims often judge the *albergues* laid out in the guidebook by the number of beds and try to stay away from those with larger volumes. Daniel had stayed in one *albergue* where ninety people were housed in one room. The combined snoring alone was enough to break a man's eardrum.

"That's a shame," Daniel says. And then, "I wasn't after sleeping very well either."

"Too many dreams of the pretty Ginny from California?" Rob asks him with a knowing look.

"No," Daniel protests. "I mean, it's not like that." Geez, will people just lay off him with the romantic innuendo.

Rob holds up his open palms toward him in the universal gesture of no harm–no foul. "Don't worry, Daniel. I understand. I have a woman friend on the Camino like this, too. A Canadian."

"Where is she?" Daniel asks.

"Oh, I don't know. Nearby, I am sure. We walk together sometimes and sometimes alone. It is a relaxing relationship, but we are very close."

"Did you know her before you came on the Camino?"

"No," Rob laughs. "You are like my wife with this question."

Daniel is not surprised that Rob's wife would ask such a question. He doesn't think Petra would have much appreciated it if he had gone around getting close to other women while away for over a month in another country.

"But it is like sister-love, I explain to her." Rob turns and looks at Daniel to see if he gets his meaning. "The Camino, it is like what you Americans have, what is it called, summer camp?"

Daniel didn't grow up with the American experience of summer camp, but he knows what the Dutchman means.

"You get attached to people fairly quickly," Daniel says.

"Yes," Rob replies, pleased to be understood. As they crest the top of the gradual incline they've been walking, he cries out like a man on a ship sighting land, "And there she is!"

Daniel looks out across a flat bowl of a valley. He can make out the small village of Cirauqui perched on the other side of it on the next hilltop. From this vantage point, he can see the groove carved by the winding narrow road as it makes its way into the village and then back out into the countryside going west. At the base of the elevation, a tall woman with a red-and-black backpack sits on a bench at the side of the trail sipping from a water bottle. She waves, and they both wave back. The Dutchman is grinning with such intensity that Daniel thinks it must hurt his face.

"Only sister-love, so?" Daniel asks, raising both eyebrows.

"Yes, well. I love my wife," Rob tells him. "But sometimes she asks too many questions."

Daniel leaves Rob behind with his Canadian sister-friend at a café in Cirauqui. The relationship appeared to be no more than platonic affection, despite the Dutchman's bravado. He hadn't struck Daniel as the philandering type anyway, whatever that type was. Daniel always got the term mixed up with philanthropy, as if benevolence held ties with infidelity, both giving till it hurt.

The woman seemed pleasant enough, though, even if she hadn't said a word to him as they walked up the hill to the village. To be fair, the steep inclines could make conversation tough. It was hard enough to regulate your breathing as you hiked up to some of these medieval hillside towns without adding talking to the mix. The villages had been built that way so the inhabitants could see an enemy coming from a long way off. Daniel wonders if the real trick was that half of their enemies dropped dead of a coronary before they reached the top. When they were climbing the last bit, Daniel had made a nervous sideways glance at Rob, remembering what he'd said about his heart. But the Dutchman didn't even seem to breathe hard with the effort.

After leaving the couple, Daniel passes through an arch off the main square and exits the village onto a single-span Roman bridge, curved and solid. The engineer in him admires these classically built-to-last structures. The poet in him appreciates the irony that they long outlasted the Empire for which they were built.

Daniel has been walking for a while on his own when he sees another example ahead, this one spanning two arches over a limited river. Some low-lying brush sits on either side, including those bushes with the dried-up yellow flowers that, even this late in the year, overwhelm him with their sweet fragrance. He saw flowers like these before coming to Spain, in France in early spring, his honeymoon spent with Petra. The scent was so intense through the window of the broken-down *pension* where they stayed, that his new wife had thought her floral body wash had exploded in their suitcase.

It had been so easy then. Lying under the sparse bed-spread, exploring each other over long days and endless bottles of French wine that somehow never made them drunk. Instead it fortified them just enough to get up out of their rumpled bed by evening to go out in search of dinner. "Look," she had said, on the way to the restaurant, pointing out the yellow arrows that would lead a person all the way to Spain and Santiago. They had made love so often his hips twinged when he walked.

"I know I took off and everything, but that doesn't mean you have to hunt me down like you're some kind of bloodhound."

Ginny is sitting on the grass at the riverside, twisting a small branch with yellow flowers in her hand. It takes Daniel a moment to process her presence as well as her comment. He had been standing there with his eyes closed, sniffing the scent of the fading flowers like a dog. He decides he could make a living out of looking like an ass in front of women.

"The flowers," he says in weak explanation.

Ginny nods, glances down at the ones she holds in her hand.

"Listen, I'm sorry about the way I left things." She stands up and walks over to him, dropping the branch on the ground. "But that old woman and that place. It just freaked me out."

"Sure, I understand," Daniel agrees, remembering the flies and the gnarled finger punctuating foreign Spanish words in the air. "The old girl at the desk."

"Now there was a weird one," Ginny says, turning away to squint into the sunlight.

"What harm, but she told me we were being followed," Daniel tells her. "Then she made the sign of the horns."

"Are you serious? Did she consult her Ouija board or her magic eight ball for that information?" Ginny asks. And then that smile again, and he can't help but return it.

Is it sister-love, like the Dutchman said? Maybe. He finds himself no longer wanting to talk about yesterday. They walk over and stand on the middle of the Roman bridge together. The shallow water moves lethargically beneath them.

"Do you know what this river is called?" he asks her, bursting at the seams.

"*Rio Salado*," she says, not missing a beat.

"That's right," Daniel says, turning to her surprised and more than a little disappointed. "How did you know?"

"It means Salt River. It's toxic," she says, wrinkling her freckled nose a tiny bit.

"Sure, but do you know what they were after doing here?" he says, trying to out-fence her with facts. Then feeling a tad self-conscious, adds, "Sorry, I'm what you might call a trivia junkie."

"That's all right. I want to know. Tell me."

"Okay," Daniel says, encouraged. He extends his arm out toward where she was just sitting. "In the Middle Ages, the Basques would wait for pilgrims to come and water their horses here. After they died, they would skin them for the meat."

"The pilgrims or the horses?" Ginny quips.

"Funny girl."

They stand on the old stone bridge and watch over the side together.

"You already knew the story, now didn't you?"

"Yeah." She giggles. It's a sound that has always delighted him in women.

Ginny raises her eyes from the slow-moving water, starts scanning the other side of the riverbank. She turns when she sees he has noticed.

"Just making sure I didn't forget anything," she explains. "I hate when that happens."

"Aye," Daniel agrees, remembering how he got lost in Pamplona and had to retrace his steps. When you're walking twelve miles a day, you don't want to add even a dozen yards due to stupidity. "Nobody wants to go back on the Way," he says.

Ginny looks down at the water and nods slowly in agreement. The sluggish current gurgling over the rocks is the only audible reply. He has hit a nerve, it appears. Daniel stands and waits for the pensive moment to pass. When it does, they cross together to the other side of the bridge and start back on the trail without comment.

"So, are you a history teacher, or just well-read?" he asks after a few minutes, trying to draw her out. He is also curious. Not many people know about things like the Salt River.

"I'm a librarian," Ginny tells him.

"You're having me on."

"What, you expected the bun, the glasses, a pair of sensible shoes?"

It is a very warm day for the fall, and Ginny has rolled up the sleeves of her fleece and zipped off the bottoms of her pant legs, converting them to shorts. He can see the sleek defined muscles of her calves, the tautness of her forearms. She holds her body with a sinewy strength, not unlike the horse his sister kept during her Black Beauty phase. Not the type of body he'd expect to see behind a returns desk.

"You'd have to be fairly thick to come on the Camino without sensible shoes," Daniel tells her. He's trying to be funny, but has ended up sounding like a maiden aunt. He moves on to something else, hoping she didn't notice. "Sure, but your knowledge seems a bit skewed toward medieval barbarism. Massacred knights, skinned horses, and the like. Why is that?"

"Well, it might have to do with the library I work in," she says as she reaches her hands behind her back and lifts and lowers her pack from the bottom in an effort to redistribute the weight.

"Really now," Daniel says. "Where is it that you work?"

"San Quentin."

"The prison?" Daniel almost chokes on the beef jerky he was snacking on.

"Well, it's not the all-inclusive resort." She pauses. "Although, maybe it is. But I'd give it a really bad review on TripAdvisor."

"No doubt. What's it like working there?"

"I have to wear a pendant with a panic button around my neck, but other than that pretty much the same as other libraries," she says, taking her aluminum hiking poles from the little loop on her backpack and extending them to be used for the upcoming incline. "The thing is, we get quite a few requests for books about murder and mayhem, if you know what I mean. We don't like to give them the more modern stuff. Too stimulating. So we bring in a lot on the Spanish Inquisition and other medieval history. Sometimes I get bored and read them."

"I'll keep an eye on my horse."

They walk for a while without speaking, their paces well-matched, but soon the conversation between them begins to flow with the current of the trail. They move up the inclines ending in hilltop villages and down again into the surrounding countryside, remarking from time to time on architecture or the natural beauty surrounding them. Each tries to one-up the other with *albergue* horror stories of snoring and stinky feet. They compare notes on what they packed for the trip, how much weight they carry, and the status of blisters: Daniel still without any; Ginny admitting to a minute one between pinky toe and the one beside it. He tells her a bit about growing up in rural Ireland, how he left the farm to get his engineering degree at Trinity College in Dublin. She owns up to a suburban childhood in Orange County, where her parents were neither divorced nor former hippies, making her the odd girl out among her peers.

When they come to Estella, a larger town where Daniel had planned to stay the night, they both agree that the *albergues* are too crowded, the urban scene not their style. They stop and eat their simple packed lunches on a park bench before continuing on through the city centre and back out of it. They set their sights on Villamayor de Monjardin, where the views are supposed to be spectacular, even though it is still five miles away and their shadows are getting longer on the path. That would turn out to be a big mistake, but they don't know that now, too at ease with the day and each other's company.

Daniel looks at his watch and realizes they have been walking together for hours, but it doesn't feel like it. They have been so engrossed in sharing their various experiences. His grandfather always told him that "two shorten the road." He supposes he was right about that, as he was about most things involving the subtle observation of human nature. His grandmother claimed it came from a lifetime of sitting on his arse watching the world go by.

Ginny's gone quiet. When he looks over, he notices her lips are held tightly together, suppressing a grin. She's up to something, but Daniel isn't sure what until they reach the narrow end of a large rectangular building with a brushed silver-plated recess built into the outer stone wall. Two spigots jut out from raised images of scallop shells, all below a large Spanish coat of arms. The Cross of Saint James with its telltale pointed spade at the base, as if you could pound it into the earth, is etched between the two taps. Ginny had told him earlier she doesn't like these crosses; they look too much like daggers.

She rushes up to the wall and stretches out her arms like a girl about to turn letters on a game show. Daniel can read some of what is written around the coat of arms now, bronze on silver, *Fuente de Irache*.

"The monastery of Irache was established here about a thousand years ago," Ginny tells him. "It was built for two reasons. One was to take care of the increasing number of pilgrims that came through on their way to Santiago."

"And what was the second reason?"

"To perfect the recipe for a kick-ass shiraz," she says.

Daniel examines more closely the spigots embedded in the wall. He realizes they each have a plaque with a Spanish word mounted above them. One says *Agua*, the other *Vino*. He also remembers now what the word *Fuente* means.

"Sure, is this what I think it is?" he asks her, not believing what he's seeing.

"Yup," Ginny says, dropping her pack, pulling out her plastic water bottle and dumping the contents out to make room. "It's a wine fountain."

"Aye, now that's grand," Daniel says.

They both fill up their water bottles. And not from the spigot marked *Agua*.

Afterward, they make their way up the path behind the fountain laughing, confident in their ability to make it to Villamayor de Monjardin.

Later, Daniel will wish they had stayed where they were.

＊

It is starting to cool off as they walk up the hill on a close path through the trees. The warmth of the wine keeps them from putting on their jackets, even as the day starts to fade and the trees block the sun. Ginny bursts out in giggles when a branch pushed aside by Daniel comes back and whacks her in the face. He apologizes but laughs himself. The physical work of walking all day and their increased fatigue have combined with the alcohol to give them both a fairly comfortable buzz.

"I cannot believe a man can get free wine out of a fountain in this country," Daniel says. Back in his Trinity days, such a thing would cause a riot. "Did you find out about it through your study of murder and mayhem in the prison library?"

"No, I'm a California girl. We have the uncanny ability to detect the scent of complimentary wine from a hundred paces."

"And I'm Irish, but we can't sniff out free Guinness, no matter how hard some of my forefathers may have tried."

"I read it in the guidebook," she says. "You really should do more than look at the pictures," she teases him.

"Sure, the pictures are the best part," he teases back.

They make their way out of the trees and emerge on a wider country road skirting cornfields. The field has not been harvested yet though it is late in the year. Tall stalks of bleached-out yellow leaves rustle with the breeze. No one else is around. Just the two of them. His buzz is starting to fade with the daylight.

"Why are you here, Daniel?" Ginny asks him, after she swallows another sample of the tart red wine. As she lowers her water bottle, a colourful beaded bracelet with little silver shells trembles on her wrist. It sets off the deep tan of her arms and makes him think of the California beaches she must have grown up on.

"On the Camino, you're saying?"

"I guess so," she replies.

Daniel finishes off the wine in his own bottle and then decides the best way to answer is with brutal honesty.

"My wife died." It sounds so flat, so insufficient, using those three loaded words to sum up so much. He thinks he can feel the brown burlap bag at the bottom of his backpack shift with disappointment. He hadn't thought about Petra or her ashes since he started walking with Ginny this morning. Guilt sets in.

"I'm so sorry," Ginny says.

Daniel clears his throat a few times, but he can't form the words he wants to say. It would do him good to unload it all to this virtual stranger. But his fear and the guilt in his backpack won't let him do it.

He decides to deflect the conversation onto Ginny's domestic situation. A serpentine move, but the best he can muster on short notice.

"You married?"

"I was," she says, her playfulness at bay for once. "But it's over."

"That's a shame. What happened?" he asks, trying to keep the focus on her.

"We were out celebrating our anniversary over dinner, and I suddenly realized I couldn't think of even one reason why we were together. When I asked him, neither could he." She watches the western horizon as they walk. The sun is low in the sky, almost touching the tops of the cornstalks. "There's not much point in staying in a marriage when nobody knows why they're there." She shrugs her shoulders. "That and he never laughed at my jokes."

"And you being such the card."

"Yeah, hard to believe, isn't it?"

"Is that why you're after walking by yourself?"

She straightens her shoulders, juts out her chin. He'd been trying to keep things light, but the tension in her body denotes a seriousness not present before. Maybe he should have asked if she had any pets instead.

"I was supposed to come with a friend, but she pulled out at the last minute," she says, scanning the horizon and the setting sun again. It will be dark soon and they are still two miles from Monjardin.

"Is that so?" Daniel says. He means the question as empathetic surprise rather than a challenge. But she takes it the wrong way.

"What, you think I couldn't get someone to come with me?" Her voice is sharp. For the first time, Daniel's head starts to suffer from the wine they drank.

"I only meant, it must be tough, now. To have had to come on your own," he says, backtracking. He really should shut his mouth. Surely, he had lived with a woman long enough to know when to do that.

"You're alone," she points out.

"Well, of course, but you're a woman."

The expression on Ginny's face causes his testicles to retreat slightly.

"You sound like my mother. Jesus." She picks up her pace. Her head down, as she walks on ahead of him.

Shite, Daniel thinks, falling in behind. *Next time I'll just ask if she has a cat.*

✳

They stop so that Ginny can zip the bottoms of her pant legs back on and to put on their jackets. It is hitting dusk, and they are still nowhere near the *albergue* they were shooting for. Daniel has finally consulted the guidebook and realizes he misjudged the distance to Monjardin back in Estella. The road has become steep, but the endless rows of drooping cornstalks continue beside them up the hill. His head is truly throbbing now, with the remnants of the wine and his own exertion.

"Do you have a flashlight?" Ginny asks him. "I was going to bring one, but I didn't want to carry the extra weight."

Daniel opens the zippered pouch on his hip belt and extracts what he grew up calling a torch. He pushes the rubber button on the side and a weak beam appears on the road ahead of them. It bounces on the dirt and gravel with each of his steps.

"Listen, about earlier," Ginny says, in delayed apology for her outburst. "I guess I'm just tired."

So is Daniel. He figures it has been ten hours since he left the little *albergue* in Obanos. His boots feel as if they're cast in cement, as he lifts them one in front of the other up the never-ending hill. Since they can't see to the top in the dark, it really does feel like it could go on forever.

"No harm," he tells her. He is less concerned about their squabble than he is about their progress. They need to get somewhere, anywhere, and soon. He thinks he can make out the deep purple outline of buildings off in the distance for a moment, and then decides it's only wishful thinking. His lips feel dry and cracked. He is thirsty as hell. The two water bottles in his pack went dry a long time ago.

The night is completely silent, none of the twilight sounds he remembers in the fields of his youth. The reassuring low of cattle as his father called them in from pasture. The noisy chirping of rooks settling in for the evening. The only noise here is the crunch of their footfalls on the hard gravel.

He is casting his flashlight in its limited range up the road when he sees the crouched human figure in the corn. It runs across the path in front of them and behind a crumbling rock fence.

"What the fuck was that?" he cries out, looking over at Ginny. She is not moving.

"Oh shit," she says.

The figure runs in front of them again, loping awkwardly back into the cornstalks. Daniel cannot discern much in the dwindling light. A mass of tangled hair, a pair of heavy hiking boots.

"Oh shit, oh shit, oh shit," Ginny repeats over and over, backing away.

"Wait here," he says to her, and takes off into the corn. He moves before thinking. Ginny calls out for him to stay, but he is too furious to respond. He has been walking for miles, it's late, and his skull feels like it holds back a mushroom cloud. Now some tosser wants to play games with him in the dark. He is not sure what he is going to do as he roughly parts the corn and plunges inside, but it's not going to be sportsmanlike.

The quiet night is amplified inside the dense corn. He can hear Ginny faintly, shouting from the road to come back, but the tall dry stalks seal him in with their tight silence, like a vacuum or the lid of a coffin. He continues to move deeper through the rows, holding up the next-to-useless flashlight, watching for bent leaves or other hints of where the figure has gone. He is about to give up when he hears breathing, laboured and raspy, as if the wind pipe were obstructed or had undergone an emergency tracheotomy. His sister had told him about one she had performed in the field, cutting open a man's throat with a knife and inserting the shaft of a ballpoint pen. Doctors Without Borders were nurses, too.

Daniel slowly pushes through toward the rasping sound. The outline of a figure in a red fleece sweater comes into view up on his left, standing still in the corn. Is it a child? No, not that small, but not that big either. Probably around the same height as Ginny. Maybe a teenager? Daniel's anger softens a little. Bloody kids.

"I don't know what you're at, but you scared the hell out of us back there."

No response, no movement, just that beleaguered breath. Daniel moves closer, tries again.

"Listen, I don't want any trouble, but it's late, all right?" He takes a deep breath and sighs. Jesus, he's tired. "Why don't you clear off home and quit frightening people, mate."

Still no response. *Maybe the guy doesn't speak English*, Daniel thinks. Although, the young people here were more likely to be bilingual than their parents. He takes a step closer and raises the flashlight beam to the kid's face.

Except he can't see the face. Only what's left of it, through stringy clumps of hair. A thick protruding tongue sticks out, swollen and bulbous, the cracked lips and teeth only partially visible behind it. Just before Daniel drops the flashlight he sees a large shiny black beetle crawl out of the mouth, then back in again, using the slack grey chin as a bridge.

He turns and runs through the tall corn with no idea where he is going. Back to the path or farther into the field, he can't tell. He is moving on primal energy, not toward anything, only away from what he saw. The blade-sharp edges of the scorched leaves cut into his hands, their pointed tips stabbing at his face, as he plunges through the rows of dried-up stalks in the dark.

When he bursts out onto the road, Ginny is ahead of him, mounting the hill as fast as she can, tripping at times in her haste and exhaustion. He runs after her, catching up just as they enter the walls of the hamlet of Azqueta. When she threatens to fall again, he grabs her by the arm and steadies her. Together they stagger down the only street of the tiny village. The stone houses that line it are closed up for the night, cool and silent. Daniel can see a dimly lit sign up ahead, a black shell with white lettering, *La Perla Negra*. Hung above it is a blue square plaque with a white letter A, the accommodation symbol for *albergue*.

Ginny is openly sobbing now as he pulls her up the street and in through the arch of the entranceway. Just before he slams the heavy oak of the door behind them, he sees the dark figure across the square, hovering at the edge of the village. The head hangs low as it drifts above the moonlit farmer's field. The tips of its slack hiking boots drag on the feathery tops of the withering corn.

Daniel holds both of his hands fast against the rough wood planks of the door when he shuts it, as if he can hold back what he has seen with his own brute strength. He can feel splinters beginning to embed in his palms. He only takes his hands away when he hears the *hospitaleiro* call from up the stairs. Daniel turns to face him, the terror still in his eyes, but the middle-aged man in his house sandals doesn't seem to notice.

"*Dónde has estado, peregrino?*" the man says.

Daniel doesn't understand him, of course. He looks all around the foyer of the *albergue* for Ginny to translate. He cannot see her.

"I don't understand," Daniel says. Not able to conjure up any of his limited Spanish. He looks up the stairs. Ginny must have run up to the top floor while he was trying to hold hell back with his bare hands and an oak door.

"*Dónde has estado, peregrino?*" the man repeats again. The canned laughter from a television drifts out from a room off the landing behind him. His private flat. A son in his twenties steps out through the doorway and stands alongside his father.

"He said, 'Where have you been, pilgrim?'" The young man translates using perfect English.

And Daniel must admit to himself that in that moment, he no longer knows.

CHAPTER 4
Azqueta to Torres del Rio

IN THE MORNING DANIEL paces back and forth on a thick braided oval rug in the common room of the *albergue*, waiting for Ginny. He hadn't even made it to a bed in the men's quarters last night. After settling with the *hospitaleiro* and going upstairs in a daze, he had dropped his pack and collapsed on the overgrown loveseat a few steps away. Beyond that he remembers nothing until he woke up and saw the spackled whitewashed walls of the common room glinting in the morning sun. Earthy clayware and rustic Spanish accents surround him on all sides. It feels like being trapped in a Bonanza-themed window display for Pottery Barn. Up in the far corner of the room a bird's nest is built into the wall where it meets the adobe ceiling. He imagines the windows thrown open in summertime to allow barn swallows to fly in and out, a calming, pastoral thought. Then he remembers what he saw in the corn and goes to make sure the sashes are locked.

Frustrated, he drops heavily into a wood and leather armchair, pushing aside the colourful striped blanket draped over the back. Azqueta wasn't even supposed to have any lodging for pilgrims. Daniel had checked earlier in the guidebook. That's why they had set their sights on Monjardin yesterday.

He wishes he could go see what is keeping Ginny, but he is barred by the invisible line drawn across the entrance to the women's bedroom. Pilgrims aren't usually divided by gender, but the *albergue* is under capacity, allowing for separate quarters. A treat for the women, he's sure. The two Spanish guys in Obanos had waited outside the communal showers with their junk hanging out the day before yesterday. Daniel considers himself more of a gentleman than that, so he waits impatiently outside the bedroom door.

A porcelain jug of water has been set out on a long oak table by the stairs. He goes over and pours himself a glass, choking down a couple of Aspirin for his growing headache. What he really needs is coffee and some breakfast, but there is nowhere to get food in Azqueta. He's asked. Even if there were, he can't step out and run the risk of missing Ginny. He needs to talk to her about what happened last night. Who else can he discuss it with? The *hospitaleiro* is already giving him suspicious looks and not just because he knocked over a large potted cactus before he passed out on the loveseat.

The bedroom door finally opens and a spindly middle-aged woman emerges. It is hard for Daniel to believe she has the muscle mass to walk the Camino. Her limbs look like twigs that might snap at any moment. Between that and her deep mahogany tan, she bears a startling resemblance to the beef jerky in his pocket.

"Excuse me," Daniel says, standing.

"Yes?" the twig woman answers. Her stiff accent is laced with a faint hostility. He recognizes her now. She had poked her head out the bedroom door when he checked in the night before, asked what time it was, first in German and then in English. He had ignored her, too scattered inside his own mind to form an answer in any language. She obviously has chosen not to forget the slight.

"I was wondering if you might see if my friend is still sleeping?" Daniel asks her, plastering his best winning smile on a face lined with stress. "Her name is Ginny. She has a backpack same as mine." Daniel indicates his turquoise pack still propped against the couch.

"There are no more women left," the German lady says as she picks up her hiking poles from a sizable unglazed urn at the top of the stairs. For a second, Daniel thinks she means in general. As if all of her sex has disappeared off the face of the earth, or at least off of the Camino. She misinterprets his reaction as a challenge.

"Check for yourself," she says, indicating the open door to the bedroom.

Daniel walks over and has a look inside. There are four beds in the small room. Only one appears slept in. The others have rough grey blankets pulled up tight on the bed frames, the pillows undented. *Somebody must have made up the other bed*, Daniel thinks although that doesn't make a lot of sense. The sheets were stripped and washed daily in the *albergues*, not for aesthetics, but to avoid the much-feared spread of bedbugs. It was redundant to make your bed.

Daniel rushes out of the bedroom and catches the German woman as she is making her way down the stairs. "When did she leave?" he asks her, leaning over the banister.

"When did who leave?" she says, looking up from the landing, annoyed at being delayed.

"The other woman who was with you, in the ladies' quarters. She came in late last night with me."

"There is no other woman. Only me," she says, turning to continue down to the ground floor. He listens as her hiking poles click away like a metronome on the hard tiled steps.

Daniel returns to the bedroom and looks again, scanning the floor, the deeply recessed window. He checks under all three of the beds as if Ginny were a misplaced sock. Nothing. He finds another bird's nest built above the inner door frame with two black swallow silhouettes painted on either side. They are rendered shadows of the real thing he had imagined in the common room this morning.

Leaning against the wall, he feels the cool adobe plaster against his temple. The angle gives him a new perspective out the window. He sees the sharp edges of black metal steps hugging the outer wall of the *albergue*. Stepping out to the hallway, he tries the door that he previously assumed led to another bedroom. Opening it, he is hit by the bracing freshness of the outdoors. A fire escape criss-crosses its way down to spill out in a side alley connected to the main street. He braces himself with one hand in the doorway, looks out across the rooftops of Azqueta to where the Camino exits the village and disappears in the distance. He tries to picture Ginny darting out into the night without him, vanishing into the air where the sky meets the trail, with that dark figure floating above the fields behind her.

Like the shadow of a bird in flight.

*

The road to Villamayor de Monjardin is even steeper than the road to Azqueta. Daniel's shirt is damp with sweat despite the chill of the morning. On the outskirts of the village, he passes by a thirteenth-century pilgrim fountain no longer in use. Under a set of impressive double arches, the water stagnates in a murky pool. A white film floats on top and the odour is not a pleasant one. It doesn't improve his headache.

Walking alone with only his own thoughts, he cannot help but become obsessive. He turns over the events of the last few days in his mind, like numbers to a combination lock. *There must be some logical sequence to explain things*, he thinks. Mistaking Ginny for Petra or hearing screams that aren't there, both of those could be written off to tired eyes or a suggestible mind.

Seeing the wretched creature in the farmer's field, though, now that's a whole other level of madness. Daniel wants to blame the wine fountain, dehydration, fatigue, anything for that. Anything, that is, except the failing of his own mind. And yet, that laboured breathing in the corn, the tongue bloated and black in his flashlight beam. He could have sworn to it. As he would have sworn to what he'd seen hovering on the outskirts of Azqueta just before he slammed the door of the *albergue* shut behind him last night.

He can't imagine Ginny going back out into the night after seeing that half-human thing following them. And she must have seen something. She was obviously frightened. In his experience, a woman doesn't normally repeat the phrase "Oh shit" over and over like a mantra unless something is definitely out of sorts. Why did she leave the *albergue* without him? And what if something had happened to her? He'd overheard a conversation that morning in the *albergue* about a woman who'd gone missing on the trail. Perhaps what they'd seen was somehow responsible. It sends his worry up another notch.

All of this is coursing through his mind as he comes to the gates of Monjardin. Above him, a high rock wall spirals around the conical peak that holds the ruins of the village *castillo*. Daniel can just make out the remains of the castle keep from his vantage point as he mounts a wide stone staircase to the village square. He wonders who the Castilians had sought to keep out with the sharpened rock edges notched into the top of the defensive walls. *Who*, he thinks — *or what*. When he cranes his neck to get a better look, a fresh burst of pain blossoms in his brain. He still hasn't gotten that coffee he needs, or any food, and as he tops the staircase to the *Plaza Mayor*, it doesn't look like he's going to get either. Everything is closed until lunchtime. He has missed the morning rush. The plaza is abandoned, except for a man with a painter's cap sitting at a round zinc table in the sun. He is eating a large banana.

"Hellooo, Daniel," the Dutchman calls out to him. He takes one last bite and then tucks the banana peel away into the zippered pocket of his hip belt. Daniel hadn't realized the Dutch were so careful with their trash. Must be the influence of his Canadian friend, a people more likely to crush a hand in a bench vice than litter.

"Hello, Rob," Daniel calls back, relieved to see him. There are times when it is good to be alone on the Camino. This morning isn't one of them. He waits while Rob straps on his backpack and walks over to join Daniel in the middle of the square.

"Here, I cannot finish this." Rob holds out a large coffee in a travel cup to Daniel, mostly full. There is a God.

"Thanks," he says, taking a deep swallow. It burns going down but tastes brilliant. Black and highly caffeinated, just the way he likes it when he needs to clear his head.

"Where's the Canadian sister-friend?" Daniel asks, trying to stay casual, as the two walk in the direction of a yellow arrow painted on the cobblestones. It takes them toward an alleyway off the square.

"Oh, her," Rob says, shrugging his shoulders. "She has left the Way to be with her family." He leans on his wooden walking staff, a piece of leather at the top looped around his wrist. "Some are like this here. A princess pilgrim." He gives Daniel a wink.

Serious pilgrims make fun of the ones who can't make it on the Camino, people who hire a service to carry their backpacks or who are too squeamish to stay at the *albergues* and opt for hotels. Even Daniel had spent a night in an upscale *casa rural* with a turndown service once after a particularly difficult day. He hopes the Dutchman didn't see him.

"That's a shame," Daniel says, identifying with the sudden loss of a walking partner. He watches for the next waymark and finds it placed high on the brick wall of a private home built off the alley. The sign has a bright yellow scallop shell with ribs fanning out from the base on a blue background. Someone told him the direction of the ribs points toward the cathedral in Santiago, but he's not convinced. Rob has now pulled a chocolate-covered Danish and another banana out of his backpack for him. The man is like a walking grocery store. Daniel accepts each offer of food with gratitude. The roar in his head retreats with each well-appreciated bite.

"And what about your Ginny?" Rob asks him, turning the subject around.

"Don't even ask," Daniel says.

Rob nods his head as if agreeing to something, and perhaps he is. The two men exchange a silence that speaks volumes on the complexity of women. Crossing onto a rural access road, they leave the village behind.

"Rob, would you mind if I asked you something?" Daniel begins. He needs to talk to someone about this.

"Ask away, my friend. Although if you are wondering if I sell drugs because I am from the Netherlands, the answer is no. A man asked me this in the queue for the showering once. It offends me."

Daniel thinks of the Spanish guys and decides offensiveness in a shower lineup knows few limits on the Camino.

"In all fairness, I hadn't been thinking of that, but good to know," he tells the Dutchman.

"Then what is it you wish to ask?"

Daniel hesitates for a moment then dives in. "Have you been seeing anything strange-like — on the Camino?"

"In what way strange?"

"Something not easily explained." He can't believe he is saying this. "A manifestation, for example." Daniel is not sure if the Dutchman will understand the rarely used English word, but he surprises him.

"Do you mean like these people who see the image of the Virgin burnt into their breakfast toast?" Rob asks.

"Uh, I would say no," Daniel says, relaxing a bit. The Dutchman has that effect.

"This is good. I am not liking believers in such things. They are too religious for me," Rob says.

Daniel agrees. Growing up in the country that he did, Catholicism is a big part of who he is, but he wears his faith like a comfortable coat that has seen him through a few winters. Anything flashier than that, his granny would have said, smacked of grandstanding or even worse — Presbyterianism.

"I mean more like an apparition," Daniel tells him. This time he has stumped Rob with the unlikely word. "A ghost," he clarifies, feeling like an idiot.

"Oh, a ghost. Boo, and like this. I understand. Now this is something the Dutch know something about. Much more than drugs." Rob glances over at Daniel and asks, "Do you know of *De Vliegende Hollander*?"

Daniel doesn't speak Dutch, but he took some German in secondary school, and the two languages are similar. He makes an educated guess.

"The Flying Dutchman?" he asks.

"Yes," Rob answers, impressed. "In the Netherlands we don't have just one ghost but a ship full of them."

Daniel doesn't know what he would do if he had to deal with an entire boat crew of what he saw last night. He is not interested in finding out. "Isn't the Flying Dutchman after being a harbinger of doom?" Daniel asks him. He knows the legend. Any sailor sighting the ghost ship would soon find himself sleeping with the fishes, literally.

"Yes, doom, but more than this," Rob explains. "If asked, the crew of *De Vliegende Hollander* will send messages."

"To who?" Daniel asks. Then wonders if he is setting a poor example in English grammar.

"To the dead, or perhaps to the living because you may soon be dead," Rob says, smiling.

"Aye," Daniel says, mulling this over. "But surely the crew is being punished? Forced to sail forever, never making port. Why would they trouble themselves with the sending of messages?"

"Even the damned need a purpose. Don't you think, Daniel?"

Daniel doesn't know what to think. He's not sure how the Flying Dutchman relates to his situation. It is, after all, just a myth. But the story passes the time, two people shortening the road, as his grandfather had said.

"Surely," he says. Though Daniel is honestly sure of nothing. Feeling unmoored from reality, like the fabled ship set adrift, he is circling an endless course around what happened last night, just as he does around the day of Petra's death.

Rob hands him his wooden staff to hold and reaches inside the front of his jacket. After a bit of searching, he pulls out a burnished copper heart a little bigger than the average coat button.

"My wife gave this to me before I left for the Way. It stays on like this." Rob shows him how the small magnetic back piece holds the metal heart in place on the breast pocket of his shirt. "It is to protect me, my health, my spirit."

Daniel hasn't seen a heart like this before, but he has an uncle who swears by his magnetic copper bracelet for his golfer's elbow. It was the kind of jewellery that was supposed to ward off everything from high blood pressure to hemorrhoids. He was not sure where you were supposed to wear it for the latter.

"Does it work, so?" he asks Rob.

"It does not matter if it works," Rob tells him, putting the heart back under his jacket, taking back his walking staff.

"What matters is my wife believes that it works. And so, I am protected, by something I cannot see or understand. Do you think this is any stranger than finding the Virgin in breakfast toast?"

"A little less strange."

"I agree," Rob says, and they share a smile. "In any case, the world is full of curious things," Rob says, adjusting his cap, looking out at the long trail spread out in front of them.

As far as they can see, well-ordered rows of plucked vineyards line either side of path. This is the beginning of Rioja country. The fall air here still holds the heady scent of a few wizened grapes left behind on the bare web of vines.

"Do you see the ghost of your wife, Daniel?"

It takes him a moment to realize what the Dutchman has just said.

"No. I mean, I don't believe so," he stammers, not sure of the answer. And then, "How were you knowing about my wife?" He is fascinated more than suspicious.

"I sometimes have a way of knowing such things," Rob tells him.

"Curious things, so?" Daniel asks.

"Curious things," Rob confirms.

Daniel goes along with this. Maybe Rob had met up with Ginny and she had told him about the ashes. He wants to ask, but decides to let it go. After all, he might have given his widower status away himself without knowing it. There are those who are highly astute at reading other people. He can imagine the Dutchman would be one of them, his empathy that well-developed.

They skirt the sinking rubble of a ruined agricultural outbuilding. The Dutchman reaches down and picks up a small stone piece that has fallen onto the trail. He walks ahead to a cairn set up at the crossroads. The stones are piled next to a display case filled with aged flowers in a dusky vase. Daniel stands a respectful distance away though he can still see the two dates separated by a dash etched into the glass. Birth and death.

"We all are having our ghosts, Daniel," Rob says, as he stoops to place the stone at the base of the cairn. "The question is not if they exist." He rises and leans into his walking stick with both hands as he turns to address Daniel. "It is what message do they bring."

The two start back on the rolling path that cuts through an infinite earthen carpet of spent vineyards. When Daniel passes the cairn, he crosses himself without thinking.

✳

They stop to eat their lunch in a grassy spot just outside of Los Arcos. Daniel has a huge cheese *bocadillo* that he bought from a take-away in the busy market town. The woman behind the counter had used a whole stick of bread to make it then warmed it in the oven. The grease from the rich, tangy *manchego* soaks through the paper it is wrapped in. It tastes better than anything he has eaten yet on the Camino, and he savours it slowly.

Rob has finished his packed lunch already, a picnic reminiscent of the day Daniel and Ginny had met him at *Santa Maria de Eunate*. He had insisted on sharing his fruit again. Daniel initially protested then ended up taking an apple anyway. Now the Dutchman lies under a wide-trunked tree, relaxed in the grass. He uses his backpack as a pillow, gazing directly up into the blue of the sky, laughing lightly under his breath.

"You don't find this funny?" he asks Daniel, hands laced beneath his head. Directly across from them is a cemetery with an ironwork entranceway. The arch is inscribed with Spanish words. "You understand what this means, yes?" he says, gesturing to the inscription. When Daniel doesn't respond, Rob consults the Google translator on his phone and reads aloud the English result. "You are what I was, and will be what I am now." He bursts into fresh laughter as he drops the phone back in the grass.

"I reckon I'm not in the mood," Daniel says, apologizing. He takes the last bite of his sandwich, resists the urge to lick his fingers.

"But this is the most depressing thing I have ever heard," Rob says, wiping his eyes, still chuckling.

Daniel had heard the Dutch had a peculiar sense of humour. He'd watched a subtitled film once from the Netherlands with Petra and hadn't realized the dark story of a family caught in an avalanche was a comedy until she told him afterward.

But there is more to his attitude than a lack of appreciation for Rob's black humour. He has made the conscious decision to put last night behind him. He needs to focus on what he's here for. To get serious, or he's going to lose more than his mind. When a slight wind threatens to blow the greasy sandwich paper away, he wraps up his apple core and throws it all in a plastic bag. "I think I'll go back to Los Arcos to light a candle," he says, hoping Rob won't take his departure the wrong way.

"For your wife?" Rob asks. The Dutchman doesn't sit up, just lies still with his hands folded across his chest.

"Yes," Daniel says. "Perhaps I'll see you in Torres del Rio." This is where Daniel plans to stop and stay over for the night. Rob hasn't shared his plans.

"Perhaps you will," Rob says, closing his eyes now like he might take a nap. "Goodbye, Daniel," he says. "Good luck with your ghosts."

"*Slán*, Rob," Daniel says, reaching for his backpack, then putting on his hat. Rob doesn't ask for a translation of the Irish word for goodbye. Some phrases are understood no matter where you hail from.

After taking a few steps in the direction of town he turns around, walking backwards as he speaks. "And Rob …"

"You're welcome," the Dutchman says without opening his eyes. The breeze blows a piece of grass into his beard. He leaves it there, content.

＊

It is only a couple of minutes to walk back to Los Arcos. Daniel's breaking his own rule about never going back on the Camino though he doesn't feel too badly about it. It was great walking with the Dutchman, but he needs to be alone with himself for a while. Alone with Petra. He still hasn't found the right spot to spread her ashes. Then again, he's not sure how hard he has been looking.

The parish church borders on the main square. As Daniel approaches the entrance, he can see a man in a worn green suit standing outside. A long white beard rests on his chest. Keen eyes betray his age as far younger than one would suspect. A rolltop backpack sits broken down next to him, hung with the white scallop shell that marks him as a pilgrim. The iron-bound exterior doors of the church are opened wide, but the man's dusty felt hat is upturned on the concrete stoop. It blocks the way in. You can't pass without paying the toll.

Daniel has heard about the homeless that walk the Camino. They stay in many of the *albergues* for free or a modest *donativo*. Spain's unemployment rate has been shockingly high since the recent downturn. Many people are victims of the country's tanking economy. This man appears to be one of them, walking the long road to Santiago just to put a roof over his head each night. Daniel reaches into his pocket for a few euros but finds nothing but the twenties he got out of the bank machine in Estella. He digs deeper and actually pulls out lint.

With embarrassment, he steps over the hat and into the doorway, trying not to look at the man or at his fedora sparsely filled with change. As a result, he smacks his shin on the door jamb and starts off his visit to the Church of Santa Maria with a string of swear words in the vestibule. If the homeless pilgrim is off-put by this, he doesn't say so, only stares at the ground, his long, carefully trimmed beard tucked covertly under his chin. Behind it, he is probably laughing his ass off.

Once recovered, Daniel stands up from rubbing his shin and starts down a poorly lit hallway leading to the sanctuary. It takes awhile for his eyes to adjust, but eventually he is aware of musty woollen tapestries that line the walls on either side. Each one depicts one of the stations of the cross, Christ heavily burdened with a heavy wooden crucifix in most of them. When Daniel reaches the last station, he realizes only seven of the fourteen images are depicted. That means the tapestries are probably pre-seventeenth century. He can't remember why the Catholic Church decided to increase the number of stations of Christ's agony in the last few hundred years. Not enough suffering, he gathers.

He exits the corridor into a small narthex with a marble font mounted on the wall. When he dips his fingers in the holy water he leaves a piece of lint behind in the basin. Fishing it out, he touches his forehead with the furry drops then steps inside the nave.

As is the case with many churches of the Baroque era, the wall behind the altar looks as though lava from a gold volcano has erupted and hardened on every available surface. The overall effect appears cheap to the modern eye though it surely would not have been. Local nobles made hefty donations to finance both the precious metals and the artwork for a church like this one. This got them not only bragging rights and a good pew, but also a shortened term in purgatory, sometimes even a free pass if the priest was feeling generous.

Daniel looks closely and can see some classical as well as Romanesque features in the interior, meaning the church has had several incarnations over its long lifetime. His first work as a civil engineer had been in Italy and France, restoring architectural relics like this one to their former glory. Or at least to the point where they wouldn't collapse on the people inside. Petra had been there on a gap year after university, studying religious art. They had met when she couldn't get a pay phone to work and he had offered up a coin. Life is such a matter of chance. It feels so long ago. Ancient history, like the Roman columns he can still see hiding inside the open door of the sacristy.

Electronic candles light up the altar rail. As he approaches them, he remembers he has no change to put in the metal slot to turn one on for Petra. He wonders briefly if the homeless guy would make change. The fake candles flicker, seemingly to mock him.

He sits down in the front pew feeling useless, unable to do anything for the living or the dead with his lack of small change. The artwork of the *reredos* behind the altar towers above him, its subjects either in abject suffering or blissful adoration depending on their position in the Christ story. A painted wooden statue of the Virgin Mary, her sacred child on her lap, smiles benevolently from her section of the screen. Daniel uses his secondary-school Latin to decipher an inscription written underneath the two of them. "I am black, but I am beautiful." Looking back up at the blue-eyed Mary and her pale skin, he figures he must have made a mistake. Although, a *morena* or dark Virgin was probably closer to the truth if you looked at the racial makeup of Nazareth at the time of Christ. Daniel had seen a black Madonna once before in Switzerland, but they were rare. White Christianity preferred porcelain-skinned mothers of God and favoured Jesuses that looked like West Coast surfer dudes taking a year off college.

"They painted her white." A voice comes from behind Daniel.

He turns around to see a woman sitting in the pew. He hadn't noticed her when he came in, but she must have been there all along. He would have heard her sit down.

"The Virgin Mary," she continues, when he doesn't respond immediately. "She used to be black, *el Virgen Morena*, but they painted her and the baby white in the 1940s."

Daniel turns back to review the small but exquisite statue. He gets up, his mouth held in a tight line. The gold-plated altarpiece looms above him, while the filaments in the fake candles crackle faintly with electricity. He moves into the woman's pew and leans in, whispering fiercely in her ear. It is the question he has wanted to ask ever since he woke up this morning and found her gone.

"Where the hell have you been, Ginny?"

✳

Passing through the *Portal de Castillo* out of Los Arcos, they are still arguing.

"I don't know what you're talking about," she says, not for the first time.

"Cop yourself on," Daniel says to her. "You saw someone running across the path, same as me."

"I did, but it was just someone fooling around. I don't know what the big deal is." Ginny walks and talks quickly, kicking up gravel.

"The big deal is that you were ready to shit yer caks. And so was I," Daniel says. This isn't even an Irish saying. Daniel picked it up when he worked construction one summer in Newcastle-on-Tyne in northeast England. He doesn't usually resort to such grand displays of coarse cultural idiom, but he's upset.

"I was just tired," she says, sounding like she still is.

"Is that why you were after running?" he asks, taking her elbow, stopping her from walking on.

"I was running because you were. You frightened me, Daniel." She adds lightly, "You're sort of frightening me now."

Daniel sees his hand holding her arm, becomes aware of the tense set of his jaw, the threat of his body. He feels a hot bloom of shame. He's never been the type of man to be rough with a woman.

"Sorry," he says, releasing her. Neither of them says anything. They start walking again. When they pass the cemetery, Rob is long gone. The wind has already erased the flattened grass where he took his catnap.

After a few minutes, Ginny breaks the silence. "It was just the wine and the night playing tricks on you."

"I know what I saw," Daniel says emphatically, but now he is no longer sure.

"Do you want to hear about Torres del Rio?" she tries. "They have a Knights Templar church there like the *Santa Maria de Eunate*. It's even smaller, but the original ..."

"I don't want another feckin' history lesson, all right?" Daniel shouts, stopping on the trail, surprising himself. His anger carries on the wind between them, whistling through her. She closes her eyes, as if to absorb the force of it, then opens them, annoyed.

"Listen, Daniel. I just went on to the next town, like we said." She's trying to talk him down, despite her crossness with him — a gift many women seem to possess in abundance, in his experience. They should use women more often for hostage negotiation.

"We did say we were going to Villamayor de Monjardin?" she says. "Didn't we?" She waits for him to answer.

After a few beats, he does. "How can you remember the feckin' names of all those places. I forget them all once I've passed through." Except Azqueta. It'll take awhile for him to forget Azqueta.

"Look, Daniel. I like walking with you." She glances down at her feet and then back up at him, shielding her eyes from the sun, no saucy baseball cap today. The light freckles across her nose set to multiply. "But I've been walking for a long time without anyone." She hesitates like she wants to say more, but doesn't.

"You shouldn't have gone off on your own like that," he says in a normal voice, more in control now. "It wasn't safe." This is the true source of his anger. He'd been worried about her. He expects her to be touched by his concern. He couldn't be more wrong.

"Is that what this is all about?" Ginny demands, her own fury starting to loosen. "This 'little woman' thing again, unable to protect herself alone on the big bad Camino?"

"Sure, I didn't mean ..."

"Because I tell you what, buddy, I am fully capable of walking the Way by myself."

She leans down and tightens the lace of one hiking boot. Daniel watches as she ties a fierce double knot.

"I saved for two years for this trip," she says, standing up again. "Piled up my vacation time, paid someone to take care of my damn cat." She pokes a furious finger in his chest.

Daniel has seen his sister in a state like this on occasion. Not usually directed at him, thanks be to God.

"And then you come along with all this bullshit trying to scare me." She yanks the hiking poles from the side of her backpack, almost breaking the strap.

Daniel gets out of her way, afraid he may be on the receiving end of one of the poles' pointy ends.

"There is no way anybody or anything is going to stand in my way of finishing this — of getting to Santiago," she says, leaning into him, so close he can see the flecks in her hazel eyes. Then she turns and storms off and away from him, her hiking poles flying in front of her in a blur.

"Aw, don't be like that, Ginny," Daniel says.

"Piss off," she calls back over her shoulder.

"Sure, I didn't mean it like that."

She speeds up and around the corner of the next bend in the trail, kicking up dust behind her.

It mustn't have rained here like it did when I came out of the Pyrenees, he thinks. The ground here is bone dry. He realizes that they have walked straight through into a different climate zone. This is what Daniel thinks about as he watches her leave him — the weather and the trail — rather than wishing she wouldn't go.

✳

They are all gathered around a table at the local hotel in Torres del Rio, a Spaniard, two Austrians, some Americans, and Daniel. There's a young pretty French girl, too. Daniel had thought she was from France, but it turns out she is Québécoise. For a country with a population less than the state of California, those Canadians were bloody everywhere.

The wine flows freely, but Daniel stops at one glass. He learned from that fountain. The others are already getting loud and animated with the *vino tinto*, a delectable red wine you can buy in this region for less than the price of water. None of them are staying at the hotel, including him. They all have bunk beds at the *albergue* across the street, where they paid for the supper at the hotel restaurant when they checked in. Each has a pilgrim dinner voucher for a meal that will probably consist of an overdone piece of pork and a smattering of soggy french fries. Coming from a race of people that lived through their share of famines, Daniel doesn't care much what is served, as long as there are potatoes.

The French girl gently touches his forearm with long tapered fingers, leaning in close to say something. She smells earthy and warm, a faint hint of smoke in her hair. He makes sparse conversation; although, later he will not remember about what. Looking out the broad window at the front of the restaurant, he watches the late-day pilgrims trudge up the brick-paved road where the Camino runs outside the door of the hotel. The light is fading, and the pilgrims appear like sepia versions of themselves, walking with heavy steps up the incline.

He is watching for Ginny, focusing his eyes across the room into the increasing dark as each tired shape moves past the window. He looks for her baseball cap or the distinctive gait of her walk. He scans for a silhouette that matches what he knows of her, soft curves blending with hard lines of muscled determination.

He keeps having to apologize to the French girl, asking her to repeat what she is saying. It is not the first time. The Spaniard across from him reaches across the table for his attention.

"And you, my friend, will you go to Finisterre?" he asks, his large square teeth bared broadly. The French girl drops her hand from his arm and grins in return. Daniel has never seen people smile as much as on the Camino.

"Finisterre?" Daniel asks. He has missed this conversation as well. They are going to start thinking he is partially deaf. "It's on the coast, I understand." Daniel has heard of the Spanish beach town. The name means "end of the world."

"It is only a three-day walk from Santiago. The original destination of the Camino. They worshipped the sun gods there long before Saint James." The Spaniard looks around the table, knowing he has the floor. "Some still do."

"The most western point of Spain, is it?" Daniel asks, always thirsty for facts.

"The worshippers thought it was, but they were wrong," he says. "But it is beautiful there. Much better than the walk into Santiago, filled with fat people and graffiti."

Daniel has heard this about the final stretch before the Holy City. That it would be overrun with churro vendors and souvenir hawkers. It was said to have a bit of a carnival feel, like Coney Island for Catholics.

"I would love to go to Finisterre," the French girl says, lifting one perfectly arched eyebrow.

"Then it is settled," the Spaniard booms, pounding his fist on the table. "We will all go." He orders another two bottles of *vino tinto* for the table, as he strikes up further conversation with the French girl. She beams at him with wine-stained lips, leaving Daniel to his distracted mood. He reckons a woman can only fathom so much of a man's inattention.

Excusing himself, he gets up and goes to the bar to get a Coke. When the bartender pops the tab, he glances out the window to the top of the street, sees a humble stone church. It is shaped like an octagon.

"Is that a Knights Templar church?" Daniel asks the bartender.

"*No entiendo*," the bartender says, obviously fed up with tourists who refuse to learn Spanish.

But Daniel knows that it is. He recognizes the octagon shape, just like *Santa Maria de Eunate*. He also recognizes the shape of the person sitting on the ground outside it.

Bolting out the door, he leaves the unimpressed bartender and his Coke. He slows as he approaches the church, afraid to spook her. He is trying to make amends, not convince Ginny he is the madman she has probably decided he is. As he gets closer, the seated shape takes on details in the fading daylight. A shabby green suit, a white beard, an old fedora hat held out in sunburnt hands.

"*Buen Camino, Americano,*" the man says. His missing teeth make the words come out with gummy consonants. Daniel stares at him dumbfounded. He had been so sure. Maybe he needs glasses. A weak lamp turns on above the church door.

"*No Americano. Irlandes,*" he says, finally finding his Spanish. He doesn't know why it is important to make the distinction to this man. To let him know where he is truly from. But somehow it seems important to be brutally honest in this moment, as the sun begins to disappear behind the octagonal church and the man smiles up at him with his young old eyes. Daniel sees the upturned hat up close now, dark with sweat around the band. It is empty. He drops his dinner voucher in it and walks back to the *albergue*, no longer hungry.

✳

When Daniel falls asleep that night, he sees Petra lying in the tall grass like the Dutchman. He is leaning over her, playing with her hair. He closes his eyes to heighten the sense of touching the rich strands, buries his mouth in the nape of her neck. She brings her lips up to brush his ear, whispering something, but is cut off with a rough inhalation of breath. He raises his head and opens his eyes to find that she is choking, and it is not Petra after all.

It is the figure from the cornfield, and he sees his own hands surround her throat, strangling her. Choking off the message she wants to give him.

CHAPTER 5
Torres del Rio to Logroño

DOWN A FRESHLY SWEPT side street in Viana, Daniel Skypes his sister over a wide-mouthed cup of *café con leche* and a cooked brunch. The day is warm and he sits outside, close to the doorway of the cantina so he can still catch the free Wi-Fi signal.

"What are you eating?" Angela asks.

"Tortilla," he says, lifting the oval ceramic plate up for her to see through the video feed.

"Sure, that looks like an omelette."

"'Tis," he tells her, shovelling another forkful into his mouth for effect. He is trying to convince her he feels more normal than he does.

"Are you certain you're okay?"

"I am sure, Angela."

"You'd tell me if you were feeling poorly, Daniel?"

"Jesus, Angela, will you lay off," he tells her, not really snapping, but coming close.

"All right, all right," she says. "No need to give out to me. I'm just the long-suffering sister, you know. Taking your phone messages and doing your dirty work."

"You were born for the dirty work, so you are, Angie," he says, teasing, trying to make up for his earlier shortness.

He props the smartphone against his coffee mug so he can have both hands free to finish his tortilla. "Now, what's this business about Gerald?"

"It's not him. It's his wife, Cynthia. She's been at me three times now asking for you to ring her."

Angela never had much time for Daniel's business partner or his wife. The couple had asked her once over dinner if she was a lesbian. She was, of course, but she didn't fancy being queried about it between salad courses.

"It's probably about the paperwork for the sale, Daniel. Honestly, I don't know why you didn't take care of it before you left."

But of course, they both know why he didn't take care of it before. For the same reason, he has a half-installed wet bar in the family room. His procrastination is driving Gerald around the bend. The money they are being offered by Triton Corporate is enough to set them both up for a very long time. Enough to rejuvenate his father's failing farming equipment, maybe even to expand, ensuring another five hundred years of Kennedys on the land. Angela had confided in him that they lost quite a bit of equity when his father's dairy herd had to be culled due to one cow with BSE, the lethal mad cow disease. His father was cagey about how much of a hit he had taken, and Daniel is beginning to wonder if his father's anxiousness for him to come home has less to do with not selling the farm and more to do with saving it.

"I still don't understand why Cynthia would be wanting me."

"Maybe she's wondering if they have gluten free on the Camino."

"Now, Angie ..."

Cynthia was a nice enough woman, but not Angela's type. Petra had called her a "yoga mom." Daniel's still not too sure what this means, except maybe that you take all your own food everywhere.

"I don't know why, but would you please ring her? The woman's in a right state."

Daniel borrows a pencil from the waitress as he settles his bill, starts writing the cell number for Gerald's wife on the back of his receipt. He's inscribing the last number when he decides something.

"Listen," he says. "I may have found a place."

"A place for what?"

"A place for Petra," he says. "Finisterre. It's on the coast."

"Is that on the way to Santiago?"

"No, it's three or four days' walk from there. I thought —"

"You're saying people keep walking after Santiago? As if five hundred miles isn't enough. What are you people, daft?"

"Finisterre means 'end of the world,'" he tells her.

"Well, that's what you'll be wishing for if you don't get home here soon. Dad and Mom are in a right panic." She softens a bit. "It sounds nice, Danny, but the family need to know when to expect you. Dad's getting ready for the calving season, and he doesn't know whether to get a hired man or …"

"I know, Angela. I just need to take care of this first, so." He is looking past the propped up phone to the main thoroughfare when he sees the flash of a familiar ponytail walk by in the crowd. "Listen, Angela, I got to get going," he says, grabbing his backpack from the spare metal chair beside him. It makes a loud scraping sound on the cobblestones as he pulls it toward him, almost falling over.

"But you still haven't told me —"

With a click, he cuts his sister off, feeling bad only for a moment. He rounds the corner of the alleyway and gets back onto the main Camino route through town. Uphill, he has to work to catch up to Ginny. He doesn't want to lose her in the twists and turns of the narrow streets, or among the locals who seem to move like glaciers on the sidewalk. He could call out to her but doesn't. Instead, he works to bridge the distance between them until the cobblestones open onto pavement and they enter Viana's large main square. A Gothic brick church takes up the entire far end. A stone-columned *feunte* with four flowing spigots sits in its tall shadow in the centre. When Ginny stops there to fill up her water bottle, he sees his chance.

"Ginny," he says cautiously, standing behind her but not too close. She doesn't turn around.

"Hello, Daniel," she says, the clipped words her only reaction to him. Otherwise, she keeps filling her water bottle as though he isn't there.

"I saw you pass by."

"I saw you, too," Ginny says, removing the plastic bottle from the stream of water, more of a dribble really. If the state of water quality matches the plumbing, she's in trouble.

"Are you sure that water is all right?" he asks her, watching the sluggish flow out of the rusty spigot.

"Still trying to take care of me?" she asks, screwing the cap on and popping the top before taking a good long drink from the bottle. He watches the rhythmic contractions move down the column of her throat as she swallows. She wipes her mouth with the back of her hand and smiles at him like a cat that got at the cream, even if that cream might contain E. coli.

"You going in?" she says, gesturing toward the overbearing church at the end of the square. There are stunted trees with naked branches planted at intervals around it, like prisoners held behind a high fence of stone pillars and wrought iron railing. The only means of escape, or entry, is a gated archway visible down the north side of the building.

"Okay," he says.

"Okay," says Ginny, nodding, as if a larger agreement has been settled.

"I gather we're not talking about it," he says as they walk together toward the edge of the square, down the external cloister to the church's side entranceway.

"No, we're not."

She runs her open hand along the iron fencing as she walks by, making a soft vibration with her fingertips each time they strike the metal rails. Daniel can see flying buttresses running along the top tier of the building at the far end. Knows they were built to keep the walls from collapsing under the pressure of high arches and vaulted ceilings. He wants to point them out to her but manages to keep his mouth shut. Not the time for an architectural lesson, he senses.

As they turn in the gate, Daniel sees a white stone block laid into the grey pavement. The reflected glare from the sun directly overhead forces them to shield their eyes in order to read what is written on it. He may not know Spanish, but he can translate the year in Roman numerals inscribed along the bottom, 1507. He also recognizes the name engraved in capitals at the top.

"Cesare Borgia," he reads. "Lovely family, I hear." He inspects the bronze-studded doors of the church held open by heavy black chain, thinks about the infamous Borgias mounting the stone steps and passing through into Mass, Spain and Italy's original crime family. "Your man Cesare not only murdered his own brother but bedded his sister, along with half the prostitutes in Rome."

"Being the illegitimate son of Pope Alexander VI has its perks, I suppose," Ginny says, not to be outdone. "I heard he even ran an orgy in the papal palace, put on performances of naked gymnastics there."

"Fair dues to him," Daniel says. "I understand they were after giving out prizes." He is eager as always to tell what he knows, but then worries about the inappropriateness of complimenting a man on his debauchery. He backtracks. "I reckon a lot of those stories are a bit dodgy. Male fantasy meets legend, or what have you."

"The evil thoughts of men?" Ginny asks him.

"More like the Renaissance's version of internet porn."

"Same thing," she says, walking across the memorial stone, dismissing in one step the most feared of the Borgia bloodline. "Anyway, I'm not here for him," she says. "Or for the evil thoughts of men." She opens the door and motions to him. "Let's go have a look around."

Inside is the vaulted ceiling Daniel had anticipated from the buttresses outside. The massive stone ribs span out like a giant arachnid above a three-storey altarpiece filled with polychrome statues overlooking the nave. He can see Saint James depicted on the right, with his pilgrim staff, *Santiago Peregrino*. This is in sharp contrast to *Santiago Matamoros*, the Islamophobic version, who is typically shown decapitating invading Muslim hordes, a feat he managed despite having died a dozen or so centuries prior to their occupation of Spain.

After giving the altarpiece a quick once-over, Ginny moves down the side aisle toward the ambulatory that runs behind it. Daniel continues to look up, admiring the domes and ellipses that hold up the seven-hundred-year-old roof, the beauty of lateral thrusts and counter-resistance. When he has had his fill of the technical splendour of well-designed applied science, he goes in search of her.

Three side chapels are built behind the round end of the polygon sanctuary. Ginny stands by the railing of the closest one, twisting her body over a low barrier railing trying to get a better look at what is inside. When Daniel gets closer, he realizes she has a smartphone in her outstretched hand, taking pictures. It is the first time he has seen her use it.

"Isn't she awesome?" she says as he comes up behind her.

Daniel sees a statue of a woman central to the chapel. She is bare breasted with a tightly woven skirt down to her ankles.

The gold weave of the skirt criss-crosses her lower body like caramel-coloured scales. She looks like a mermaid with a large crucifix in her hand and a pained expression on her face.

"It's Mary Magdalene," Ginny tells him. "This is her chapel."

Daniel sees the sign on the wall, *Capilla de la Magdalena.* The "other" Mary.

Ginny takes a few more photos and then pockets her smartphone. "She's my favourite," she says.

"Yeah, I have all her hits. Fallen Women of the New Testament. Penitents on Parade."

"Ha ha," Ginny says, overpronouncing the consonants to show her sarcasm. "Actually, there is no real evidence that she was a fallen woman. That's just something Western Christianity created. Makes her racier. The Bible's original pin-up girl."

She's right. Daniel has observed two constants when visiting churches on the Camino: the statue of the Virgin Mary is usually bigger than the one of Jesus; and Mary Magdalene always looks like a tramp.

"Have you always had a thing for her?" he asks.

"No," Ginny says. "I wasn't even raised Catholic. My mother felt any discussion of religion was in poor taste, like passing gas in public."

"That's a shame." Daniel remembers arguing both politics and religion at the supper table with his parents and siblings while growing up. Heated debates that made them all raise their voices and sometimes ended with his dad pounding their long wooden kitchen table in earnest. Daniel still loves the mental fencing of a good argument.

"My family was a bit like the Borgias," Ginny admits, pursing her lips for a moment. "Well, without the sexual depravity." She looks at him directly for the first time since their fight, as if evaluating him, then goes on. "My sister was a bit of a nightmare."

"Was?"

"They caught her trying to strangle me in my crib once."

"Sibling rivalry," Daniel says, thinking of his sister and he, the youngest, teaming up against their two older brothers. He had nicked one of them in the neck with a homemade wooden sword once when he was three. His brother had wailed while their mother pulled the splinters out with tweezers. Daniel had wailed later when she took the sword away.

"Something like that," Ginny says, turning back to the statue. Mary Magdalene sits atop a pedestal under a domed marble roof, surrounded by columns streaked gold and blue. The colours pick up the rich caramel of her reed skirt. "Then again, I was a bit of problem child myself. Spent most of my teens looking for ways to piss off the world."

"Testing the boundaries," Daniel says.

"More like blowing the boundaries off the fucking map," she tells him, with some embarrassment and just a touch of pride. "I had to grow up young, though. Left home when I was sixteen and never went back." A cloud moves across her expression, then floats away. "That's why I love Mary Mag so much," she says, turning to the saint. "She's a woman with a history. Like me. Like the Borgias." She grabs the railing and leans back, making a V with her body and the barrier. Her neck hyperextends, ponytail meeting backpack. She closes her eyes as she stretches.

"I'm sorry about what happened before," Daniel says, watching her. The supple bend of her torso is laid out in front of him like a spring set to pop. As with most men that find themselves admiring a woman, he isn't aware he is staring.

"That's okay, Daniel," she says, pulling herself slowly back to an upright position. She turns to face him again. "You've got a history, too," she says, raising her eyebrows slightly before walking away toward the next chapel.

Mary Magdalene watches Daniel from across the barrier, and they both know that she's right.

✳

They hear the parade before they see it. The buildings in Logroño remind Daniel of Dublin, not very tall, but close together with narrow streets. You can't see anything coming until you're in danger of being run over by it. That's how Daniel and Ginny have come to find themselves blocked at an intersection by a marching band. Young people dance in brightly coloured clothes and wave oversized red-lace fans in the air to the steady beat of drums. It looks like a Spanish rave.

The two are still shocked by the size of the crowd rounding the corner, the loud whistles and drumbeats. They have spent so many days walking in open, empty spaces that it is hard to not feel overwhelmed by the teeming procession.

"Look!" Ginny cries. Raised at least four feet above the crowd are giant papier mâché heads, bobbing and twirling down the street. When Daniel looks closer he sees that they have bodies as well, decked out in elaborate costumes designed to provide the maximum amount of swing when the person hidden underneath spins around.

"Who are the characters supposed to be, do you think?" Ginny asks.

He was about to ask her the same question. There is an old-fashioned bewigged British court judge draped with a beauty queen sash. A traditional Spanish girl surrounded by brilliant orange petticoats that bounce and twirl. A Muslim beauty behind a sheer gold veil that flows to the bottom of her skirts and ripples with her operator's movements. He cannot recognize any of them, unfamiliar as he is with Spain's cultural icons. The only character whose significance Daniel feels he does understand is the monsignor with the black domed hat and long black cassock, made famous during the Spanish Inquisition. He's seen them in Monty Python sketches.

A man slides open a small door below the roped belt of the puppet clergyman and peers out, as if checking in visitors at a speakeasy. Someone in the crowd reaches out and places a cigarette in his mouth, and he takes a long appreciative drag. Smoke spews out from the crotch of the cassock. Daniel makes a mental note to tell Angela about what it was like to see that.

"There's a king and queen," Ginny says, pointing farther up the street.

The stately couple dance less than the others, walking together as if surveying the procession. Ginny steps out into the street to get a better look, not noticing the woman waving a flag on a metal pole. Daniel manages to grab her by the backpack and pull her back just before she is beaned on the head with it. The woman continues waving the broad black-and-red flag in wide hand-over-hand arcs, as though she never even noticed them.

"That was fairly close," he says, still holding on to Ginny's backpack.

"Yeah, no one likes a parade injury. It's such a buzzkill."

When the parade thins out a bit, they join in the procession, enjoying the beat of the music and the mesmerizing "Big Heads," as they later learn the papier mâché figures are called. The crowd, the music, the dancers, they all snake through the city streets with Ginny and Daniel at the tail, the two pilgrims far less colourful and exotic in their dusty hiking boots and beige sun shirts. It is getting hot, not just from the warming trend of this late fall weather but also from the pressing of so many bodies in an enclosed space. The constant beat of the drums is so different than the marching bands they are used to back home, far more tribal than military. The tempo and flight of the dancing red fans pulls the two of them along. Daniel watches Ginny as she bends and sways to the music, lifting her arms above her head, so that her smooth, flat belly shows when her shirt hikes up.

Just as she requested, they have not talked about what happened in Azqueta. He is starting to think he blew the whole thing out of proportion anyway. It probably was just a kid fooling around, with a mask like those Daniel can see all around him in the parade. Maybe they had used one of the Big Heads to make it look like an apparition was floating above the corn, just as they floated the characters above the throngs of people in the parade. He and Ginny had walked almost twenty-five miles that day. He had been so drained and dehydrated that he might have seen an entire chorus of milkmaids lifting skirts in that field. He turns and smiles at Ginny, who is moving side to side with the rhythm of the music. She responds with a gentle hip check when she sees him looking.

"Come on," she says, beckoning him to join her. He gets ready to make excuses, like he has been making for the last year to his family, to his friends, to himself. Then he thinks, *What the hell.*

He grabs her hand in his and holds both their arms high in the air as he dances down the street. He sways and shimmies and hip bumps like a man released. If his friends back home were here, they would rib him for a week for even knowing how to dance like this. And even then, Daniel thinks, as they blend into the throbbing crowd — he still wouldn't let go of her hand.

After several blocks, the frantic drumbeat of the parade starts to get repetitive. Daniel sees a wine bar in a small open plaza off the main street and points it out to Ginny without words. She wouldn't be able to hear him above the music if he spoke. When she nods, they pull out of the crowd, collapsing into two chairs set outside next to a round patio table.

"Those people have more energy than me," he says, pulling out his water bottle, waving down the waiter for a Coke. He needs sugar as well as liquid.

"Well, we *have* walked about fourteen miles today," Ginny says, loosening the laces on her boots and then taking the boots off. She wiggles her toes in her thick wool hiking socks, legs stretched out straight in front of her in a not so elegant but entirely captivating way. Daniel longs to take off his boots as well, but he is afraid of offending with the odour that might be unleashed in the process.

"So, what do you think that was all about then?" he asks her.

"The parade? Damned if I know," she says.

"I thought you were after knowing everything," he says.

"Coca-Cola," the waiter says as he drops a glass tumbler in front of Daniel with a clatter and pours in the black fizzy drink. He then places the can on the table with an air of distaste, as though he has been forced to serve a dead fish.

"Why don't you ask Mr. Sunshine here what the parade is all about," Ginny says.

Daniel tries asking in English, but the waiter just stares at him with an air of distrust. Doesn't even grace him with a "*Que?*" or "*No entiendo.*" Ginny provides Daniel with some basic Spanish words with which to ask his question.

"The parade?" the waiter says, suddenly finding his English. "This is the wine festival, *peregrino*, you are in Rioja country." He says this with the same look of disgust for Daniel as when he served him the Coke.

"I guess it must be a sin not to drink wine during the annual wine festival," Ginny says, grinning.

"Sure, I wouldn't want to contribute to the further blackening of your soul." He turns to the waiter, still standing there looking suspicious. "*Una bottella de vino tinto, por favor*," Daniel tells him. Ginny smiles at his increasing Spanish. "And two glasses," he adds as the waiter walks away.

"*Dos vasos,*" Ginny whispers, giving him the translation.

"*Dos vasos, por favor!*" Daniel calls after the man. The waiter looks back, and then continues to walk away shaking his head.

"I don't believe he likes pilgrims much," Daniel says, taking another long draw on the sweet coolness of the Coke. "Oh, forgive me, I mean *peregrinos,* he's not after liking *peregrinos.*"

"Speak for yourself, I'm a *peregrina,*" Ginny says, leaning back farther in the chair, lifting her face to the sun, eyes closed, as she had leaned back from the railing of Mary Magdalene's chapel.

When the waiter comes back, he asks if they want tapas. Along with its wine, the region is known for these delicious appetizers that line the local bars under glass, like bakery windows. You pick from an array of delectables featuring fresh olives, tangy cheeses, and salty cured meats. Tapas, however, would require the two of them to get up and go inside to select their choices, and neither is up to it. It is strange how a person can walk for so long and then simply cannot walk anymore, as if the body goes on strike. When they refuse the tapas and ask for a menu, the waiter is visibly appalled by their lack of culture. He places the bottle of wine and both glasses in front of Daniel and marches off in a huff.

"Do you think he fancies me a drinker?" Daniel says as he pours a glass of wine for Ginny and pushes it toward her.

"Wouldn't that be a form of racial profiling?" Ginny says.

"Indeed, it would be," he says, filling his own glass and bringing it to his lips. His first thought is that it tastes so much better than the wine fountain. His second thought is that it tastes better than any wine he has ever had. Even in France. No wonder the town has a whole bloody festival for it. "People talk about avoiding stereotypes," he says to Ginny, taking another sip. "But nobody seems to have a problem with assuming I'll be paralytic before noon every Saint Patrick's Day."

"And are you?" Ginny asks, baiting him.

"I come from a family of teetotallers. One year, a friend brought me a six pack of Guinness for Christmas and there were still two of them left come Easter."

"An Irish guy that doesn't really drink," she says.

While Daniel nods, he feels secretly ashamed, thinking about the uncharacteristic hard drinking he had done in the last year and the reason behind it. "We aren't always what people expect us to be," he says, looking across the plaza.

"No, we're not," Ginny says. "I guess that's why we often disappoint people."

"You're not after disappointing me."

"Give me a chance," she says, rolling one sleeve of her T-shirt to reveal a defined shoulder. "Gotta maintain my tan," she says as she rolls up the other one as well. The silver shells of her beaded bracelet catch the sun and seem to set off sparks.

"Where'd you get the bracelet," he asks her. It is a lot less tacky than the ones he has seen in the souvenir shops. He's thinking it would be something his sister would like.

"A little stall in one of the villages," she says, biting her lip. "Were you thinking of buying one for a girl back home?"

"There are no girls back home," he says, knowing what she is really asking.

It all seems so smooth and uncomplicated in the warm sunshine, as though only the two of them exist, him and this pretty girl with the easy laugh. But as with the crowd in the street, Daniel is always aware of the hidden horde that lurks around the corner. He is a penitent, like Mary Magdalene, always waiting for the judgment of his fall.

✳

Hours later when they leave the wine bar, pleasantly filled with the spicy seafood paella they ordered, he will see one of the Big Heads from the parade down an alley off the main street. The Spanish girl with the orange petticoats is slumped against a brick wall, lifeless where a burly young guy with tattoos has discarded her heartlessly on the pavement. Daniel cannot help but stare until the guy looks up at him, wondering what he wants. He and Ginny turn away and move on.

It is late and all the *albergues* are full for the night. They even knock on the doors of some of the *pensiones*, prepared to pay the extra money for upscale accommodation. Everything is at full capacity because of the festival. Ginny sees a *casa rural* ahead that they haven't tried. It looks pricey, not to mention noisy, overlooking an expansive three-tiered fountain and a plaza filled with clamouring party revellers. However, at this point they are getting desperate.

Thankfully, the proprietor of what Petra would have called a B & B speaks English. "There is one room, *peregrino*. You are lucky. I had a cancellation."

How the hell does everyone assume right away we are pilgrims, Daniel thinks. Then he looks at their hiking pants, the backpacks. Who is he kidding?

"Do you have two rooms?" Daniel asks.

The innkeeper scratches his head, thinking. He must have assumed they were a couple.

"Sorry, man, just the one. Fifty euros for the night."

Daniel and Ginny exchange exhausted looks. They both answer together.

"We'll take it."

✳

It is getting dark when the two of them sit on the balcony with their feet hanging over the side. They are on the third floor and have a panoramic view of the city. Daniel has finally taken his socks and boots off and showered in the shared bathroom down the hall. They both drink water now, trying to replace the fluids they lost during the day out in the sun, as well as from the dehydrating effects of the exceptional wine. They had ordered a second bottle before they were done. The wine was so cheap, and it went down far too smoothly. Daniel thinks the alcohol content must be lower than conventional wine because, while he feels relaxed, he does not feel drunk. This is good; he'll need to have his wits about him tonight.

Ginny has showered and changed as well. She is wearing a pair of running shorts she uses as pyjamas. She dangles her long legs through the balcony railing over the crowd below. They kick back and forth in the night air, strong and sleek like the rest of her. Honey-brown hair hangs down free of the ponytail. She appears fairly relaxed as well.

"You're surprising me," he says, looking out into the evening. Lights turn on to illuminate the fountain in the busy square below. He can see flowers and trees carved into the stone like fancy embroidery. A roar goes up from the crowd.

"Why?" Ginny says, once things have quieted down again. "Because I would bunk down with a man I barely know rather than risk sleeping on the street?"

"There are two beds in there and I'm after giving you the big one." He must admit, he had breathed a sigh of relief when he saw the small single bed in the corner.

In the centre of the room, there is a queen-size bed with luxurious duvets and pillows, and something that looks like mosquito netting hanging over it from the ceiling. Ginny had said that it was just for decoration. He knew that but had fun pretending to her that he didn't.

"I reckon I'm just surprised you're still with me. After everything."

She ignores the subject he is trying so delicately to breach. "See over there," she says, pointing toward the hills just outside of town.

He can barely make out the faded green bumps of grass on the horizon, just outside the walls of Logroño. They are quickly fading with the diminishing light.

"Aye," he says. "I see them."

"That's where the witches used to meet," she says. "They would dance in the field by the river naked."

"Are they out tonight, so?" Daniel pretends to crane his neck to get a better look.

Ginny gives him a swat on the arm. "I'm serious," she says. "Logroño was famous for its witch trials during the Spanish Inquisition. They arrested thousands of people and charged them."

"We don't have witches in Ireland," he tells her.

"What do you mean?"

"Sure, we had the occasional tale of some old crone eating children during the famine, of course." He can't believe he's saying this. "Oh wait, tell a lie, we do have witches," he says. "Butter witches."

"What did they do?"

"They stole butter."

"Wow, what a hardcore lot. Makes the Spanish Inquisition seem like a bunch of pansies."

"Sure, I told you we didn't really have witches. Just fairies and that nonsense."

"Did the fairies dance naked?" Ginny continues to kick her legs absentmindedly in front of her.

He thinks about the big bed behind them in the room. How those ivory sheets would slide down the silky skin of her thighs. He tries to change the subject to a safer topic than naked women.

"Enough with asking me questions. Let's hear more about the Spanish Inquisition."

"Well, it was pretty grim, as I'm sure you know." The legs stop swinging. "They'd do unspeakable things to get people to confess, to turn on their family and friends. That's how they ended up with so many witches — everyone kept accusing each other."

"That's a terrible thing." The lightheartedness of their earlier conversation begins to dissipate. He wishes now they'd stuck with the butter witches.

"They'd lock them into a metal figure shaped like a bull," Ginny says. He can barely hear her now over the noise in the square below. "The snout had the only air holes. I read about it." She takes another sip of water, gazes out into the night. "They'd set a fire underneath. The person would force their mouth into the air holes and scream and try to breathe. It made them sound like a bull before he charges." She shivers as she turns to him, her eyes wide. "They did this as entertainment."

Daniel is silent. He doesn't know how to respond. He can picture the horror of the scene, as well as the fascination of it. It's one of the paradoxes of the human race; both our revulsion and our attraction to agony.

"I mean, a person would say anything under those circumstances, don't you think?"

"Agreed," says Daniel, his thoughts of the bedsheets now diminished.

"People never know what they will do if faced with that kind of fear," she says. "They think they know, but they don't."

She's trembling. He hadn't noticed before, but she is.

"I believe there may be more to that story." Leaning in, he gently puts what he hopes is a non-threatening hand on her nearest shoulder. "Perhaps you need to be telling it," he says.

She is holding something back. A dark shadow of a secret. Much like himself. Maybe that's why they are attracted to each other.

She turns to him and her lip quivers a bit like she's going to speak, then instead she lowers the side of her head to his shoulder. He can smell the soap she used in the shower, a combination of ginger with sweet vanilla. He saw the body wash in the bath. He loves ginger, fresh and spicy. It gives an edge to the vanilla, makes it less ordinary. He wants to touch that scent, and not just with a brotherly hand on the shoulder. He wants to hold her in his arms. Maybe even pull her down on the cold mesh metal of the balcony and kiss her while the people below watch her bare legs kick out above them in a whole different way.

As if hearing his thoughts, the crowd cries out in unison. The lit fountain is changing. Daniel looks down and watches as the clear flowing water turns blood red, spraying streams and droplets all around the circular stone basin, staining the sides dark. Some of the people below jump into it, and let the crimson liquid saturate their hair and clothes. It pours down their faces as they laugh and scream, holding their mouths open, bright red currents flowing down their chins. They dance around like kids at the beach or extras in a horror film.

"Oh my God!" Ginny shrieks, scrambling off the balcony. She runs into the bedroom. Daniel runs after her. She is trying to get the door to the hall open but forgets she needs the heavy skeleton key that the innkeeper gave them to get out as well as in. It still sits on the bedside table next to their backpacks. She begins to yell and pound on the door to get out like the tortured witches in the Inquisition's metal bull.

"It's all right, Ginny," he says, pulling her toward him and away from the door. "It's only red dye." He lowers himself to her height, looks directly into her eyes to make sure she is processing what he is saying. "The innkeeper told me about it when you were in the shower. It's for the red wine festival."

She stares at him blankly, then appears to understand, looking over his shoulder out into the night and then back at him for reassurance.

"I, I just ..." She begins but can't seem to finish her thought. She glances down at his hands held fast above both of her elbows, her own hands clinging to his forearms so hard he can feel her short but sharp nails dig in. "I'm just so tired," she says, explaining things away, releasing his arms, staring down at the carpet of the room, a deep shag reminiscent of the seventies that Daniel always associates with porn flicks. A strange mental connection, but given what he was thinking before Ginny flipped out, maybe not an entirely unexpected one.

"I'm sorry," she says, regaining composure.

He releases her, with a touch of regret. "Maybe you should be adopting some lighter nighttime reading than the Spanish Inquisition," Daniel tells her, working to lighten the mood. He cannot believe no one has come to bang the door down, thinking Ginny's being violated or worse. He's glad that they didn't though. He imagines himself trying to profess his innocence in broken Spanish, like a misunderstood monster.

Outside, the fountain continues to flow a bright red. It will do so until tomorrow night, when it will turn a softer rose and then pale gold to depict all the types of wine the Rioja region produces. The innkeeper told Daniel all of this. He is wishing now that he had told Ginny.

"I think I'll go to bed," she says. She fetches the key off the bedside table and lets herself out to use the toilet. The door makes a metal click as she releases the knob from the other side.

He walks over to the single bed and lies down on top of the duvet fully clothed, listening to the muted hum of the crowd in the square as they talk and sing songs he doesn't know. When she comes back through the door, he shuts his eyes tightly, like a kid caught after lights out. He listens to her turning the key in the lock again, and then to the sound of her slipping between the cool sheets of her bed. There is a slight rustling of the netting above he can hear even with the noise going on outside.

He thinks about Ginny lying so close to him. Listens to the evenness of her breath as she falls into the deep slumber that takes all pilgrims after a full day of walking the Spanish countryside, no matter how inconducive the environment may be for sleep. The body takes what it needs, and what hers needs is rest.

After Ginny's reaction to the red fountain, he knows he is not the only one with a past that still haunts. Ginny carries a burden on her Camino, too. Something as terrifying as blood from a fountain, or a witch in a cornfield. Maybe even as horrifying as what happened to Petra.

He slowly drifts off, remembering how it feels to have a woman's soft skin next to his. What it is like to reach your leg over to rest a thigh on her hip. Arms wrapped around a taut torso, with the curve of a breast held protectively in one hand. He is ashamed of these thoughts but too tired for self-recriminations. He wonders what Ginny's secret is, but at the same time he doesn't care. He pictures her beneath him, giving herself up like a woman born of witchcraft, dancing in a field naked to the rhythm of drums. He falls asleep to the roar of the crowd, feeling guilty and aroused all at once, like a good Irish Catholic boy.

The evil thoughts of men, his mind warns, as unconsciousness takes him. *The evil thoughts of men.*

CHAPTER 6
Logroño to Azofra

IT'S STILL DARK WHEN they pack up and leave the *casa rural* the next day. Both had woken up early. Neither had slept well. Daniel had lain in bed awake at four in the morning, staring at the ceiling, counting Ginny's even breaths — until he heard her clear her throat and sigh, and he realized that she was awake as well. At dawn, they leave by the back door of the building, like thieves, avoiding the fountain out front. Daniel is not sure if this is intentional, but it probably is.

It is still dark enough for the streetlights to be on. They illuminate a Logroño littered with Rioja festival leftovers. There are streamers and torn red fans curled up on the pavement, and discarded bits of food and broken bottles washed up on the curb like seaweed and shells.

"Watch out," Ginny warns, just as Daniel is about to step in a Technicolor pool of vomit outside one of the seedier-looking bars.

"Thanks," he mutters, holding his breath as he steps over the mess.

They both breathe a little easier once they exit the city into the expansive tract of parkland built at its limits. The moon provides just enough light in the grey-streaked dawn to lace the ripples of the artificial lake they walk beside. It has been built as a centrepiece for the green space, and the trail looks dusty and dark next to its gleaming edge. Later, when the sun comes fully up, Daniel will see the path they walk on is stained red, a mineral idiosyncrasy of the soil that clings to the grapes and impregnates the wine of the region. This is what gives it that otherworldly taste, the seeds of mercurial dirt.

Daniel and Ginny tread softly along the Way while everyone else sleeps, letting the sun rise up on their backs and tint them with the shades of a new day. Daniel tries to relax into the Zen school of silence and steps. But he finds he is too tense to let go. He is ashamed of the thoughts he had last night. The ones he still has. Whenever he glances over at his walking companion he can't help but admire the swell of her lower lip as she bites down gently on it, or follow her eyes so he can steal a glimpse at what she is seeing. Ginny appears oblivious to his study of her. She yawns widely without covering her mouth, wrinkling her nose unattractively afterward. She is like a woman watched unknowingly through a lit window at night, unaware she has left her blinds up.

Maybe she had sensed his thoughts, and that's why she couldn't sleep. But he doesn't fully believe that. Not after the way she reacted to the fountain. Ginny has her own reasons for being kept awake at night.

Once they make it to a high ridge that looks back out over the city, they stop for breakfast, packed cheese and crackers bought from a vending machine earlier. Daniel still has an orange he bought the day before at one of the roadside stands. The juice leaks over his hands as he peels it. He offers a dripping wedge to Ginny, but she declines. They make polite conversation, suffering from their new-found awkwardness. After eating, they continue along the trail, remaining quiet and reserved. He feels like a kid in high school — or what he imagines high school would have been like had there been girls. He'd been sent at twelve to an all-boys boarding school run by priests. He'd joined the stamp-collecting club just for the opportunity to meet the opposite sex at off-site exhibitions. To this day, the smell of self-adhesive stamp glue can make him uncomfortably aroused.

The Camino leads down and along a wire fence that separates them from the highway. They walk parallel to it, expecting cars, but there are very few. Into the wire fence pilgrims have woven hundreds of crosses made of strips of bark from the scraps of a nearby sawmill. Ginny stops and fixes in her own cross from what she finds on the ground.

"Do you want to make one, Daniel?" she asks, holding up some extra pieces of bark.

"I don't," he says. "I mean, thanks, but I'm fine."

"Not a religious guy?"

He shrugs. "I am, I suppose," he says, still standing back. "I just don't feel in a state of grace at the moment."

✳

When they start walking again, crossing the *autopista*, she puts on a pair of earphones, and a faint overspill of music leaks out. She seems fully recovered from her fright the evening before, content to walk and listen to her playlist. He recognizes Alanis Morissette. Later, Pink Floyd, *Dark Side of the Moon*. He is puzzled when he hears the Beastie Boys come on. She sees him looking and turns down the volume self-consciously. He wishes she hadn't. The tinny seepage of the song had been just annoying enough to distract him from his deeper thoughts. Like a radio tuned a bit off-station. He prays they bump into Rob so the Dutchman can carry the conversation. Then Daniel could just walk and listen to the sound of their voices, crowding out the ones inside his head. Those voices remind him he is here to make amends, to forget, to finally bury his wife. Not to get laid, for Christ's sake. What the hell is wrong with him?

As they sit over lunch in Najera, he still has his guard up, trying not to give anything away while still observing Ginny for clues. She talks about her work at the prison library and the eccentricity of her cat. He counters with his own shallow conversation. The business he helped build with his partner. The motorcycle he had thought of buying once but never did. Safe topics that skirt around his life with Petra and her death, like pieces of a puzzle purposely left out of the box. Harbouring his own missing pieces, watching for hints of hers.

"Is everything okay, Daniel?" she asks when they are waiting for the bill. This is the most perplexing of questions for a man from a woman. Men never ask it of one another. Just as they do not ask what each other is thinking. However, he has enough experience with her gender to know the standard answer.

"Sure," he says, wiping his mouth with a paper napkin. He crumples it up and leaves it on the table next to his half-eaten lunch. "Everything's grand."

※

It is just past noon on the last part of the day's journey. Most of the landscape out of Najera has been treed, a nature reserve saved from agriculture. Lofty pines provide some shade from the sun that hangs directly overhead, but not enough. It is unseasonably hot again today, and Daniel forgot to change his socks midway as he usually does on warm days. He thinks he may have developed his first blister as a result. He'll have to tend to it when they get to the *albergue*.

"It's only a few more miles to Azofra," Ginny pipes up, noticing his discomfort. He hadn't thought it was that obvious.

"It's not a big place, is it?" Daniel asks. After Logroño, he is hoping for a sleepy little town with a little less excitement, or at least less vomit.

"Only three hundred people," Ginny says, consulting the guidebook she keeps in her waist bag. "Wouldn't exist if it wasn't for the Camino."

Many of the towns and villages they pass through wouldn't have survived without the trade brought from the Way. In some, the population had dwindled to single digits, the pilgrims outnumbering the locals like invaders outfitted by the Outdoor Store.

"But look," she exclaims, pointing halfway down the page of the guide. "The *albergue* there is awesome. You only have to share your room with one other person."

Daniel nods. He reckons that one person better not be Ginny in his case. He doesn't know if he could trust himself for another night. It would be like stamp club all over again.

"Oh my God!" Ginny cries out, looking up from the book.

"What?" Daniel asks, startled.

She tucks the guidebook into the side pocket of her backpack. "They have a swimming pool."

"You're full of shite."

"No, I'm not," she says. They quicken their steps in anticipation, despite the increasing incline.

It is not until they reach the top of the rise that he sees her. The figure from the corn. By the light of the full day, he can make out her features more clearly, her head slumped down chin to chest, her long hair hanging over her face, tangled with what appears to be hardened dirt. He can also see the slight strain of the hiking pants along the hips, the faint curves underneath her red Columbia sweater. A woman for sure. He hadn't been certain until now. She stands in a graveyard nestled among mature trees where the trail levels off at the bottom of the rise. A faint wind mixes with the heat rising off the ground, making the outline of her body waver. He stops and turns to Ginny.

"Do you see her?" he asks. He needs to know.

"Yes," Ginny says. She has stopped as well.

Daniel starts walking again, moving quickly down the rise.

"Daniel, wait."

He can hear Ginny but keeps on regardless. Her hesitant footsteps follow behind him. She must be wondering what he is going to do. He has only one task in his mind. To reach the woman at the graveside and lift her hair up in order to confirm for himself what lies beneath. Something easily explained. A trick, instead of a nightmare. He is furious that anyone or anything might try to make him live through another one of those.

"Hey!" he shouts, as he nears the graveyard entrance, a simple five-bar farm gate. The tombstones behind it are decrepit, the crypts crumbling with age and neglect.

"Hey," he shouts again as the woman lifts her head but doesn't answer. She walks purposefully toward the back of the cemetery, moving over stones and grave mounds with a surprising grace and speed in her heavy hiking boots. Daniel quickens his pace.

When he gets to the entrance, he discovers the gate has a sturdy piece of wire looped onto a post to keep it closed. He'll have to pry it off where it has bitten into the wood. Reaching underneath, he pulls, and when that doesn't work, he begins to claw with his short fingernails. Little flecks of rust flake off onto his hand when it finally breaks free. As he slips the wire off the post, Daniel sees that the woman has disappeared into the woods at the back of the cemetery. Or so he assumes. It is the only way out other than the gate. He doesn't think she could have hopped the fence.

"What are you doing, Daniel?" Ginny asks from behind him. She stands well back, watching. He hadn't noticed her there when he struggled with the gate. Just as she hadn't noticed him watching her earlier.

"You saw her," he says. "I'm going to ask what her feckin' problem is."

"She's just visiting a grave, Daniel."

"The hell she is. She's the same one who was messing with us at the cornfields in Azqueta." He's not about to let this go.

The graves, on closer inspection, are even more poorly kept than he thought. Many of the markers have fallen over, lying in pieces in the sparse faded grass. Some of the grave mounds have begun to collapse, the ground sinking around the monuments and leaving holes for things to scurry in and out. He thinks he sees something mangy and earth coloured rush along the forest floor, where it disappears under a dank patch of leaves. The woman peeks out from behind the thick cover of an old pine tree where she appears to have been waiting for him. Then she turns around and disappears into the glut of needles and branches. They swallow her up like a pine-scented black hole.

Daniel marches toward the woods, not wanting to lose her again. When he reaches the forest, he goes to push a collection of prickly limbs out of the way and they snap back and hit him in the face. He swats at them like a man attacked by bees. It would be funny if he weren't so angry. He has spent the last few days thinking he is losing his mind because of this woman. He wants to unmask her and get on with his damn Camino.

The dense branches obscure his view of the ground as he finds a small overgrown path through the trees. He sees too late that the woods have overrun the oldest part of the cemetery. Low grave markers and mounds of disturbed earth litter the forest floor. When the tip of his boot catches on a broken gravestone, he falls and smashes the side of his head on a rock half buried in the dirt. He can feel the tickly heat of blood running down his scalp and behind his ear as he lies on his side, winded. Dry pine needles stick him when he tries to move, and mouldy leaves get stuck to his cheek. He curses out loud and a metallic taste in his mouth tells him he has also bitten his tongue. When he licks the blood off his lips and opens his eyes he spots it, a rat — only a few inches away in a sunken hole at the base of an old tombstone. He makes the painful effort to roll over onto his back in a weak attempt to get up.

The smell of her reaches him before he can look up and focus. The stench is worse than the slaughterhouse where he used to drive the cattle in the truck with his father. She is standing over him, waiting, like the furry rat skulking in the hole. Her body appears in negative against the bright light of the sun through the trees behind her, like a poorly planned photo taken inside against a daylit window. She sighs with an open maw of a mouth, and the vileness of her breath hits his stomach like a vicious sucker punch. He turns to the side and retches, unable to lift his head and shoulders to vomit properly. The sick dribbles out of his mouth onto the pine needles. When he's finished, he turns to look up at her again, involuntarily swallowing the foulness that burns the back of his throat.

He sees now that her hair is caked not with dirt, but with the dried remnants of blood and brain matter. She raises one hand to lift the strands away, as if she anticipated his earlier wish to see what lies underneath. Reddish-brown clots flake off her chin as she reaches up, falling at his feet like the rust that fell from the wire at the gate.

"No," he pleads. He can't look anymore, but can't turn away either. It is like rubbernecking at a car accident or watching a too-young girl walk away in a short skirt. He just can't stop himself.

As she lifts her hand, he sees it. The sleeve of her jacket pulls away at the wrist and the little silver shells there catch the sun, winking at him. They set off the green and purple bruise of her skin the same way they had set off the tan of Ginny's arms. The colourful beads of the bracelet dig into her where she has swollen with bloat, like stained pearls embedded in spoiled bread dough.

His peripheral vision is already beginning to go as she draws back one half of the curtain of hair. His sight is a dwindling circle that only serves to highlight the unveiling of her face, as if he is trained on her display with a telescope. He sees the long gash weeping down from her temple, exposing the bone of her cheek, the gristle glistening where the jaw was broken off. Her earlobe is torn completely; the jagged remains make it look as if she's been viciously bitten.

He reaches up with his own hand now, as if to touch her, to see if she's real. But all he wants is to stop her before she raises the last of her hair. She has no mercy for him as she lifts the final strands to expose the deep socket, dark and empty, its former contents hanging down from a stringy piece of meat onto what's left of her cheek. He groans, and the tunnel of his vision fades to black.

In the darkness of his mind, his body and his consciousness morph and fold in upon themselves. He is falling, down deep into one of the holes between graves, where he shrinks and grows fur. He crawls feebly underground in the dirt, searching for a way out.

But every time he thinks he has found an escape route, a light shining from the surface, his way is blocked. The woman with the hair twists in front of the sun, from a tree branch above, the beaded bracelet with the little silver shells hanging brightly from the deadness of her arm.

He cannot move anymore down below, under the ground. Cannot even call out. He looks up to the light above and hears a scraping sound before he feels something soft and cool hit him in the chest to run down the sides of his paralyzed body. The same sound, and another soft splash of coldness across his torso, then his legs, and finally into his open mouth which fills up, choking him even as he is just beginning to realize the taste.

Dirt.

Each shovelful punctuates a new sentence of terror, as he watches the light and his life disappear above.

✳

"So, are you saying I'm mad?" Daniel holds a dressing to the side of his head. When he takes it away, it has fresh blood on it, but less than the last time. The wound is finally starting to clot.

"I am saying no such thing," Ginny says. "What I am trying to tell you is that you are most probably concussed. Even the nurse thought so."

The nurse had cleaned up the wound a few minutes ago then doused him with antiseptic. His hair smells like someone spilled paint thinner on it. He and Ginny are in one of two treatment rooms of a small clinic in Azofra, waiting for the doctor. It is cramped, but the floors and the walls are spotless. The waiting area outside doubles as a bakery. They had sat out there earlier with pilgrims sporting various complaints, shin splints and infected blisters being the most common. Others just wanted to buy churros. The proprietress had taken down Daniel's medical insurance details at the counter, getting flour on her pen.

"Sure, even you saw her, Ginny," Daniel says, sitting up on the examination table, the ridiculous paper beneath him crackling as he shifts his weight. He hates sitting up on the table like an invalid or a child, but Ginny has taken the only chair in the corner. His backpack sits beside him, taking up its own spot on the paper like a second patient.

"Of course, I saw her," she tells him. "But she was just standing by a grave, Daniel. You can't fault her for that."

"It was the same woman as before," Daniel says. "She's after following us."

"Seems to me you were the one following her," Ginny says. "And you probably frightened the hell out of her barrelling into the cemetery like that."

They have been over this before, in the waiting room. Daniel turns away from her, getting tired of the cyclical nature of their discussion.

They hear the sound of shuffling paperwork just outside the door before it opens. The doctor walks in with a clipboard tucked under his arm. He has a white lab coat on, but other than that he looks the same as the *hospitaleiro* at their last *albergue*. Daniel notices he wears dirty work boots with hay stuck to them, like his dad's. In a town this small, people hold multiple roles. This guy is probably the mayor as well.

"*Buenos dias*," the doctor says. He moves immediately to examine Daniel's head. No preliminaries. He's a busy man, judging by the number of pilgrims waiting to see him out in the bakery, and he doesn't even turn around to acknowledge Ginny.

"*Buenos dias*," Daniel says, wincing as the doctor palpates with one latex-gloved finger the impressive goose egg on the right side of his head. When he's finished, he takes the same finger and moves it back and forth in front of Daniel's eyes. He follows it without being asked to do so, having been knocked around enough playing sports as a kid to know the drill for checking out head injuries. Once in middle school he got hit so hard playing rugby that he lined up with the wrong team after the scrum.

"How did this happen?" the doctor asks, snapping his gloves off and throwing them skillfully into the trash bin in the far corner.

"I fell," Daniel says. "Sure, am I all right to go now?"

Ginny had made him go to the clinic. If it had been up to him, he would have just cleaned himself up with a washcloth and taken a few Aspirin.

"How did you fall?" the doctor persists. His English is excellent. Daniel almost wishes that it weren't. Then he wouldn't have to explain the situation further. All he wants is to get to the *albergue* and lie down.

"I thought I saw someone," Daniel says, looking around the doctor at Ginny, challenging her to say otherwise. She rolls her eyes at him. The doctor turns in her direction and then back toward Daniel without comment.

"Someone that you found necessary to chase through a graveyard?" the doctor asks him. Daniel looks at him, confused, and then realizes.

"You heard me talking in the waiting room," he says.

"My wife did," the doctor says, smiling. "She runs the bakery."

Daniel remembers the woman with flour on her hands who also acted as the clinic receptionist. Feck it, did everyone understand English here? He had thought she was staring at him because she was afraid he'd get blood on the pastries. Turns out she thought he was so unbalanced she had to mention it to her doctor/farmer husband.

"Right then," Daniel begins, "I'm not at all sure what I saw, but I saw something." Daniel figures he might as well be honest. "I've seen it before," then he adds, "on the Camino." He wants to make sure that the doctor doesn't think this is something he carried with him from home, like a communicable disease he could spread. "It's a woman. I think she may be following us."

The doctor looks hard at Daniel, then moves over to the sink to wash his hands. He closes the tap with his elbows and then turns to him with arms raised. The water drips down into the sleeves of his white coat.

"*Santa Compaña*," he says to Daniel. "Do you know what this is?"

"I don't," says Daniel, wishing for the hundredth time that he knew more Spanish. If Ginny knows what it means, she's not saying. He sees her sitting in the chair, twisting a piece of thread coming off from the seam of her hiking pants.

"It means 'Holy Company' in English," the doctor says. He turns in Ginny's direction and then back to Daniel, lowers his hands. "They are also called the 'Night Ones.'"

"I was after seeing this in the daylight," Daniel tells him.

"They are called this because they are of the night, not necessarily because they are seen at this time. In Spain people believe they are the tormented souls of the dead. They follow the living."

Daniel raises an eyebrow at the doctor. Now who is the crazy one.

"You think this is a ridiculous superstition?" the doctor says, smiling. It is a statement more than a question. "I have travelled to many countries that have stories that are the same. In your own country they have beings such as this that accompany death or suffering."

"Banshees," Daniel says, colouring a bit.

The doctor nods then turns and begins rifling through the cupboard behind him. He pulls out a small plastic bag, which he fills with antiseptic wipes, gauze, and some surgical tape. He measures out six white pills from a large bottle and drops them in.

"Go on, Doctor, you're an educated man, surely you don't believe in the likes of that," Daniel says.

The doctor closes the cupboard and gathers up the bag of first-aid supplies along with Daniel's Irish passport with the medical insurance card tucked inside.

"I was educated at Oxford, Mr. Kennedy, but that is not where I learned to believe." The doctor hands Daniel his things. "There are some painkillers in there. No more than two at time. Take it easy with the walking for a few days." He picks up a clipboard and ticks off a few boxes with a pen tied to the top with a string.

"The Way of Saint James is a mystical place," the doctor continues, pausing again before he goes on. "So many would not be drawn here over the centuries if it wasn't. It may show itself to each pilgrim differently. But my experience has been that the Camino always provides."

"Provides what?" Daniel asks.

Ginny seems to be paying attention now, having forgotten about the thread.

"Provides what you uniquely need," the doctor says as he puts the clipboard under his arm. "But not necessarily what you came for."

He grasps the door handle and opens it. The fresh yeasty smell of the bakery drifts in. The doctor stops and turns to him before he leaves.

"Only some can see the *Santa Compaña*, Mr. Kennedy," he says. "If you are one of these, there is a reason for it."

He walks out, closing the door behind him. They both watch him go. A few seconds later they hear him speaking fluent French to the patient in the next room. Daniel zips the supplies and his passport into his pack and gets down from the exam table.

"Let's go," he says, opening the door. Ginny grabs her own pack and follows him out. They walk past the doctor's wife behind the bakery counter as she eyes them suspiciously over freshly baked bread. Daniel keeps on walking, banging the bakery door behind him on the way out, the little bell attached jingling.

*

At the *albergue*, Daniel checks in. Ginny already has while he was being cleaned up by the nurse. She had been afraid the *albergue* might fill up and she would have to sleep out in the lean-to they had built next to the parish church for overflow. Luckily, it is not that crowded, and Daniel gets a room. After taking showers and hanging their washed clothes to dry, the two wander into the large kitchen off the common room. A German man has made a huge pot of chipped beef and mashed potatoes, which he shares around. Despite Daniel's earlier stomach issues, he cleans the plate, his body taking charge and demanding the calories he needs to cover a day's worth of walking. Neither he nor Ginny says much. Ginny picks at her meal, meticulously separating the beef from the mashed potatoes with the tine of a plastic fork.

Afterward they go out back and sit with bare feet dangling in the cool water of the "swimming pool," an example of false advertising that turns out to be an unheated six-by-three-foot cement tub with an anemic fountain at its centre. Still, it is a nice place from which to watch the sun go down with their hiking pants rolled up, the bracing water taking the swelling down in their overworked legs and feet. Daniel's head still hurts, but he has taken a couple of the painkillers the doctor gave him, and they are starting to work their magic. He pulls out one foot and checks for the blister he was sure he developed earlier, finds just a reddened "hot spot" on the outside of one toe. He'll have to be more careful tomorrow, apply some petroleum jelly to keep it from chafing further.

"How are you feeling?" Ginny asks him.

"All right, I suppose, all things being considered," he says.

The muffled clang of a cowbell sounds in the distance. They don't have cowbells in Ireland. Or at least, they never had them on his farm. When he hears them now he keeps expecting a town crier to come around the corner.

"That's still quite the bump," Ginny says.

She brings her hand up and gently rests it on the side of his head, her fingers catching in his dark curls. He feels embarrassed at her closeness.

"Sure, I've had worse," he says, shrugging it off. He waits a moment, then asks her, "What did you think about your man, the doctor?"

"About what he said about your head?" Ginny says, still with her fingers in his hair.

"About what he said about the bleedin' *Santa Compaña*," Daniel says.

"I think it's a bunch of horseshit." She takes her hand back.

"A bit of a cynic, you," Daniel tells her, though not unkindly. He's not surprised. He thinks it's a bunch of horseshit, too. Well, at least 90 percent of him does. He did grow up in a country where fairies stole children, or so his granny would threaten when he showed up after dark for dinner.

"I'm not so much a cynic, as a pragmatist, Daniel. Santiago is still over three hundred miles away. I don't have time for things that go bump in the night."

"I saw something, Ginny," he says.

"This woman?" she asks.

"Aye, but more than that." Daniel hesitates. He's been keeping one detail from her. He takes a deep swallow before he goes on. "She was after wearing the same bracelet as you, Ginny." He reaches out and lifts the beads and shells hanging from her wrist with one finger. "The very same one. Sure, I saw it when she was standing over me."

Ginny stares at him holding up her bracelet. She says nothing for a moment. He takes his hand away after a few seconds but holds her gaze.

"Daniel, when you fell, I came running," she tells him. "I was the one standing over you."

He hears her but cannot process what she says right away. It makes no sense.

"The bracelet you saw was the same because it was me, Daniel."

"It wasn't you," he insists.

"You'd hit your head. You were totally incoherent when I found you."

"It wasn't you," he repeats more quietly, turning away. He'll believe he was hallucinating from a head injury, but there is no way he will believe that his mind turned Ginny into that creature with the hair. He couldn't have hit his head that hard.

She doesn't say anything more, only gazes out to the horizon. Eventually, he does as well, and they both sit, stoically watching as the sun dips below the rolling silhouette of hills. The cowbells fade with the day and go silent. Daniel thinks how romantic a scene it is — that is, if they hadn't just been arguing about whether he saw a woman with a dangling eyeball.

"I think I'll turn in for the night," he tells Ginny just as she reaches for his hand.

❋

Back in his room, Daniel pulls the prescription bottle he got in the States out of his pack and opens it for the first time. He throws two of the little blue pills into the back of his throat and swallows them down using the warm water left in his bottle. Lying down on the bed on top of his sleeping bag, he shuts his eyes and waits for sleep to come. Between the little blue pills and the painkillers he took earlier, that release comes quickly.

He doesn't hear his roommate come in to bed. Nor does he hear Ginny say goodnight through the door. He doesn't see the woman or think of Petra or of Ginny or of anything at all. He just sleeps without dreams, while those that are of the night lie in wait, their reasons still secret, guarded until he is ready to hear them.

CHAPTER 7
Azofra to Grañón

"HELLO, DANIEL!" The Dutchman walks across the *Plaza del Santo* still carrying his carved wooden walking stick.

Daniel and Ginny have stopped for lunch at one of the patios on the square.

"Hi, Rob." Daniel rises from the table, relieved to see his calming friend. They shake hands and Daniel pulls out a chair. Rob leans his stick against the rubble wall of the café behind them and sits down. He greets Ginny then turns and notices the bandage on Daniel's head.

"What have you done to yourself, my friend?" His easy smile has turned to a frown of concern. He looks to Ginny, as if she might provide an explanation, and then back at Daniel.

"I fell," Daniel says, touching the bandage, feeling embarrassed.

Ginny might like to say more, but Daniel's quick look in her direction makes it clear that she shouldn't. The Dutchman waits for a beat or two of silence and then tries to make light of what he senses is a touchy subject.

"You should be taking better care of him, Ginny from California," he says with a wink in her direction.

Ginny winks back, then takes another sip of her coffee. Crisis averted.

"Apparently, he is the one taking care of me," she says, giving Daniel a cautionary glance.

"Chivalry is a right terrible disability," Daniel says, and she laughs then. So does he. The tension of the day before is starting to fall away with the sunshine and the exercise from this morning's walk to Santo Domingo. The additional pills he's taken this morning don't hurt either.

The medieval town is in keeping with the others but full of modern amenities. The original monastery pilgrim hostel has been made into a Parador hotel with extravagant rooms and a nightly price tag that approaches the cost of Daniel's plane ticket to Europe. This combined with the busy plaza, shops, and cafés makes the *Santa Compaña* and the woman in the graveyard seem very far way. They are shadows from the past that don't relate to this sunny modern world any more than the formerly stark monastic pilgrim hostel bears resemblance to the opulent rooms of the Parador.

"Where have you been, Rob?" Daniel asks him. He is surprised they haven't bumped into one another over the last couple of days.

"Oh, many places." The Dutchman adjusts his painter's cap and squints into the sun. "Such warm weather for the fall. I slept outside last night in a field."

"Aren't you worried about sleeping out in the open?" Ginny asks him, toying with the salt shaker on the table in an attempt to make her inquiry appear more casual than it is.

Daniel has learned she is a woman ashamed of fear, which is why he thinks she is lying about the woman following them. She might not be *Santa Compaña*, but she's something to Ginny. He just hasn't yet figured out what.

"Afraid?" Rob tilts his head and looks pensive. "I have not really thought of this. What should I be afraid of?"

"Sure, around here, perhaps being trampled by cows," Daniel says, taking a sip of his Coke. He never was a fan of soda but it seems to hit the spot these days. He'll have to drop the habit when he gets back home, or he'll end up with the spare tire he teases his older brothers about. Home. It seems so far away. Does he really have a home anymore with Petra gone?

"I had not thought of cows, but of course this could be a problem." The Dutchman appears to be taking Daniel's comment about cattle trampling seriously.

Then again, he should. Daniel and Ginny have been surprised by large herds crossing the trail more than once, and they often hide in the early morning mist of the mountains. You didn't see them until they were practically stepping on your hiking boots. Daniel remembers how the sound of cow bells in the Pyrenees would warn him like a ship's foghorn before an animal suddenly appeared, a huge furred prow with horns emerging out of the dense white clouds.

"I was thinking more of a human threat," Ginny says. Both the men glance at each other. They live in a world where women must be more uneasy about these things than they are, and they know it. It's not fair, but it's the truth.

"I used to worry more about this," Rob says kindly, not dismissing Ginny's concerns but mirroring them. "But I do not worry anymore. This is what they call blind faith, I think." He chuckles to himself. "I love these English sayings."

Ginny smiles. "Yes, why not deaf faith," she says, getting into the spirit of the Dutchman's pun. "Or mute faith?"

"Or faith with no sense of smell at all," Daniel adds. He sniffs the pizza he purchased in the café to underline his comment then takes another bite. It tastes as if it came frozen in a box — nothing like the fresh *bocadillo* he had savoured with Rob that day in the grassy field. Cuisine can be up and down on the Camino, just like the terrain.

"Speaking of faith," Ginny says, reaching for her guide-book. She flips through with her thumb and stops on a page that has a little blue pen mark at the top. "I want to take a tour of the cathedral." She locates a passage with her index finger.

Daniel peers over her shoulder and makes out *Capilla de la Magdalena* printed in italics, not without difficulty. His vision is getting blurry. "Visiting your favourite saint, are we?" Daniel says, nudging her.

She gives him a playful push in the arm. The change in him from last night makes him feel bipolar. Yesterday his concussed brain had thought she was a decomposing corpse standing over him. Today he's a primary-school boy yanking at her pigtails. It could be the painkillers that he took before setting out this morning or the prescription from home he downed on a visit to the café's toilet. Still, he feels saner — even a little detached, but in a good way. He is safely distanced from the frightening scenes of the last few days, like when you watch a thunderstorm from indoors or a prize fight on the television. He hates the idea of safe barriers and other crutches, particularly the pharma-ceutical kind, and once his head is better, he'll dump the pills. He can handle his own nerves. Plus, he stumbled a bit when he went to get pizza.

"Sure, there's more in the cathedral than the chapel of Mary Mag. There are chickens," he says, chuckling to himself.

Ginny looks at him strangely. He thinks he may have spoken this too loudly, makes a mental note to up his self-monitoring.

"Yes, I have heard of these chickens," Rob chimes in, rescuing him. He has remained quiet up until now, observ-ing the interaction between Daniel and Ginny. "They live in the cathedral, yes? There is a shrine?" He clasps his hands together and waits for confirmation.

"Aye." Daniel leans back dangerously in his chair. "And a legend to go with them."

"I'm intrigued," Ginny says. She gets up and bends over to put the guidebook away in her backpack. Her body creates an attractively rounded ninety-degree angle that Daniel never remembers learning about in math class.

"Let's go then," Daniel says as he takes the last bite of his cardboard pizza and reaches for his pack.

"This church I will go see," the Dutchman says, standing to join them.

"I thought they were all the same," Ginny teases.

"They are," Rob says, retrieving his walking stick. "But in this one, if a chicken crows while you are there, they say you will have a blessed Camino."

"You're having me on." Daniel looks at Rob. He knows the legend but not this part.

Ginny leans in and cups one hand around Daniel's ear. Her lips dance dangerously close to the sensitive lobe. "C'mon, we can use all the help we can get," she whispers, before pulling away and starting in the direction of the cathedral.

Daniel can still feel the closeness of her breath after she walks away. It sends a delicious chill through his increasingly sedated body as he and Rob follow her through the square.

✳

The two chickens are held in a brightly lit gilded box, high up and recessed into an inner wall of the cathedral. A cock and a hen. The coop resembles an old-fashioned circus cage more than a functional pen for farm animals. The closely arranged iron bars are ornate, bent into fancy twists and curls along the front with a Plexiglas divider laid on top, a practical addition to prevent the chickens from kicking hay and excrement onto the cathedral floor below. Even divine animals have bodily functions.

"I cannot get a picture," the Dutchman says, trying to adjust the camera settings on his smartphone. "The light is too strong."

Daniel views the image Rob shows him on the screen. It is true, the light from the chicken coop has got to be a couple hundred-watt bulbs' worth. The rest of the cathedral is not well-lit. Whenever Rob tries to take a picture, the surroundings are lost in the background of the bright light, making the chicken shrine appear to float in a sea of blackness.

"I got some good pictures of Mary Magdalene," Ginny says, returning from around the corner where she had gone to observe the chapel noted in her guidebook. She holds out her phone to Daniel and he sees first a picture of a small room with an arched opening, not unlike the one they saw in the church where the Borgias were buried. She moves to the next photo, a gorgeous close-up of the saint painted in sumptuous reds and blacks. Mary Magdalene holds an urn in an awkward hand-over-hand manner. It's as if the artist meant to paint the Virgin Mary holding the Christ child and then changed his mind midway, turning the baby Jesus into a vase and the Virgin into the local harlot. The two women do share a lot of physical characteristics as well as a first name, Daniel has noticed. Except Magdalene wears a knowing look while the mother of Jesus is most often depicted as beatific and amazed, like Audrey Hepburn coming out of Tiffany's with two fistfuls of shopping bags. He laughs to himself, and Ginny looks at him strangely, wondering what the joke is.

"I like that one," Rob says, admiring the portrait on her phone as well.

The painting is done in the traditional Dutch style of the Golden Age, and Daniel wonders if that influences Rob's tastes. He's surprised he can remember this bit of art history even though his brain is becoming increasingly fogged.

Petra had schooled him well. She had made sure he learned to appreciate the great masters housed in the buildings he was restoring that summer when they met. Introduced him to the world of Rembrandt and Raphael. It was a gift she gave him, the ability to slow down and take in the details of beauty that he had previously passed by without noticing. Right now he is feeling so loose that he doesn't think he would notice if an eighteen-wheeler drove through the sanctuary.

"So, why chickens?" Ginny asks, gazing up at the lit rectangular cage above them.

The proud cock walks back and forth in front of the bars. The hen sits unimpressed.

"They're here for the miracle of Santo Domingo," Daniel says, waking up at the opportunity to relate another fact.

They move toward another shrine surrounded by tourists. Many of them have audio devices held up to their ears listening to an explanation in their native language of the contents of the twelfth-century building. *Ginny doesn't need an audio device*, he thinks, *she has me.*

"This is his tomb, so," Daniel says dramatically as they approach the raised and railed-off display. It contains an alabaster sarcophagus. The Egyptians weren't the only ones to use them.

"What was his miracle?" Rob asks as he joins them at the railing. He has given up on getting a good picture of the coop. He also has opted out of the audio device. "They never are having the Dutch language anyway," he had complained earlier.

"There was a family making their pilgrimage on the Camino," Ginny begins, surprising them both.

"Sure, you *do* know the story," Daniel says, feeling proud of her rather than upstaged. He leans against a marble column, hoping to look casual but really needing the support.

He watches as she pauses and bites lightly on her lower lip in reply. It is just a quirk of self-consciousness, but it stirs something in him despite his anesthetized state.

"They stayed with a local nobleman and, apparently, the young daughter of the house made advances on their son," Ginny says. "Okay, now your turn," she says, looking at Daniel.

He wants to continue the story in tandem but finds himself highly distracted by her lip. It takes a few clearings of his throat, but eventually he manages to speak. "The devout young man rejected her advances," he says, trying to focus on the carved details in the alabaster sarcophagus that has begun to appear in double. It starts to give him a headache and he turns away. "She accused him of stealing the family silver," he manages to choke out. Christ, he needs to get a hold of himself.

Ginny walks toward the far wall that leads down to the side chapel corridor. A display is housed in a shallow alcove there behind yet another barrier. Daniel can't make out the contents. He moves unsteadily toward it for a better look. So does Rob.

"Of course, he was charged and convicted. The girl was from a noble family, remember. Not much hope there." Ginny keeps on with the tale as they approach the display. He can see the painting at the centre of the exhibit now. A man holds on to the lower half of his son in a grief stricken embrace. The body is dressed in white and the feet dangle a few feet above the ground.

"He was hanged," Daniel says, standing resolutely in front of the painting as best as he can. His head is really starting to pound now. He sees the robed medieval figures standing at the gallows in the painting, weeping. They begin to appear in double just like the sarcophagus.

"The mother and father were devastated, of course," Ginny says, keeping up her part of the tale. "But still somehow made it to Santiago. When they came back, they visited the place their son had died and found him hanging where they left him."

Sweat has begun to break out on Daniel's forehead. He can feel the little beads gathering, welling up from somewhere inside him like a fever. It makes the wound at his temple throb. He leans against another column.

"They found him still alive. A miracle." Ginny waits for the question that sets up the ending of the story, but only the Dutchman asks it. Daniel can't.

"What is this to do with chickens?" Rob asks, looking hard at the painting. Ginny waits and doesn't answer, knowing it is Daniel's turn.

"The parents went after the local reeve." He pauses, wets his lips. "They told him the miracle of their son's survival." Daniel forms the words slowly, still trying to gain his composure. Nobody seems to notice his distress. He closes his eyes tightly and takes a deep breath.

Ginny takes the pause as permission to finish the story. "The reeve was in the middle of his meal and told them that their son was no more alive than the chicken on his plate." She turns around and delivers the much-awaited punchline to the Dutchman. "And the cock got up off his plate and crowed. They've kept chickens in a shrine here ever since."

She grins and turns to Daniel for approval. He has opened his eyes again, but his face is ashen. She drops her storyteller air.

"Are you all right, Daniel?" Ginny doesn't move toward him, but even Rob turns around when he hears the apprehension in her voice.

Daniel stands at the entrance of the dark corridor staring at the painting of the boy in the tight noose. A slight twitch starts at the corner of his mouth. Aware of the unwanted spasm, he speaks in an attempt to cover up the strangeness of it.

"What did the reeve do then, so?" he asks, his voice breaking, even though he knows the answer. He looks down at the block floor of the cathedral and then back up at Ginny, swallowing hard.

She hesitates and then answers him gently. "He took them to the gallows and cut down their son," she says. "He was alive, just like they said."

"A miracle," Daniel says, looking up at the painting again, seeing not the young boy but Petra in the noose, her blue swollen face with the life choked out of it. It hangs down, a dead piece of meat, like dinner on a plate. The figure of the reeve floats up and cuts into the lower half of her jaw with a knife and fork. He lifts the bloody flesh to his mouth and bites down on a piece of lower lip he has cut out with part of her chin.

"Daniel," Ginny says again, "are you sure you're ..."

Daniel stumbles out of the cathedral before she can finish. He staggers through a side door and out into a small churchyard garden. He doesn't notice the nun sitting on a bench until he lifts his head from vomiting in the flower beds she planted in the spring. She points an accusing finger at him as she scolds in staccato Spanish.

He doesn't know what she is saying, and he doesn't care. He is going mad. And madness has its own language. He wipes the sick off with the back of his shirtsleeve and meets the nun's angry glare head on. Her face goes white to match his own and her mouth drops open. The desperate look of him betrays what he is capable of. The nun sees what is inside of him and hurries away through a low archway in the garden. Her long black robes make a swishing sound as she disappears from sight. From behind the closed door of the cathedral someone slides a bolt into the lock. Daniel can hear the cock crow from inside, lurid and lonesome, a divine prisoner crying out for justice within its gilded cage. He staggers away from the sound before vomiting one more time in the garden. Then he looks for the road, not knowing where it leads.

*

Miles away, in Grañón, Daniel is pulled up the back stairs of an old church. All the churches are old here. The word really loses its meaning after awhile: ancient, antiquated, archaic. Everything is old on the Camino, or perhaps everything is lost in time with no real age at all.

Daniel can't think straight although his head is clearer than it was back in the cathedral. He doesn't even know how he got to Grañón. He remembers hopping over a short wall of the churchyard onto a back street where low-hanging trees robbed the light. He had walked aimlessly from there until he left the city behind him, faintly registering the cars that honked and braked in his midst. They could not touch him. He was invisible. He was damned. He was a ghost.

By the time he came into Grañón, he had started to come back to himself, noticing the change in scenery. His head began to clear, either from the painkillers wearing off or from the shock, perhaps. That is when a fast-talking group of Italian girls had grabbed him by the arm and led him into the stairwell of *Iglesia de San Juan Bautista*. When he first walks in, he is in such a daze he thinks the twelfth-century church is named after a baseball player.

"Welcome, welcome, *peregrino*."

Daniel had expected a priest, but instead a short middle-aged woman in a flowery print skirt greets him at the top of the stairs. She has frizzy red and grey hair held down under a bright kerchief, and Birkenstocks with socks on her feet. Her accent is American. She reminds him of the teacher in those children's science books, Ms. Frizzle. Petra used to read those books to her pupils. Sometimes he stole a look at them, enjoying the basic lessons about electricity and the solar system.

As Ms. Frizzle leads him into the foyer, he sees a common room off the hallway. It has a fireplace, low couches, and a set of long tables stacked against the wall. A small kitchen emits steam from a doorway. Stairs lead both up and down from the space. The Italian girls appear to have dispersed along one of these; he's not sure in which direction. Aged buildings such as these contain many twists and turns. You could hide an entire football team among them.

"Thank you," Daniel manages to cough out. He shakes his head, as if to put something back to rights. Like one of those games where you tilt a box to slip the little ball bearing back into place.

"Would you like a drink of water?" The woman can sense his distress.

He nods, and she disappears into the steamy kitchen, returning shortly with a tall glass filled to the top. He takes it and drinks it all down in one go, belching heavily afterward. The laughter of the Italian girls peals out from another room. Daniel doesn't know which is worse, the taste he just brought up in his mouth, or his mortification at having belched in this woman's face.

"Excuse me." It doesn't seem like enough, but it will have to do.

The woman smiles and tucks a red and grey frizzy piece of hair into her kerchief. "That's okay. You must have been very dehydrated." She clears some clean linens from a bench beside him. "Please sit down. You need to rest, I think."

He sits down, and she helps to remove his backpack. Her adept fingers unbuckle the straps when he fumbles with shaking hands. He feels the delicious release of the heaviness being lifted off his back. You never know the weight you're carrying until it's taken from you.

"How far did you walk today?" she asks him as she props his backpack against the wall with the others in a perfect line. Daniel looks over at a deep windowsill halfway down the stairs he just came up. Dozens of hiking boots are stacked there, ordered by size like a used shoe sale. This woman runs a tight ship.

"I'm not sure," he says at first, and then concentrating harder he comes up with a name. "Azofra, I walked from Azofra."

"Well, that's far enough," she says, reaching for the glass still in his hand. "Let me get you some more of that." She disappears back into the kitchen and Daniel leans back against the wall and shuts his eyes.

How many miles had he walked since he left Ginny and Rob in Santo Domingo? It felt like he'd walked for days, but he knows it is not even dark yet. He senses he travelled in circles before he came to enough to see the yellow arrows pointing up the hill and back onto the trail. He followed them even when he didn't realize he was, faithful in their guidance. "Good Orderly Direction," he supposes. That was the new trendy word for God. *More like dumb luck*, Daniel thinks, coming more and more back to himself as he rests on the bench. He opens his eyes and sees the woman standing in front of him with a replenished glass. He takes it from her with thanks and introduces himself.

"My name's Daniel. Forgive me, I reckon I got a little too much of the sun." *Or I may be going stark raving mad*, he thinks to himself, *but don't worry because the only people I scare are nuns.* Then it occurs to him this woman may be one.

"I'm Patrice." She folds her hands in front of her in a way Daniel associates with little girls reciting poetry. "I'm a volunteer here. I used to be a pilgrim myself. I came back for a few months to give back to the Camino what it gave to me." Her hands remain clasped.

He wonders if he is supposed to say something or just nod. He goes with nodding.

"We are a parochial *albergue,* run by the church. You can pay whatever donation that you can." She narrows her eyes at his brand name backpack, expensive hiking boots. "I suggest fifteen euros."

"Of course," he says, reaching into his pocket. He pulls out some crumpled bills, stuffing them into a gift-wrapped shoebox she has presented before him with the word *Donativo* written in black marker down the side. He manages to do this while balancing the slippery glass of water in one hand, a concerned Patrice looking on. She does not appear to be a woman who takes kindly to spills. He gulps down half the water to set her mind at ease.

When she asks for his passports, both pilgrim and Irish, he fishes those out as well. She takes them to a table in the hallway with the shoebox and enters his name in a black ledger with precise block letters. After she hands his documents back to him, she carries on with her prepared monologue.

"There are mattresses on the floor for sleeping. One bathroom for both the men and women. Your room will be down the stairs and to the left. Mass is at five o'clock and afterward Father Matias will conduct a tour."

"A tour?"

"Yes, there are some significant religious artifacts and artwork stored here. A sixth-century baptismal font was uncovered in one of the last renovations." She is proud telling him this. He wonders how she manages to explain all this to the people who don't understand English.

"After the tour, we will all return here and prepare dinner. We eat together in the common room." That explains the tables against the wall.

Daniel rubs his thumb on the sleek condensation of the glass and waits for Patrice to go on, but she appears to be finished with her script. When he drinks down the last of the water she reaches out and takes the tumbler from him before he can offer to put it away. The woman is a cross between an angel and his Aunt Breda, who never let them eat crisps in her parlour.

"Please make sure to remove your footwear before going to your room." Patrice observes his boots and he follows her gaze. They are covered in mud and a spray of tomato-red splatter. It may look like blood, but he knows it is just remnants of the crappy pizza he threw up. He leans over to undo his laces as she returns to the kitchen.

When he is placing his boots in the window well with the others, he sees them, Ginny and Rob down below in the street talking and pointing. Ginny's ponytail swishes back and forth as she chats and gestures, her hands moving expressively. She holds her arms out wide, as if to exaggerate the size of a fish she has caught. Then she laughs. He can't hear it, but he can see her body shake with the pleasure of it. The Dutchman leans casually on his walking stick, ankles crossed as he laughs with her.

Daniel turns away when he hears the sound of change clattering onto metal behind him. Patrice is emptying the collected *donativos* into a rectangular strong box. He sees his folded bills disappear inside to join the smattering of coins.

"These religious artifacts and artwork on the tour. Do they include anything at all to do with Mary Magdalene?"

"As a matter of fact, they do." Patrice's face brightens with the opportunity to showcase more about her volunteer home. "There is a tiny but exquisite statuette of her held in the rear cloisters. It was carved out of a single piece of ivory. *La Magdalena* is lying on her side in repose." She lowers her voice before she goes on. "A bit racy for the Catholic Church. It is a miracle that it survived all these years. One of the priests hid it under a floorboard during the Inquisition, apparently."

"A miracle, so," Daniel repeats before he turns back toward the window again. Ginny and Rob are gone. The street is empty, red dust whorls in colourful closed doorways.

"Will you be joining us for the Mass and tour, then?" he hears her ask from behind him. She thinks she has piqued his interest.

"No, I don't believe that I will," he tells her, walking slowly back for his pack and slipping it over one arm. He adds an explanation before he heads for the sleeping area off the back stairwell. "I reckon I've had enough miracles for one day."

✳

Daniel lies on his mattress on the floor in the dark and waits for sleep. A Japanese man snores loudly by the door. Daniel has earplugs, but he won't need them. He has taken more of the pills in a desperate bid to go to a place where these things won't bother him anymore. That is, if they don't kill him. He can't remember how many he took. Enough, he hopes, to wipe out the painting in the cathedral, the gallows, the reeve with a taste for human flesh. Enough to wipe out thoughts of Petra, and the memory of those final days when the cancer surrounded her like a hangman's noose.

But the thoughts come just the same, the pills taking their time. He had told everyone he'd been at home that day, that he'd left his bedside vigil only to fetch a few things. Hell, sometimes he told himself the same thing. The phone had buzzed from the passenger seat of the car as he drove away from the hospital. He'd returned the call when he got home, told the doctor he'd been in the shower.

"I'm so sorry, Petra," he says imperceptibly into the night.

He'd let her linger for weeks by then, unable to carry out their agreement. The cancer was ruthless as it spread through her body, taking everything from her, like the spoils of war. Each night, he'd kiss her and tell her "Tomorrow, darling, I promise." The next day would come and he would kiss her again, repeating the same lie before he left. Her lips felt like paper. He was a coward, and a product of his upbringing in a country where no life was for the taking except by God himself. They had researched other options — more humane ones than forcing a man to snuff out what little life lay trapped within his wife — but there were none.

Daniel had waited until after the nurse was gone, after she had finished going through the fruitless motions of checking blood pressure and changing the IV bag. Petra lay there so sick and wasted, in such an unfair state between life and death. A cruel joke of nature. His anger grew, as he searched for someone to blame the punchline on.

He had brought the pillow down over her shrunken face, bald and wizened, a man with no more faith in miracles. She never struggled, only lifted one or two fingers off the bed as if trying to make a point or ask for the check. Waiting for the mechanic scream of the flatline, he had closed his eyes and pretended he was hiking in Spain, Petra by his side, as they'd always planned when they first saw the yellow arrows on their honeymoon in France. He pictured them together with their backpacks looking out from atop the Pyrenees, not in that sterile room, her face buried beneath the white snow of the hard, unforgiving hospital pillow. He hadn't had the courage to deal with the attendants who would rush into the room afterward. Instead, he had dropped the pillow on a chair and walked out the door and into the night, away from his wife's still body. Away from the guilt that clung to him like a snake, paralyzing everything that came afterward.

He spirals down, the pills having their desired effect. Even from the dark well of his mind he believes he can hear her voice, alive, like the hanged boy in the painting who had come back to life. She never really died at all. He struggles for consciousness so he can talk to her, his upper body rising slightly from the floor. His hands reach out trying to touch her, to confirm what he thinks he sees. She is not dead. It was all a dream. She got better. He hadn't done what he'd done and been granted a miracle in return for his faithfulness. This is the wish that is never fulfilled, the one he keeps coming back to again and again. If only he had done things differently, been a better man. He had betrayed her in the end. She didn't realize it, but he had.

His hands grasp the emptiness of air. She is there but not there, as she always is for him. His body falls back down on the thin foam mattress on the floor, his arms drop beside him in defeat. He is heavy with the drugs and his own sorrow. His brain shuts down piece by piece, like an overworked electrical board powering down.

"Be careful what you wish for," she whispers, just before he is lost for the night. Her voice travels away on the wind mixed with red dust. He falls asleep without realizing it wasn't Petra at all.

Daniel rises above the sleeping men and women on the floor. He drifts out the door and to a place deep in the church reliquary, where an eight-inch ivory statuette lies back on her side and yawns. Mary Magdalene's eyes go wide as she sees the shadow of a woman with half a face float by the stained-glass window. Daniel sees her as well, but deep in his narcotized slumber, he will not remember the next day. This is a blessing, as death can be.

CHAPTER 8
Grañón to Espinosa

THE NEXT MORNING DANIEL drops all the pills in the trash before he leaves the *albergue*, except for his bottle of Aspirin. He pops two of that miracle drug in his mouth before he walks out of Grañón. He doesn't even wash them down with the water in his bottle, just lets the grainy bitterness of them burn down his throat. They won't kill the pain as efficiently, but they won't make him see things that aren't there, either. He blames everything on the pills, even though his strange sightings began before them. It is easier that way.

He still feels groggy from what he took the night before, and he steps along the trail with more effort and concentration than he usually needs to exert. It's like one of those dreams where you are trying to run away through Jell-O, each step seeming to occur against semi-solid resistance. Thankfully, the terrain has only moderate hills, nothing too taxing for his tedious gait. He trudges along, head down for the most part, only glancing up from time to time to briefly observe his surroundings. There are more trees than yesterday, and the farm fields and villages are poorer than the ones he has passed before. Scattered remains of wheat crops and oats have replaced the bare, harvested vineyards. Grains are not the lucrative business of wine, he supposes. Booze is worth more than bread.

This part of the Camino appears to have been torn from a history book, *Agrarian Peasant Societies of the Middle Ages*, it would be called. Many of the buildings in the villages he passes look like they hail from that era though they might only be a couple hundred years old. The style of building is what makes them appear ancient, their bent disposition. Some seem as if they may fall over and crush him as he walks by. They lean like drunken soldiers guarding the edges of the rundown villages, as they have probably done for years, passing the centuries looking on the point of ruin, but really just playing a game.

Like me, Daniel thinks. Playing the role of the grieving man who needs propping up when he doesn't deserve the sympathy. He had loved Petra more than he loved the land he grew up on and left everything he knew to be with her. His profound grief is real. Yet he feels like an unbalanced fraud. The blame he carries makes him lean precariously toward collapse, like the buildings in the town that lack the sense to fall down.

The Camino begins to run closer to the highway. It is less peaceful than the farm fields. At least the pedestrian traffic is light, with few fellow pilgrims and their well-meaning attempts at conversation to trouble his mood or his recovering head. He has ripped off the bandage, pleased to be rid of the gauze and the tape — the markings of an invalid. The dressing probably should have been left on longer, but so far the wound hasn't started bleeding again. It is beginning to heal, as is his prescription hangover. By noon the last of his haziness finally burns off along with the morning mist he started the day in. Off on the horizon he can see new mountains. He doesn't know which ones they are and doesn't bother trying to look them up in the guidebook.

Belorado is the first major town he comes to. The ruins of a castle are to his right as he enters the city proper, and soon after a roadside restaurant reminds him of a classic American truck stop. The low rectangular box of a red building and its glaring neon sign give it a nostalgic old-time diner feel. He crosses the pedestrian bridge over a busy *autopista* and opens the door in search of *bocadillo* and a Coke. He is not disappointed in finding either.

He has just sat down with his sandwich and drink when the little bell above the door of the café rings with another customer. Its discreet jingle is no match for the booming voice that comes with it.

"And then I said to him, who the hell do you think I am, Barack Obama?" The speaker has dropped the H on hell. British. Daniel turns around and sees a huge man, in his sixties probably, but in good shape. He walks in the door behind two young women and a bald man who is nervously scraping his hand across where he used to have hair. All of them seem to be trying to distance themselves from the Englishman. As soon as they are fully inside, the girls excuse themselves and make a run for the restroom. The bald guy orders a ham *bocadillo* and a bottle of San Miguel. The waitress behind the counter slices the bread and prepares the sandwich while the two men watch. She opens the beer bottle with a metal church key and passes it over. The Englishman doesn't order anything.

After paying and collecting the sandwich in its white paper packaging, the two men sit down together. After several minutes, when the girls don't return, the bald guy starts to look nervous again. He eventually gets up and walks out the door without a word to his tablemate, leaving half his meal and an almost full beer. Too embarrassed, Daniel figures, to admit they've been ditched.

When the waitress comes to clear the food and drink away, the Englishman reaches out in protest, letting his fingers linger as he clasps his mitt of a hand over hers on the bottle of lager. She starts, and drops the bottle back on the table, where he stops it just before it tips over. He leans over and whispers something into her ear that Daniel can't hear. It couldn't have been good though. The waitress runs into the backroom like a woman pursued by wolves.

Daniel has watched this whole little drama unfold. Eating alone, he doesn't have much else to do. But when he sees the Englishman get up with the beer in his hand and walk toward him, he quickly looks down as if the mottled grey Arborite tabletop is the most interesting thing he has ever seen.

"Mind if I sit down?"

The man is too loud for Daniel to pretend he doesn't hear him. He pulls out the chair opposite Daniel, then puts the bottle of San Miguel down on the table. Seated, he leans back with his fingers interlaced behind his square head, completely at ease with himself. A big man, he must be used to inserting himself wherever he wants to be. Daniel murmurs his assent, but it hardly seems necessary at this point.

"My name's Mark." He extends one of his mitt hands over to Daniel and they shake. Despite the size of man's fist, his grip is limp and clammy.

"I'm Daniel." He watches as the man nods then returns to eating his *bocadillo*, chewing faster now, swallowing with an urgency that only the girls hiding in the restroom can really understand. Daniel's not afraid of the guy. Nor does he have a problem with Brits, counting many as good friends. It's just he can tell there is no way that he and this man are going to get along.

Mark lifts the beer to his lips and takes a stiff draught — downing almost half of it in one go. A bit of foam remains above his mouth afterward and he wipes it off with the back of his hand. Almost every finger he has sports a fat gold or silver ring.

"Is this your first time on the Camino, Daniel?"

Daniel inwardly cringes from the decibel level. The Englishman seems to come with only one sound setting for speaking.

"It is."

"Well, this is my second. How's about that, Daniel? You ever heard of someone who would do this bleedin' thing twice?"

Of course, Daniel has, but he is not going to say so. He'd met more than one person who claimed to have made the trip a second time. Seemed like overkill to him.

"Yes, I know quite a few things about the Way. That's for sure." Mark takes another swig of the beer. At this rate, he is going to be done in four sips. And they say the Irish are drinkers. "Have you got any blisters yet?"

"I don't." Daniel thinks a moment and then reconsiders. "What harm, I think I might have one." Late this morning, he had felt another hot spot developing on the edge of his left foot. Maybe he'd developed it during those lost hours after Santo Domingo, but now that his body has cleared fully of the medication he is starting to feel it more.

"Well, you must *know* the trick for blisters." Mark doesn't give Daniel time to tell him anything he knows. "You take a needle and thread and you pull it through. Lets all the pus run out and keeps the wound open so it can keep on draining." The Englishman's voice overpowers the small restaurant, people turn around and stare at them and then quickly look away. Afraid presumably that the man will come and sit with them and discuss pus over lunch.

"Sure, I'll keep that in mind," Daniel says. He must admit that this is a fairly good strategy. However, he already knows it. Most pilgrims do. He notices the Englishman looking over toward the restroom and follows his gaze.

"Those young ladies would do well to be walking with someone who could protect them on the Camino." He turns his attention back to Daniel. "Young women today, they don't understand the importance of having a man with them."

Daniel hides a smile behind his Coke as he takes a sip from the can. He can imagine what Ginny would think of this conversation. He wishes she were here, and not for the first time this morning. She's probably walking with the Dutchman. They looked like they were getting fairly cozy last night.

"Oh, I don't know about that," Daniel says, finishing off his drink. "I'm after thinking the Camino is pretty safe."

The Englishman stares at him with a superior look. "You think so, do you?" He pronounces the word "so" like it has a wow on the end. "Well, I suppose you don't know that a woman disappeared off the Camino just recently."

"Aye, I might have heard something about that." Daniel stops crumpling up the white paper his sandwich was wrapped in and looks at the Englishman. "But I hadn't heard anything more, reckoned she'd been found by now."

"They're trying to keep it hush-hush." The Englishman checks around the lunchroom as if he is the one trying to keep things quiet, an impossibility for him, but he tries to lower his voice just the same. "She was an American. Disappeared one day and no one's seen her since. None of her bank or credit cards have been used either. Just vanished right off the trail."

Daniel thinks of Ginny again. Now he hopes that she is walking with the Dutchman.

"Surely, it's an isolated incident," Daniel says as he stands up, throwing his garbage in the nearby can. He reaches for his pack, getting ready to go.

"There's been other attempts at abduction." Awb-dook-shun. "Women being attacked by men in ski masks who try to pull 'em into a car." The Englishman glances over at the restrooms again, as he wets his upper lip. "Or just groped as they walk along." He turns back to Daniel. "You know, a bit of the tit and tail, that sort of thing."

One of his huge hands wraps around the beer bottle, and he slides it down the exterior, loosening the label made moist with condensation. He doesn't say anything more. Daniel uses the opportunity to get away. He nods as he stands, then walks over to the counter where they sell T-shirts and other sundry items, leaving the offensive gobshite to his beer. There, he buys more Aspirin and a headlamp to replace the flashlight he dropped in the cornfield. Trying it on, he stands in front of a mirror. He looks like a cyclops or a coal miner, but it will keep his hands free and he can't drop it if it's tied around his head. The band passes just above where he smacked his head on the rock. Once he's completed his purchases, he comes back to the table to grab the last of his things.

"I'll be on my way, then."

The Englishman nods but doesn't raise his head — not even when the little bell jingles as Daniel pushes hard on the exit door. He turns back and sees the big man still focused on the bottle, pulling at the wet label with a ragged fingernail, ripping it off bit by tattered bit.

Once outside, Daniel stops to put on his sunglasses. He doesn't usually wear them, but after talking with Mark he feels as if he needs to hide himself somehow. The glasses provide a barrier between him and the disturbing things the Englishman told him.

Daniel walks across the bridge. The traffic on the *auto-pista* below has been reduced to only a few cars here and there. It is nearing siesta, and everything is settling down for the customary Spanish afternoon nap. Daniel hurries on the trail through the streets of Belorado, as one by one the little shops and cafés turn their signs over to *Cerrado*. As he leaves the town, he passes a church built into pockmarked limestone cliffs. There are caves within it where hermits lived before they became saints. Daniel has read about them and had meant to stop and have a look. Instead he keeps on walking. No longer interested. He keeps his eyes trained on the path ahead, watching where the trail disappears into the next valley. Each time he reaches a crest, he hopes to see the familiar baseball hat and ponytail. Just as he hopes the young girls will stay in the restroom until long after the Englishman is gone.

✳

She's hanging laundry outside the *albergue* when Daniel catches sight of her. Clipping her socks one at time on a long line strung between two trees. He doesn't trust his eyes at first. He had been hoping to see her all afternoon and was frequently disappointed. Now she looks like a mirage of his own making as she bends down to get her damp T-shirt out of the basket, two brightly coloured clothes pegs held gingerly in her mouth.

"Ginny?" He stands beside the grassy triangle formed by the meeting of the Camino on one side and the one narrow street of Espinosa on the other. She stops and considers him for a moment then picks up the wash basket and saunters over.

"Hi, Daniel." She balances the basket on her hip, like a fifties housewife.

"Sure, Ginny, about yesterday …"

Ginny shocks him by raising two fingers swiftly and placing them on his lips. "Let's go find someplace to talk."

The picnic table behind the *albergue* borders on rolling empty fields, the soil grey and cracked from a summer of harsh Spanish sun. Ginny has dropped her wash basket inside the back door and come to join him there. She holds two lemonades she purchased from the vending machine inside.

"Here, you look like you could use this."

He can. Lemonade is the elixir of the gods on the Camino. It's the perfect balance of salt and sugar to restore a pilgrim's electrolytes with some vitamin C mixed in. That, and it tastes fabulous.

"Thanks." He tries to twist the top off, but it won't budge. Ginny reaches for the bottle and deftly pops the cap with the opener she had ready in her pocket. She does the same with her own. They sit with the bottles in front them, not drinking, but not talking either. Daniel doesn't know where to start.

"What happened yesterday, Daniel?"

"I went off my nut, is what happened." He reaches out and takes a sip of the lemonade. It wakes up his tongue, maybe loosens it a little. "It was the painting. The one of the hanging."

"That was pretty damn obvious." She keeps the mood light. She wants him to feel at ease.

He is grateful for this. It makes getting ready to tell a half-truth easier.

"I reckon it reminded me of what happened to Petra."

"She hung herself?" Ginny asks, surprised.

"No, no, nothing like that," he says. "She had cancer. It got fairly bad toward the end." He pauses, considers the memory of his wife wasting away in front of him. Her eyes still so alive, so her, but the rest of her body just a painful shell. A flesh prison she couldn't escape. "Sure, it got really feckin' bad," he says.

Ginny nods and waits for him to go on.

"We made the decision to take her off the life support. That was how she wanted it. We'd discussed it. Before." And they had. Petra was adamant. No heroic efforts. A DNR when the time came.

"That must have been really difficult."

"It's not like it is in the movies, of course." Daniel takes another sip of the lemonade and places the bottle down on the rough wooden table. The wet label against the skin of his palm reminds him of the Englishman, and he recoils, snatching his hand away. "She started choking, grabbing at her throat."

"My God."

"It went on for a full ten minutes, her being in distress like that. Sure, I couldn't take it any longer. I had them put the breathing tube back in." They had taken it back out again later, but by then she had stabilized, managed to breathe on her own. He'd lost his chance, as well as hers, for a faultless exit.

"Jesus, Daniel."

"The painting, of the lad hanging." He can't tell her what he really saw, so he settles for a tenuous paraphrase. "I was reminded of how she looked, choking like that. It set me off, I suppose." He takes another sip of lemonade.

"I'm sorry, Daniel."

"I should be over these things," he says, knowing that he may never be.

"It takes time." They hold that thought for a moment and then she asks, "What finally happened, with your wife?"

"She died not long afterward," he tells her. "They took her off the machines and she managed to breathe on her own for a few days, but then she finally gave in. I wasn't even there when it happened. They had to call me at home. I'd run back to get a change of clothes, so." He clears his throat of the lie, then pushes the bottle of lemonade away from him.

They sit that way for a full minute at the picnic table. Far away he can hear a farmhand calling to his livestock, then the passionate swish of a corn broom on cement steps. A child cries out and then laughs. A screen door opens and shuts. It cuts off a child's giggles behind it.

"What harm, Ginny," Daniel finally says, breaking the silence of ordinary sounds. "They let you put down an animal that's suffering, but a person ..." He stops and gazes out into the dried-up fields, unable to finish.

"Yes," she says simply, hesitating a moment before she puts her hand on one of his. "I understand."

✳

Daniel stands in front of the cracked mirror in the *albergue* washroom. He's wetted the comb in his hand with the dribbling stream of water from the faucet. Now he is trying to use it to force his curly hair into submission. It is stuck up like a circus clown's after the nap he just woke from. Rushing, he hits his healing head wound with the comb's teeth and curses. He's supposed to meet Ginny across the street at a pub for dinner. The pub. The whole hamlet consists of just it, the *albergue,* two houses, and a falling-down barn. Of the five buildings, the man who runs the *albergue* owns three of them.

He gives up on his hair and forces the door to the small washroom open. It catches on the warped floor and he has to push hard to move it. When it finally gives way, it hits the wall with a thud that shakes the whole upper floor. A small Japanese woman sitting on a twin bed looks up at the noise and then returns to the book she is reading. The title on the cover is unintelligible to him. All the Japanese characters seem like a cross between little houses and the symbol for pi. Their black strokes end in narrow points as if they were painted in haste with a fine-tipped brush.

"Sorry," he says. The woman doesn't look up from her book but waves a delicate hand in the air. He is forgiven and dismissed all in one go.

The night air feels cool on his face. It sharpens the soft edges still left over from his nap. He feels more clear-headed. More awake. He takes a deep breath and tastes moisture in it. Rain tonight or tomorrow morning. That will be good — the soil could use it. Almost two decades away from home, and he still looks at weather as a farmer would.

He spits in his palm and makes one last attempt to pat down his hair before he opens the door to the pub and walks in. It's surprisingly bright inside — not like the pubs at home where murkiness is a selling point. He walks past a well-stocked bar and into a small dining area. Ginny sits at a table for two over in the corner, a bottle of red wine already open in front of her with two glasses. He'd asked the *hospitaleiro* to have it ready for them at seven o'clock. It is at least seven thirty now.

"Hey there, sleepyhead."

"Hope you haven't been waiting long." He seems to have done nothing but apologize to this woman since he met her.

"Don't worry about it. I've had lots of entertainment." As she says this, a roar of laughter comes up from a long table at the back of the room. There are at least eight middle-aged women sitting around it, each in various states of what Daniel's mother would politely refer to as "tipsy" and his sister would call "completely bladdered."

"They're Australian," Ginny says as Daniel takes the seat opposite. "I think they've been at it for a while. Before you came in they were trading war stories."

"What kinds of wars are they after fighting?" Daniel says. "They look like members of the Catholic Women's League. All they need are the pillbox hats."

"No." Ginny giggles. It bubbles out of her, natural and easy. "More like battle of the sexpots. They are trying to one-up each other with tales of embarrassing one-night stands. The last one involved hand puppets. I'm glad you weren't here to hear it."

"Gather I'd be shocked, do you?" He takes the second glass and fills it halfway with red wine.

"If you weren't shocked, I'd be concerned about you."

The waiter brings a menu, and Daniel leans over to share it with Ginny, but she's already eaten. He feels guilty again for being so late. Ordering a seafood paella, he hopes it will be as good as the one he had at the Rioja festival. They talk a bit about the towns they walked through and the things they saw that day. The castle ruins. The roadside stands selling air dried *embutido* and rich, ripe fruit. Daniel's paella comes quickly. This most likely means it was made in the microwave. He attacks it lustily with his knife and fork just the same.

Another peal of laughter rises from the group of women at the long table. One of them falls out of her chair. The proprietor runs over to help — then brings back shots of grappa on the house for each of them, in an act that can only be described as enabling. When he offers one to Daniel, he waves it off. A glass of wine will be enough for him.

"So, what happened to Rob?" Daniel has been wondering where the Dutchman is since he got here but was afraid to ask.

"He wanted to go on to the next town. More choices for places to stay and eat."

A countdown begins at the long table. When they reach blast-off, they all down the grappa. One of the younger ones burps loudly into a napkin. Ginny rolls her eyes.

"Maybe he had the right idea."

"Oh, I don't know. I'm getting right attached to them." Daniel pops a rubbery but well-seasoned shrimp into his mouth, grinning at her. He feels so much better than he has the last few days. The nap. The meds out of his system. "Then again, I've always enjoyed the company of women."

"Is that so?" Ginny arches an eyebrow over the rim of her wine glass.

"Not like that," Daniel protests, shovelling in another forkful of rice. "I spent the better part of my childhood growing up on an isolated farm and the rest of it in an all-boys boarding school. By the time I got to university, women seemed like an exotic species I'd never had the opportunity to observe up close." Daniel remembers their differentness, walking in packs between lecture halls, all soft voices and round edges.

"And what happened once you got close?"

"Well, most of them told me to feck off, if you must know."

"I don't believe that for a second."

"I wasn't always the smooth character you see before you." He wipes his mouth with his napkin then throws it down on his plate. "Though I always liked chatting women up." That didn't come out right. He tries to explain. "What I mean is, I get on with women." Jaysus, what is wrong with him? "I have a sister," he finally ekes out. "We're very close. Perhaps that's where it comes from."

She rescues him from himself. "Do you have any other siblings?"

"Two brothers, a fair bit older than me. They always found me a bit of a tagalong, I reckon. What about yourself?"

"A sister," Ginny says, her brows knitting briefly together. Daniel remembers now her mentioning this, how they didn't get along. Ginny reaches for her wine glass and changes the subject. "Tell me more about your family."

"Well, my parents are still alive and living on the farm, back home."

"And where is back home?"

"Carn N'Athair. I'd say you've never heard of it." She hadn't.

"They must be getting up there. Your parents."

"They are," Daniel answers, feeling a twinge of guilt knowing his father might have to hire help, with money he possibly didn't have.

"What's it like, where you grew up?"

Her question conjures up images of the home farm for him, the stone courtyard by the house where his mother kept roses, the sweet smell of hay as he walked down to milk the cows in the morning. "A fair bit like here," he tells her. "But greener. We raised dairy cows so it's mostly hills and valleys for grazing." He coughs a bit from the spiciness of the paella and takes a sip of water to offset it before going on. "The area gets its name from the hill overlooking our farm. You can see hundreds of acres of pasture in the vale from it. We'd always be up there when we were young, searching for wild mushrooms for supper or just messing about, you know, kid stuff."

He pauses, remembering his last trek to the peak. Petra had loved hiking up the heavily wooded slope whenever they went to visit his folks. They'd made love at the top, dangerously close to an open clearing, hurried and excited against a tree. She'd gotten sap on her hands and then on his boxers. His mother had asked him about it when she did the wash. Petra started to laugh so hard she had to leave the room.

"What does the name mean?" Ginny asks.

Daniel doesn't understand her question at first, still lost in the memory of that sweet, sticky tree sap. "You said, 'The area gets its name from the hill,'" she prompts.

"Aye, Carn N'Athair," he says, coming back to himself. "It means 'Hill of our Fathers.' Probably the better part of my mouldering ancestors are buried up there somewhere."

"Will you go back?" She asks the question innocently enough, not realizing how loaded it is for him.

"I said I would," he admits. "After Petra died. Both my brothers are doctors, so there's no chance they'll be taking over the farm."

"So why haven't you?" she asks, pausing. "Gone back, I mean."

"You're after sounding like my sister." He hadn't meant for it to sound so curt. He makes a point of softening his tone. "I'm a bit slow in getting ready to go, is all," he explains. "Petra's illness, her death. It happened so quickly." He holds the fork suspended in his hand for a moment.

"Was there ever any hope?" Ginny asks gently.

"No, no, there wasn't." He lets that hard truth sit between them for a moment, then adds, "She was a tough one, though. You'd never have known what she was up against."

Daniel remembers the diagnosis, the feeling like his stomach had sunk into his feet at the doctor's office. Petra had taken his hand but otherwise remained composed throughout the conversation of chemo and months remaining. She had been adamant with him after they left the office. She wasn't afraid to die.

"She was trying to be strong for you," Ginny says matter-of-factly.

He looks across the table at her with his mouth open, quickly shutting it when he realizes there is still some paella in there. Remarkably, what Ginny said has never occurred to him. That his wife might have been putting on a mask of strength for his sake. He had been too busy with his own deceptions during her illness — trying to act like he wasn't ripping apart inside all those months.

"I thought I was after being the strong one," he tells her. But he knows in the end he was weak.

"Have you spread the ashes yet?"

"No," he admits, a bit defensive. He takes a long sip of wine so he doesn't have to look directly at her. "I don't believe I've found the right place." He doesn't tell her about Finisterre. It sounds too much like he's procrastinating. Instead, he toys with what's left of his rice and adds with emphasis, "And if you haven't noticed, I may be losing my mind."

"Oh c'mon. It's not that bad."

"I'm after seeing zombies in cornfields, Ginny."

"Just the one."

"One is surely enough."

"Daniel, you were exhausted, and it was dark. And all that wine we drank couldn't have helped."

"And what about the cemetery?" he reminds her. His stomach is starting to tense up with the discussion. He puts down his fork.

"I told you, Daniel, you hit your head really hard."

"Enough to go bleedin' mental in the middle of the chicken cathedral?" He has raised his voice. He picks up his fork and stabs at a particularly tough shrimp that bounces off his plate and skitters across the tile floor. The Australian women turn in their chairs to look at him. He and Ginny stare at one another for a few seconds not knowing what to say.

"Okay, that was pretty strange," she says, and starts to giggle again. The Australians go back to their grappa. The waiter covertly retrieves the wayward shrimp. "The Dutchman thought you had a thing about birds."

Now they are the ones to burst out laughing. Perhaps it was all explainable after all. The last incident just a weird interaction of the meds. *All doctors are quacks*, Daniel thinks, remembering the country physician and his *Santa Compaña* story. He decides even his brothers are a couple of prats. He's glad he threw all the pills in the garbage.

"You're tougher than you think, Daniel. I wouldn't worry so much," Ginny tells him, leaning back in her chair, relaxed. It makes him feel relaxed, too. He no longer worries about what secret she may be hiding. Everyone has secrets. It doesn't matter to him if she wants to keep part of herself to herself.

"Sure, you might be right about that."

The Australian women start to break up their party. Noisy chairs scrape the floor and the whole stumbling throng walks past them and out of the bar. They watch Daniel and Ginny and snicker behind their hands like schoolgirls. Ginny picks at what is left of Daniel's paella and pops a rubbery scallop into her mouth.

"I'm right about a lot of things."

Stepping outside after dinner, they are surprised by how late it's gotten. The street is silent and dark. Clouds have moved in and covered the moon. Daniel had been right about the rain. The only light is what leaks from the draped pub window. Ginny holds Daniel's arm and lets him guide her across the grass triangle between the street and the *albergue*. They don't see the big man until he steps out of the deeper shadows where he was smoking behind a crumbling stone garden wall.

"Hullo!"

It's the Englishman, Mark. Daniel feels Ginny stiffen beside him.

"Is that you, Daniel?"

"It is."

Daniel stiffens as well. Mark has stepped out and blocked their way. The butt of his cigarette glows in the dark.

"Who's that you got with you?"

Ginny grasps Daniel's arm more tightly. He can't see her face clearly in the darkness, so he's not sure whether she's frightened or annoyed.

"Is this the one you ran out of the café for, Danny?" The big man takes another drag on his cigarette. The red-dotted ember flares then floats to the ground. "I'm not surprised." The outline of his enormous head moves up and down regarding Ginny critically in the weak light.

Everything the man does drips with something unclean, Daniel thinks. Like the sour stench of a train station toilet. "We were just on our way back to the *albergue*," Daniel says.

He goes to lead Ginny around, but the Englishman steps out in front, coming far too close. Daniel wants to knock him back on his arse, but he knows this would be overreacting.

"I know you." The Englishman is addressing Ginny. "How are you, young lady?"

"Fine, thanks." She crosses her arms protectively.

"How's your friend?" The Englishman takes a long drag on the cigarette, lets it out too near to Ginny's face.

She cringes. Even from where Daniel stands, he can smell the grappa on the man's breath.

"Listen, mate, why don't you clear off." Daniel steps in between them, pushing the big man ever so slightly aside.

"I think the lady can speak for herself, don't you?" Mark smirks.

"I think the lady would prefer to be left the hell alone," Daniel says, even and threatening.

The big man ignores him, focuses on Ginny again. "So, you have a new walking partner now, have you, dearie?" He looks briefly at Daniel and then turns away, dismissing him. "I'm glad. Can't be too careful. There's women going missing on the Camino, don't you know?" He switches the cigarette to his left hand, then reaches out with his right and tousles Ginny's hair.

"Right!" Daniel shoves him hard across the grass. The big man staggers but doesn't fall. He's dropped his cigarette, though. Daniel can see the ember burning in the grass. Mark retreats unsteadily into the shadows, like a lazy trained bear, all raised fur and no claws. Daniel takes Ginny by the arm and hurries her back to the *albergue*. The Englishman calls out from the dark.

"Watch out for that one, Danny boy."

Daniel can hear him fire up a lighter for another cigarette in the dark.

"This isn't her first time on the Camino either."

CHAPTER 9

Espinosa to Hotel Las Vegas

"WAKE UP, DANIEL."

Daniel looks up into the half-light of the *albergue* bed-room and sees Ginny standing over him, dressed for the road.

"What time is it?"

"I don't know. It's almost dawn, I guess." She searches around the room, as if expecting the dawn to creep up behind her. "I just want to get started early. I was hoping to make it to Burgos today."

Burgos is a lot farther than Daniel had planned to walk — close to twenty-five miles — but he doesn't want to be left behind. He sits up in his sleeping bag and runs a hand through his unruly bed-head hair. "Give me a second to get ready. I'll meet you outside."

The coolness of the mist strikes Daniel as he opens the front door of the *albergue*. The temperature has dropped significantly overnight. He can't see the pub across the street and can only barely make out Ginny in the road waiting for him, fading in and out in the curls of heavy fog. He has little time to snap on his new headlamp before she starts making her way west along the cobblestone street.

"Is everything all right?" he asks her, catching up.

"Yeah, I just want to get out of here. That guy gives me the creeps."

"The Englishman?"

"Yeah, him. Mark. He's such an idiot."

"What was all that nonsense he said about your friend?" They hadn't had a chance to talk after last night. Ginny was so upset she went straight to bed.

"He must have seen me with Rob and then he saw me with you. I guess that makes me a Camino-slut or something in his eyes. The guy's full of shit."

Daniel nods in agreement. The light from his headlamp bobbing up and down. "You're right. He is that."

A farm animal makes an explosive snort close by, but neither of them can see where from. Between the darkness and the mist, visibility is reduced to just a few yards ahead as they walk, even with his headlamp.

"Sure, he wasn't wrong about that missing woman, though," Daniel continues. "I was looking it up on the internet last night." Even in a blip on the map like Espinosa they had Wi-Fi. "She disappeared at the end of the summer, outside Mazarife."

"Probably got sick of the trail. Some people can't hack it. They'll find her holed up at a resort in *Costa del Sol*, drinking sangrias with the cabana boy."

"Perhaps," Daniel says, unsure. "I reckon it's a still a good idea to stick together, in any case." He treads carefully with this last comment. He doesn't want another lecture on how she doesn't need him to take care of her.

"That's cool with me," she says, although her full concentration is on the path rather than the conversation.

She is moving quickly, with long confident strides through the poor visibility, like a car overdriving its headlights. He needs to hurry to keep up. It must have been quite a run-in she had with the Englishman for her to want to put this much distance between them.

"Ginny, was something after happening, you know, with your one?"

"With who?"

"With the Englishman." He doesn't usually push people with personal questions. But if there is something going on here he thinks he needs to know.

"He tried to grab me once," she says matter-of-factly. "After we all came back from dinner one night. Went to cop a feel when he said goodnight."

Daniel feels a twinge of guilt over his own grasping thoughts the night they shared a room. "Jesus, Ginny. You should have told me."

"So you could have really got into it with him, like a couple of Neanderthals? I don't think so."

"What if we meet up with him again? You need to let me at least have a word with him, Ginny." Have a word was a euphemism for Daniel here, meaning "smack upside the head."

"Please don't," she says. "He was drunk, like he was last night. Not like that's an excuse."

She looks behind her and so does he. There is a faint ball of light being dispersed through the haze. The sun is coming up.

She turns to him, slowing down a bit. "Just leave it, Daniel, he's not worth it."

"You shouldn't have to feel like you have to run away from him," he tells her, trying to keep his Neanderthal-ness in check.

"I'm not running away from him. I'm just not a big fan of conflict."

Neither is Daniel. Although in this case, he'd like to make an exception. "You're surely moving fast for someone who's not running away."

"I just don't want to have my Camino spoiled by a jerk like him, all right?"

She is silent after that. Daniel knows he should let it go, but there is one more thing he feels compelled to ask her.

"What was he meaning by that last comment?"

"Huh?"

"About it not being your first Camino."

"I told you, Daniel, he's just a dick." She steps up the pace again.

He nods and keeps up with her. On this point, he is in full agreement.

They continue at a rapid rate, even as the fog mixes with fat drops of rain. Even when the increasing warmth of the day makes them sticky inside their tightly tied jacket hoods. Between the water dripping down his face and the murky morning drizzle, Daniel is missing most of the waymarks. Sometimes he's lucky enough to spot a watery flash of yellow floating out of the gloom on the side of a tree or painted onto a rock. But he would have to walk over and stand right in front of it to determine which way the arrow is pointing. Ginny keeps them on course, despite her frenzied pace, never stopping to watch for markers. Or so it seems. He turns his headlamp off after awhile. She doesn't appear to need it, and it makes little difference for him in these dense conditions. Her behaviour seems a bit overblown, but he's willing to let it pass. He's hardly the one to make judgment on erratic behaviour these days. He lets her guide them both through the cloud-covered hills, not asking any more questions, as they twist and turn along the Camino, never getting lost.

✳

The rain is starting to ease up a bit by the time they hit Atapuerca. There are standing stones here, like Stonehenge but not as grand. They remind Daniel of the ones they have in the Burren, a rock-embedded part of Ireland not far from the Cliffs of Moher. He is disappointed when he finds out these ones are fakes, replicas erected to mark the spot where the bones of Europe's oldest skeleton were found.

"Four hundred thousand years old," Ginny translates from the historical plaque, finally stopping for the first time this morning. "Wow."

"I wonder why he fancied this place to settle?" Daniel observes the low-lying but otherwise unremarkable valley as he leans on one of the stones for a rest. "Though, I suppose four hundred thousand years can surely change a place."

"True," Ginny says. "This might have been a lake we're walking through and the poor guy drowned trying to catch sturgeon for dinner."

She looks at her wrist as if there might be a watch there, but there is only the bracelet, its glass beads and shells glistening wet with moisture. Daniel shudders slightly at the sight of it but passes it off as a shiver from the weather. Once more he steadies himself with the reassurance of facts.

"Aye, the sturgeon, now that's an ancient fish, dates back to the time of the dinosaurs, long before this boy came along. Now the sabre-toothed salmon, it ..."

Ginny walks back over to the path, waits for him expectantly. "We better get going," she says. "It's still eleven miles before Burgos." Four tour buses pull into a parking lot to the north of them, spewing out visitors into an interpretive centre as the rain starts in earnest again. Old skeletons are almost as big business as wine.

Daniel readjusts the weight of his pack on his back with a shoulder shrug then joins her, keeping his knowledge of the extinct salmon and its vicious teeth to himself. Some people just don't appreciate a good fish story.

The gradual rise of the sierra out of Atapuerca has become a steep, craggy slope. The stones are slippery, and Daniel is reminded of his hike down the side of *Alto del Perdón*, the day he tried to spread the ashes, the day he met Ginny. At least the fog has burnt off, and he can see what he's doing. He and Ginny pick their way up the rocky incline, testing each sharp stone before putting the full weight of a boot down. The need for concentration on the hard climb keeps them quiet. Although, they do manage to comment on a military training site they parallel. Only a barbed-wire fence a few feet off the Camino separates them from it. Warning signs with sincere exclamation points are nailed onto trees in the dense forest on the other side of the barrier — *¡Cuidado!* — which Ginny explains is Spanish for "Keep the hell out." Daniel doesn't need to be told. His last experience in a Spanish wood is enough to make him stick close to the trail, like a reformed Irish Red Riding Hood.

His calves are screaming by the time they reach the crest at the high point of the sierra. It is flat like a tabletop, as if the peak had been chopped off neatly with an axe. The evenness of the terrain is a relief, and the new angle stretches the cramped muscles at the back of his legs like a good massage. It stays flat like this for another half hour before they reach the end of the tabletop and look down on the next valley, waterlogged and hungry. Ginny finally gives in.

"Let's take a break," she says, aiming for a bench under a lofty wooden pole cross that stands watch over the valley. Daniel isn't about to argue. He drops his pack on the ground and sits on the bench beside her, stretching out his legs. Tall grass in the fields below them moves in waves with the wind. Off in the distance he can see modern buildings and concrete, the outskirts of the city of Burgos. The rain must have stopped awhile ago. You get used to bad weather after walking in it for a few hours, so you no longer notice it, even when its gone.

"Thank you," Ginny says, after they've wolfed down a couple of crunchy power bars with some water. She pulls down her hood. Her long bangs are plastered to her forehead, wet where they peek out the front. She still looks good.

"For what?" He drops his own hood, feels the pleasing warmth of sun. The clouds are clearing along with the rain.

"For not bugging me about wanting to get out of Espinosa. I know I was being unreasonable."

"I can understand why you'd want to be rid of that shite," Daniel says, wiping some water off his face where it has dripped down from his hair.

"Yes, but most guys would get all testosterone about it," she says, facing him.

"Are you after doubting my male hormones?"

"No, just appreciate you keeping them in check." Her voice sounds like there should be a wink with this comment. She clears her throat instead. "I mean, you respected what I wanted. Stuck with me, even though ..."

"Even though you were acting crackers?"

"Yes, that."

"I suppose I should be thanking you for the same favour." He stops smiling at this, starts digging into his backpack for his hat as a diversion tactic.

"C'mon, Daniel, we talked about this, I told you —"

He holds up a hand, interrupting her. He doesn't want to rehash the whole thing again either. "Some things are best dealt with by leaving them be, I reckon."

She nods. He eventually finds the hat, puts it on the bench beside him rather than putting it on.

"Besides, denial is a cultural imperative in Ireland. We're good at it. Got the lot of us through multiple famines."

"Really?" she says, challenging, but playful.

"Sure, that's why alcoholism plagued the nation for so many generations. Numb the mind. Deny the obvious."

"Even starving to death?"

"Even that."

A couple of other pilgrims arrive and the two of them raise a hand in greeting. It's a man and woman, and they ask Daniel to take a picture of them standing with the backdrop of the valley. The man wraps his arm around the woman's waist and they both pose, beaming for the camera. After they thank Daniel, they walk away holding hands and quietly chatting as they move out of sight. The woman laughs at something the man says, leaning into him.

He and Ginny watch as the two follow the serpentine path of the Camino down into the valley, the design meant to lessen the force of the decline even as it makes the trip longer. Daniel can hear the couple long after he can no longer see them. The intimacy of their conversation carries back along the open air to the two of them, sitting on the bench under the cross.

"Tell me about the good stuff."

"Pardon?" Daniel had almost forgotten Ginny was there.

"The good stuff about your wife," she says.

"About Petra?"

"Yeah. You told me last night about when she was sick. What was she like before that?"

Daniel hasn't talked about this in a while. People were always more interested in Petra's death than they were her life.

"She was an artist." He's not sure where to start, but Petra's art is as good a place as any. "She painted mostly. Although she could create anything with her hands. She used all forms of medium. Clay, metal, dirt."

"Dirt?"

"Aye," he says. "She was a force of nature. One Christmas, she used a box of old Star Wars toys to build a nativity scene." Daniel's mouth turns up in a half smile at the memory.

"You're joking," Ginny says, her eyes wide.

"Yoda was after being the baby Jesus. Our Lady was played by R2D2." He can see the little characters all lined up in the holy stable Petra created from popsicle sticks and dry grass from the backyard. "Sure, it sounds like a kid thing, but she often did things like that. She taught second grade. Was always looking for ways to delight the children. She lived for it."

He swallows after the last sentence, struck by the irony that Petra and he were never able to have children of their own, but perhaps in retrospect, it had been for the best.

"She even did magic tricks," he adds, forcing himself back into remembering good things.

"Like with cards?"

"The young ones weren't so interested in cards. You need something cleverer than that to impress an eight-year-old. Or something with animals. The kids just loved the animals. We owned a white rabbit named Ollie that got a fair bit of experience jumping out of hats."

"That's amazing!" Ginny claps her hands together in delight. "What other tricks did she do?"

"Oh, making things disappear and reappear. The little ones like that as well. Just a form of hide-and-seek really. They weren't easy to do, of course. She'd practise for weeks to get a trick working right. Sure, the one with the dove pan was pure genius. Took her months to perfect."

"A dove pan?"

"It's a metal pan with a lid, so," Daniel explains. "You pour in some flammable liquid and set the whole lot on fire. Then you put the lid on to douse it, say the magic words, and when you take the lid off again, a white dove appears. Ta-da!" Daniel mimes a dramatic flourish with his hands.

He can remember Petra working for hours in the kitchen on that illusion, the flames from the pan lighting up her face, the white dove tucked protectively under her arm. The ceiling had a scorch mark from all the practice she'd put into getting the trick right. He hadn't noticed it until long after Petra had to give up performing magic. Then he left it there as a reminder of how she used to be.

"I think I would have liked her," Ginny says.

"Aye, I think you would have," he says, picking up his hat from the bench, then holding it by the wide brim in his lap. "She was forced to give up her job when she got too ill, of course. Give up the magic. Came to a point where she couldn't even work in her studio anymore. That was the beginning of the end, so to speak. When she couldn't paint anymore." He finally puts the hat on his head, pushes a wet lock of hair off his forehead. "She had to stay in bed most of the time by then. I set up some of her oils and such on a breakfast tray, but it got where she was too weak to lift the brush."

"That would have been hard. On both of you."

"Cancer is a right cunning thief," he says, thinking of his bubbly energetic wife confined to the narrow life of the bed-ridden. "It stole Petra away long before she was gone. She lost so much of herself, of who she was, before she lost her life." He leans down and starts to fuss with the rain cover on his backpack so he doesn't have to look directly at Ginny as he speaks. "Sometimes I'd come to the hospital after work and find her stuck in the same position as I'd left her in that morning. It hurt too much for her to move." He pushes the cover back into its pouch at the base of the bag even though it's still wet. "I didn't know what to do to help. I reckon that was the worst thing. Every time I asked what I could do to make things better, she'd tell me she was fine." He pulls hard on the soggy zipper for the pouch and it catches. "What harm, I was watching her slip away and nothing I could do made a difference." He keeps tugging on the zipper.

"It must have made you angry," Ginny says.

He looks up at her, his mouth a tight line. He abandons the half-zipped pouch. "That sounds terrible. Being angry at a person for being sick." But he knows she's right. He had been angry — not at Petra though; *never at Petra*, he tells himself. Only at the desperate fuck-up of a situation they were in.

He looks down to see that the couple he'd taken a picture of earlier have reached the bottom of the trail now, two small dots with matching panama hats moving among the waving grass.

"You know my friend, the one who was supposed to come on the Camino with me?" Ginny's gaze is fixed out across the valley as well.

"Yes." He's not sure where she's going with this, but he appreciates the change of subject.

"She had problems." Ginny screws her eyes up at the sun as it makes its way fully out from behind a receding rain cloud. "We'd been good friends when we were growing up but lost touch. You know how people do."

Daniel knows. Some of the men he still calls his best friends he hasn't seen more than once in the last ten years. Men are poor at keeping up their friendships, Petra had once told him, and he supposes at least in his case it's true.

"She became a writer. Signed a three-book deal for some chick-lit crime series."

"Would I know the book?" Not exactly Daniel's genre. He's more of a Terry Pratchett kind of guy. But Petra always liked a good whodunit, as long as the female characters weren't clichéd bimbos that made her throw the book at the bedroom wall.

"No, you wouldn't know it," Ginny says, head down. "She never finished writing it. The publisher asked for the advance back, and by then she had spent it all on stuff to ease the pain of writer's block, if you know what I mean." Ginny looks up at him with a wry smile, but there's no mirth in it. "Sort of went downhill from there, I heard. That was years ago."

"So how did you meet up again?"

Ginny sighs hard before she replies, as if she needs to make space in her lungs for the answer. "I went to a party thrown by some old friends and bumped into her there. It was right around the time I was planning this trip. Made the mistake of telling her about it. She wanted to come along. I knew she was in recovery, on methadone, the whole bit."

"What did you say?"

"I told her I'd think about it. People warned me not to bring her. But we'd been so close once. God, was she ever fun back then." Ginny sips on her water bottle. "When we were teenagers we used to go out clubbing in our miniskirts and high heels. Two young things on the prowl with fake IDs. One time I got my stiletto caught in a grate and couldn't get it out. I had to leave it behind. One shoe on, one bare foot. She took off one of her own high heels and ran around with me like that in solidarity. We looked ridiculous but, damn it, did we ever laugh."

Daniel looks at Ginny and nods. He understands what it is to long for the way things used to be. "Sure, you thought maybe things would be like that again if you took her on the Camino with you."

"Yes." She holds the water bottle protectively on her lap. "But she was so different. I thought I knew her — but she'd changed so much since I ... since I last saw her." She pauses, caught up in the memory.

Daniel thinks she must be finished with the story, but then she continues, speaking more hurriedly than before.

"We tried to train before we came here. She came up and stayed with me for a week in Berkeley, so we could. But she was very tearful, needy. We'd go for hikes and have to break every few minutes for her to take a supplement or drink water to stave off one of her dehydration headaches." She stops for a second, then glances up at him. "And she had this thing about chanting."

"Chanting?"

"Yeah. We'd be out, and she would sit down wherever we were and start chanting. She had chants for strength, chants to ward off negative thoughts." She turns to Daniel and smiles. "Chants for blood-sugar imbalance."

"That's after being a bit specific."

"She said she had prediabetes. And prehypertension. Oh, and post-addiction withdrawal syndrome. I can't remember all the conditions she had, except they were all pre- or post-, like she didn't have the wherewithal to be fully ill in the present." Ginny makes a hollow laugh. "I don't mean to make fun. She wasn't well, mentally. I understood that. But after awhile it made me angry, too. Like you got angry about Petra."

"Petra wasn't like that." Daniel doesn't like the comparison Ginny's drawing with the two situations. His wife was nothing like this woman. If anything, she didn't complain enough. "Sure, Petra was really sick."

"My friend was sick, too," Ginny says, focusing on the water bottle.

He supposes she's right, but he doesn't feel like getting into a philosophical discussion on mental versus physical afflictions.

"So, what happened?" he asks instead.

"With what?" Ginny starts as if she just woke up from a dream.

"With your friend? Why didn't she come, so?"

"She overdosed." Ginny spits out the words without emotion. "She relapsed before we left, died on the bathroom floor of her parents' place."

"Jesus, that's a terrible thing, Ginny." He hadn't been expecting this ending. Assumed that Ginny had just decided her friend was too much trouble to bring along.

He reaches out and gently lays his hand on hers, feels how cold her fingers are through the thin gloves she wears. She doesn't pull away, not at first.

"Yes, it is," she says. Then she stands up from the bench abruptly, her hand slips out from under his. She takes one last hit from her water bottle, finishing it off. "Let's get going. I want to make it into the city centre tonight." She starts walking hurriedly toward the trail and then turns with a nervous laugh, returning to retrieve her backpack from the base of the cross. In her haste, she'd almost left it behind.

✳

It is hours later before the two of them give up on making it into Burgos proper. Trudging on the punishing cement in the suburb of Villafria, they cringe as planes cross low in the air overhead. Exhaust from local traffic grates on their throats. Forced to take accommodation on the seedy airport strip, they decide on the Hotel Las Vegas, a former four-star trying to keep up appearances as a one-and-a-half. The glossy marble stairway in the lobby speaks of a grander time, but the tarnished mirrors and water-stained wallpaper in the hallways tell the real story. Daniel keeps expecting to see a neon sign outside flashing *Girls-Girls-Girls*.

Ginny goes directly up to her room, citing the late hour, and Daniel grabs a stale *bocadillo* from the hotel snack bar before going up to his. He takes a bath, trying to touch as little of the tub as possible, then sets up on the bed with his feet propped up to Skype his sister.

"How far did you walk today?" Angela asks him from the tiny screen of his phone. He'd called her as soon as he was settled, catching her at the end of a *CSI* rerun.

"Twenty-four miles," he tells her, chomping down hard on the rock-like bread of the *bocadillo*. The cheese inside sticks to the roof of his mouth.

"How far is that in kilometres, you feckin' Yank?"

"Thirty-eight," Daniel says, still chewing.

"Are you mad?" Angela asks him. He winces a little at that, but she doesn't seem to notice.

"Nah, I don't think so." He swallows another lump of sandwich. "It's only Ginny wanted to get to Burgos." It is out of his mouth before he thinks about it. Ginny's name, not the lump of sandwich.

"So, it's Ginny now that you're walking with. And now you find yourself at the Hotel Las Vegas. Isn't that a fine bit of providence?"

"Listen, don't be teasing, Angela. There's been some trouble on the Camino. Women after being harassed. One even disappeared off the trail. I don't fancy Ginny walking alone at the moment."

"I'm certain you don't."

He still feels like he needs to make excuses. "And there's this *eejit* that's been bothering her. An Englishman."

"Well, he's obviously a hazard then. Can't trust that lot."

"Angela," he says, drawing her name out in warning.

"All right, all right," she says, laughing.

He can see her blow on the surface of a cup of tea, the mug held up with two hands wrapped around to warm them.

"You just mind yourself, little brother. Don't go getting the shite kicked out of yourself defending a damsel in distress."

"Sure, that wouldn't be very pilgrim-like."

"Saint James would turn over in his shrine."

They both laugh this time.

"Oh, listen," she says all of a sudden, remembering something. She takes a tentative sip of the hot tea. "Did you call Gerald's wife?"

"Shite, I forgot." Daniel puts the *bocadillo* down, starts searching for the piece of paper with the phone number on it.

"Don't bother. She's gone to her ma's. I talked to her this morning. Seems your partner's done a runner on her."

"Go on, that doesn't sound like Gerald."

"Oh, I'd wager that man has seen inside a few Hotel Las Vegases since he's been married."

Daniel knows this is true, but he didn't realize that Angela did.

"He owes money, serious. Gambling debts."

"Feckin' hell." Daniel has cursed more on this phone call than he has in the whole last week. Although, he supposes *feckin'* is a substitute swear and doesn't really count. His father always told him that only the uncreative had to replace an adjective with a curse. "But what does she expect me to do about it?" he asks his sister.

"How the hell do I know?" Angela says. "But my guess would be she wants you to sign the papers to sell the business to that New York firm that's so hot for the two of you in order to pay off the hoodlums."

There is a deep pause. He puts the *bocadillo* down on the bedside table. "I'm not at all sure I'm ready to sell," he says meekly, waiting for the explosion. He's not disappointed.

"Why the hell not?" Angela slams her tea down on the table in her apartment in Dublin. "It's a fierce amount of money. And you're coming home anyway." She moves forward, filling up the screen. "You *are* coming home, Danny?"

"Sure, I could come home and still keep my side of the business," he counters. "A silent partner, so." He had thought about this more and more in the days before he left for the Camino and since, but hadn't dared to voice it. "I built that company up from nothing, Angie. Petra, too, in the office, before she went teaching." He picks up the sandwich again and takes an angry bite. He doesn't like being told what to do.

Angela's sigh is both audible and visible on the Skype feed. "All I'm saying is it would be a fair turn to Cynthia if you were to sell now. Honestly, Daniel, the woman was right cut up on the phone. Not to mention Dad. I told you, I think the farm may need more than your presence. Things were devastating here after the downturn. They thought the banks might fail, for God's sake. I don't know if Dad ever fully recovered from it. The market's gone to shite. If he has to sell, he might not have much left afterward."

Daniel is shocked and worried about this piece of news, feels like crap about it, actually. He could still come over and help his dad, he reasons, but keep his place back in the States. The house, the business, it's all he has left of Petra. He can't abandon that any more than he can abandon the memory of the snow-white hospital pillow.

"I need to talk to Gerald."

"He's out on a tear, as I told you before. I don't know why you give a right testicle about what that man thinks." His sister can be graphic when frustrated. "Do you know he asked me about having you declared incompetent, back when you were having your troubles after Petra? He doesn't care about anyone but himself, Daniel."

"Jesus, are you serious?" He had told Gerald about the night with the Ambien. Sleepwalking into the muffin-baking Mrs. Boddis's backyard was embarrassing, but surely it hadn't made him incompetent. He realizes in the last year he had come a little unhinged, but he didn't think it showed. Obviously, it had.

Angela softens a little. "I didn't want to tell you at the time. But in retrospect, I suppose he was more interested in taking that offer than he was willing to let on. I wager he already knew he was for it at the time."

"What harm, but I was after buying a postcard to send to that bastard. You think you know a man." Gerald could be a social-climbing twit, but not a backstabbing one at last check. "Jesus," Daniel says a second time, then loudly burps up the acrid taste of stale *bocadillo*.

"Well said." Angela lifts her eyebrows at him from across the Skype feed. She takes another deep sip of her tea and leans into the camera of her laptop. "Seriously, Daniel, you're not always a good judge of people having your best interests at heart. Just mind yourself."

"I will," he says, wiping crumbs from his face with a napkin. "I mean, I am."

✳

That night Daniel dreams of the Englishman following them over the sierra like a loping wolf. He and Ginny reach the tall cross overlooking the Burgos valley, and she starts to cry. Someone is nailed to it. He doesn't want to look up to see who, even as he sees the blood dripping from the muddy hiking boots nailed to the shaft. The rat from the forest cemetery where he last saw them perches on the toe, licking at the blood.

He wakes up, damp with sweat, to hear the dying end of a scream. It could have been his own, but he is convinced it came from across the hall of the hotel. Jumping out of bed, he runs to Ginny's room and bangs on the door calling for her. She doesn't answer. Doesn't respond. Even after he has convinced the sleeping concierge to open the locked door with his master key. When he does, they find the room empty, the bed not slept in. No one is there. The pissed-off concierge trudges back down the sticky marble stairs to the front desk, cursing him in Spanish. Daniel is left standing in the hallway in his stocking feet, staring at the empty room and wondering whether it is possible to really know anybody at all.

CHAPTER 10
Hotel Las Vegas to
Rabé de las Calzadas

DANIEL FEELS CONSPICUOUS COMING into Burgos, a modern city humming with the morning commute. Women in colourful dresses look bored waiting for the bus. Billboards shout unintelligible Spanish at him from atop apartment blocks. People hurry past on the crowded sidewalk, parting around him as if he's a stone against their current. His backpack and hiking boots give him away as a pilgrim among the smartly dressed urban Spaniards, earn him an occasional half-hearted *Buen Camino*. He doesn't enjoy standing out. When he passes a uniformed employee sweeping the front steps of a three-storey Burger King, he thinks about going in, if only to hide in the branded familiarity. He decides against it when a group of teenagers in a car leaking bass pull up to the drive-through and honk at him. A man needs to draw the line somewhere on a spiritual quest.

As he crosses the street with the green light, he wonders again what he did that caused Ginny to run off. He had grilled the concierge for details of her exit but couldn't make himself properly understood. The man was either trying to tell him that she never asked for a room, or that she never ordered the fish. He wasn't sure which. He needed to use the translator on his phone to even get that far.

Or maybe the concierge was just being cagey, figuring Daniel had been left on purpose. Perhaps he had gone too far yesterday, spooked Ginny when he took her hand. Feckin' hell, maybe he's as bad as the Englishman and right now she's sprinting out of Burgos just to get away from him. He wouldn't be surprised. He has not exactly been good company on this trip with his maudlin talk of a dying wife and horror-show hallucinations. In retrospect, he doesn't blame her for wanting to distance herself. He'd leave himself behind if he could.

The city's main plaza takes the edge off his mood. It soothes him with its timelessness, an oasis of antiquity. Cobblestones replace asphalt. Traditional cafés and store-fronts replace fast-food joints. Even the locals seem on a different time continuum, lounging over coffee and pastry on outdoor patios despite the cool morning. The heavy twelfth-century stone architecture insulates the square from the fast-paced world that surrounds it. Towering over it all, grand and Gothic, stands the Burgos basilica, one of Spain's largest cathedrals. Daniel sees the two imposing barbed limestone towers that frame the main entrance and remembers the style is referred to as *squelette*, the French word for skeleton. He also remembers what lies behind those fortified walls — he'd seen it in the guidebook — and decides to take a chance.

✳

"I thought I'd find you here."

Ginny doesn't turn around at the sound of Daniel's voice, despite the hush of the empty side chapel gallery. It is early, and few tourists have arrived. *Cathedral de Santa Maria* holds many artistic treasures, and the oil painting before Ginny is no exception. *Santa Maria de Magdalena* is inscribed on the placard next to it, right above Da Vinci's name.

"Leonardo didn't even paint it," Ginny says, not bothering to turn around. "Or at least, not entirely. He probably did the outline and one of his students completed it." She tilts her head, observing the painting at a different angle. Her hair falls against her shoulder without the burden of its usual ponytail. "He might have done the face, though, I think." The face of the *Magdalena* is remarkable. Her chin and eyes are angled upward and to the left, as if she is trying to catch a glimpse of something without detection. Her arms cross in front of her bare breasts both seductively and protectively. She holds back an impending smile. If it weren't for her generous lips, she could be the Mona Lisa's sister.

"Why did you leave, Ginny?"

"I don't do conflict well, I told you that," she says flatly.

"Sure, I'm not a big fan of it myself."

"It's more than that." She tears her eyes away from the painting. "I have a history of running away from things."

"Like Mark the Englishman," he says.

"Yeah, I suppose. But more than that." She goes to sit down on one of the cool marble benches, leans over and takes her head in her hands.

Daniel joins her on the bench, his backpack wedged behind him on the seat back. The portrait of Mary Magdalene views them from the adjacent wall, as if part of the conversation.

"I ran away from home when I was sixteen," she says, still not looking up.

"Sure, that's young." Daniel imagines a sixteen-year-old girl fending for herself in California and all the low-lifes that might try and prey on her. How bad could things have been for Ginny to choose that over home? "Did you have problems with your parents?" he asks gently.

"Sister," she says.

"Aye, you mentioned you didn't get on."

"That would be an understatement." She lifts her head from her hands, narrows her gaze. "People think only men can be violent, you know, but women can be just as bad. My sister was missing something, I'm not sure what. Basic empathy for sure, but it was more than that."

Daniel waits for her to go on.

"She would think up creative ways to hurt me," Ginny says. "From the time I was little. She and her best friend, Sheena." Ginny looks across the room. "Sheena had a little sister, too. The kids called her Twitchy Trish. Only I knew why, I suppose. She was so fucking scared all the time. So was I."

"What did they do to you?" Daniel asks softly. He knows bad memories are best treated gently.

"They'd stuff us into old sleeping bags and kick us down the stairs," Ginny says, stating the facts dispassionately to distance herself. "Catch us and cut our fingers open with sharp blades of grass when we played in the sprinkler on the lawn." She runs her finger along the cool white stone of the bench as if to soothe the old injury. "Sometimes they'd perform experiments and make us participate. The two of them held me down once and covered my mouth to see how long I could go without breathing. They made Trish keep time. I still remember how her hand trembled holding the stopwatch, afraid she'd be next. Then I lost consciousness. We couldn't have been more than five."

"Jesus." Daniel had heard of sisters clashing with each other, but nothing like this.

"Once we got older and bigger, they couldn't pull shit like that anymore," Ginny says. "But they still found their opportunities. My sister would drop broken glass on the bathroom floor before I got out of the shower. Trish found straight pins buried in a jar of cream she'd had prescribed by the doctor for her eczema. I knew because we'd become close friends by then. Bound together for survival of our own siblings, I guess."

"Why didn't your parents do something?"

"Our parents were oblivious," Ginny says, showing her first sign of anger. "Mine were too busy watching their marriage disintegrate, and hers were never home. When they did notice anything was going on, they wrote it off as the usual kid stuff." Ginny holds onto the bench tightly with both of her hands, as if the force of her story might catapult her off it. "No one wants to believe they've given birth to monsters," she says.

"So, you left." Daniel speaks the words like a secret. The only way to speak in a hushed cathedral, or when discussing monsters.

"One day," Ginny begins, "when I was in the bathtub, I must have left the door open, or she picked the lock. My sister knew how to do things like that. I looked up and she was standing over me with the hair dryer in her hands. It was plugged in and she turned it on. She dangled it over the water, smiling. Then she took the cordless phone in her other hand and called Sheena. She just sat there, on the edge of the tub for half an hour, talking to her friend on the phone, the two of them laughing and carrying on. The whir of the hair dryer only inches away from me. I didn't dare move. The water got colder and colder. My teeth were chattering. I could see the blue veins under my skin."

"Jesus, Ginny." He pictures her, a terrified kid, shivering in the tub. An entire childhood spent looking over her shoulder. He knew she had been harbouring something frightening, but hadn't been prepared for something so domestically sinister.

"I don't know what would have happened if my dad hadn't started pounding on the door, demanding to know where my mother was," she says, breaking the tension slightly with her musing. "He would notice that his dinner wasn't made when he got home, but not that his eldest daughter was a psychopath." Ginny shifts on the bench, swallows hard, then sits up straighter. "So, I took off after that. Hitchhiked north, got a job, and finished school at night. I never went back. I just ran away."

"You were afraid for your life, I'd say."

"I saved my own ass, is what I'd say." Ginny raises the pitch of her voice but not her volume. Her next sentence comes out in a sharp whisper. "I ran, and I left my best friend behind, with the monsters."

"Sheena's little sister," Daniel says, and she nods. Then he realizes. "The old friend, that's who she is. The one you were bringing on the Camino with you."

"Yes," Ginny says, gazing up at the portrait again.

"Ah, Ginny, it's not your fault. You had to go."

Daniel rests a hand on her upper arm, the nylon of her jacket crinkles under his fingers. She shudders a little but doesn't pull away.

"I wish it were that easy," she says, sighing. "I can't help thinking, if I hadn't left her there. If I had been braver. If I hadn't run away. That things would have been different. For her."

"Right, like you're responsible for her becoming an addict? Or her overdose? Go on, Ginny. You can't hang that on yourself."

"But I do."

She leans away from him, and his hand falls between them again.

"And I don't want to do the same to you, Daniel. To hurt you because I can't handle things. I'm always going to run when the situation gets, you know, volatile. Always."

"Do you think I'm volatile?" Daniel asks, trying to keep his speech steady.

"No," she says, running one hand over the smooth marble of the bench. "Besides, it's not just that." She gets up and moves across the chapel to stand in front of a richly carved stone sarcophagus. A dead bishop, judging by the pointy hat. "I don't know whether I'm good for you, Daniel." She glances back across her shoulder. "You're seeing these things and this woman. Did you ever think that maybe I'm to blame?"

"That you're to blame?" Daniel gets up from the bench and crosses over to stand behind her. "Sure, what could you possibly have to do with it?"

She doesn't answer at first then abruptly turns around to face him. "Tell me, Daniel," she asks. "Do I remind you of Petra?"

He is floored by the question. Of course, there are aspects of Ginny that remind him of Petra. And there was that first time he had seen her at *Alto del Perdón*. The mistake he had made. But he had never told Ginny about that, and he isn't about to now.

She reaches up with one hand, rests her fingers lightly on his chest. "I worry sometimes that you're mixing Petra and me up. Maybe it was memories of her, at the end, that made you see that — that woman when you saw me in the graveyard."

Daniel's body stiffens, and she takes her hand away.

"Petra never looked like that." Then again, the sunken cheeks, the flesh in a state of decay even as his wife still lived and breathed. There were similarities.

"I just don't want to make things worse for you is all," Ginny says, taking a few steps back. "I don't want to make things worse for either of us." They lock eyes with one another across the silent gallery.

"Are you after being afraid of me, Ginny?" Daniel asks her, holding his breath. Suddenly, this is the most important thing to him. Not whether he is going mad, or whether he'll ever manage to spread Petra's ashes and get on with his life. Only if Ginny puts him in the category of the volatile monsters of her past.

She holds his eyes with hers. "No."

"Then it's settled, so," he says, taking back his breath. "No conflict here. Just an Irishman with an active imagination. You've got nothing to run from with me, Ginny."

"Are you sure?" she asks.

"I am," he says, feeling a new sense of confidence. If she believes in him, perhaps there is something in him worth saving. He walks over and joins her. They turn and look at the painting again. Lose themselves for a minute in the rich calm of brushstrokes on canvas. Daniel doesn't believe a student could have done such a thing on Da Vinci's behalf. He whispers sideways to Ginny.

"Besides, who will protect me from the likes of those Australian women, if I don't have you along."

"I think you are capable of taking care of yourself," she says, a hint of a smile forming on her lips to match Da Vinci's muse.

"Sure, one of them tried to flash me on my way to the toilet in Espinosa."

She turns to him, mouth open. "They did not!"

"All right, perhaps that's a lie. But she was dressed in a tattered old bathrobe and I felt like I was after being flashed."

"Scarred for life, I'm sure."

He takes a few steps toward the main sanctuary exit and crooks his elbow. "Come on, there's far more to see in here than Mary Mag."

Ginny wavers for a second, her head held as if pondering a question, then she moves forward and takes his arm.

"I hear they have a giant mechanical doll on the west wall that chimes the hour," Daniel tells her, as he escorts her across the room.

"It's almost nine o'clock," she says. "Not a Da Vinci, but worth a look."

They walk out of the gallery together, leaving the watchful eyes of Mary Magdalene behind.

*

The Camino out of Burgos is difficult to track. The busy streets and bustling commerce compete for a pilgrim's attention, and it's easy to miss the waymarks. Eventually, Daniel and Ginny find their way out of the city and onto the flatness which hallmarks the beginning of the Camino's infamous *meseta* region. Infamous with pilgrims, at least. This section of the Camino is home to vast and level open plains that last for days upon days of walking. The terrain is easier on the back of the legs than the mountains and *sierra* they left behind, but harder on the shins. Daniel grits his teeth at the blister he has developed on the side of his foot. Ginny stops to take breaks more often than is normal for her. The weather has changed. Rain from the day before has freshened the wind, and the air is cooler and crisper, more like autumn back in New Jersey, where Daniel and Petra would walk among the falling leaves and talk of learning plans and the latest crop of students. She tended to each pupil as she did to her painting, with appreciation for the different textures and hues. He can remember her laugh as she recalled the pranksters and her furrowed brow as she felt for the shy ones. All on a backdrop of cool breezes and blue sky. The sense of déjà vu is so intense that he is afraid if he looks beside him he will see Petra again instead of Ginny, substituting one for the other, as she suggested. He concentrates on the road ahead, staying focused on the never-ending horizon.

It takes hours to leave the built-up industry of Burgos and its suburbs completely behind. The scenery slowly changes back to agriculture, with flattened wheat fields and walls of stacked blond hay. The multi-lane *autopista* that has dogged them in parallel finally branches off to the north, reduced to a black tarmac snake in the distance. Daniel and Ginny mount the quiet asphalt road into Rabé de las Calzadas.

The small village on a limited rise looks down on the fleeing motorway, along with the *rio Urbel* that flows just outside its eastern limits. Most of the population is housed in a large nunnery in the lower part of town next to the *Iglesia de Santa Marina*. The remaining secular buildings are grouped at a high point circling a small main plaza with tired rose bushes planted in the middle like a life-sized centrepiece.

"Where do you want to stay?" Daniel asks. There are two *albergues* to choose from on the square, the *Libéranos Domine* or the *Casa de Michelle y Felix*. Neither appears open. That's because it is still early, only just past lunch. They were both tired from the marathon trek of yesterday and had purposely planned to make it a short day. The door of *Libéranos Domine* opens, and a large man walks out, recognizes them, and waves.

"Hey, *peregrinos!*" the Englishman calls out, his voice barrelling through the square with the precision of a bulldozer.

"*Casa de Michelle y Felix*, it is," says Daniel, taking Ginny by the elbow and leading her in the opposite direction. He leans in to whisper in her ear, "I can't believe the old codger outdistanced us."

"Just keep walking," Ginny says tersely. She opens up the door of the *albergue* and they both go in.

✳

Casa de Michelle y Felix does not contain a Michelle or a Felix, but Dores, the proprietress, is known for cooking a mean pilgrim's meal. Ginny and Daniel both oversleep their afternoon naps, a carry-over from the miles of the day before and a difficult night. Daniel never did go back to bed after his nightmare and finding Ginny gone.

When they finally do get up, they discover they have missed dinner. Dores makes them a plate of leftover pork and rice to share. They eat in appreciative silence, Ginny taking most of the rice and leaving him with the pork. Neither wanted to go out for dinner and risk running into Mark. They'd managed to dodge him earlier when he became distracted with the arrival of a couple of friends, a squat young man in a straw boater hat and a good-looking girl with a too-loud laugh. Daniel still can't believe the Englishman managed to pass them on the trail. Probably took a taxi partway, the cheating bastard of a princess pilgrim.

When she comes to clear away his empty plate, Dores hands Daniel a square of paper with the words *Peregrino bendición* written on it and a time, 2100h.

"It's for the pilgrim's blessing," Ginny explains, reading from over his shoulder. "The Sisters of Charity have it at the convent each night."

She takes a last bite of the ice-cream sandwich they were served for dessert. Daniel had eaten half and then dutifully handed it over to her to finish.

"That's what the card says, at least."

"Should we go?" Daniel asks.

"Sure," she says, crumpling up the ice-cream wrapper and throwing it basketball-style into the garbage can in the corner. A perfect shot. She turns to him and licks one last bit of cream off the corner of her lip in a way that threatens his state of grace again. "Why not?"

❋

Nuns have changed since Daniel was a boy. He remembers the sisters who occasionally visited his priest-run boarding school as diminutive women who never spoke. They drifted by in the background like shadows with their long black tunics and veiled habits. He was never quite sure what they actually did. Cleaned things, he supposed. Only now does he realize what a sexist assumption that was. The nuns at the

Nuestra Señora del Monasterio do not wear veils or robes, only black skirts past the knee as his granny did. Opaque nylons cover a variety of legs ranging from sturdy to spindly, with the exception of one ancient member of the order who wears beige wool socks that droop about her ankles. A pleasant-looking middle-aged woman with a large crucifix dominating her equally impressive bosom greets them as they walk into the sanctuary.

"Welcome, *peregrinos*. Please take a seat." She hands them a laminated blue card with a Spanish order of service on it and beams accessibility.

"Do you have one in English?" Daniel asks, hopeful.

"Welcome, *peregrinos*. Please take a seat." The nun continues to project her practised smile to match her words.

"I think she's a one-trick pony," Ginny says. "Let's sit down."

The pews are made of pale, functional maple, their style unadorned. The two find a spot a few rows back from the front. Daniel genuflects in the aisle before he takes his place, appreciating the carpeting on the floor. The chapel is simple and contemporary, more reminiscent of a corporate meeting room than a sanctuary. If it weren't for the large mahogany cross at the front with Christ hanging from it in agony, Daniel would expect someone to begin a PowerPoint presentation.

"Are you a practising Catholic, Daniel?" Ginny whispers to him sideways in the pew.

"I told you that I am." Daniel knows Ginny's not Catholic, but he assumes she is a believer of some sort. He'd seen her fashion that wood-scrap cross in the chain-link fence outside Logroño, even mouth a prayer afterward.

"I mean are you ... you know, devout?" she says.

"I'm not one for Mass every Sunday, if that's what you're saying." The last time Daniel had been to a full Mass was the funeral. He and Petra had gone to church only irregularly.

They liked the idea of taking time out to pay their respects to God, but they enjoyed sleeping in on a Sunday morning.

"Do you believe in —" she hesitates, trying to be delicate. "In everything the Catholic Church says?"

"Most of it."

"Most of it?"

"Sure, there are things I disagree with." When Ireland had a referendum on abortion, Daniel had voted with his conscience rather than his religion, albeit by absentee ballot. He doesn't think he could ever bring himself to make that decision, but he supported a woman's right to do so. This information he doesn't whisper to Ginny, for fear that voicing such a thing in a nunnery might cause him to burst into flames in his functional maple pew.

"If you disagree with it, why are you still a Catholic?"

"Are there things the U.S. government is after doing that you don't agree with?" he asks.

"I suppose."

"And yet, you don't stop being an American, now do you?"

"I see what you're saying," Ginny says thoughtfully.

"In Ireland, being Catholic isn't about religion, at any rate."

"What's it about then?"

"Sticking it to six hundred years of English oppression," he says with a wink.

Ginny stifles a giggle behind one hand, and Daniel grins like an idiot. He loves making her laugh, particularly after the seriousness of their conversation in Burgos. When the welcoming nun takes her place behind the pulpit, she clears her throat and the two guiltily collect themselves as if they've been caught passing notes in class.

"*Señor, ten misericordia.*"

"*Señor, ten misericordia,*" all the nuns repeat in unison. The nun with the slouching wool socks walks unsteadily toward the front and lights the altar candles. Daniel is briefly afraid she will fall directly into the flame of the Christ candle, but she manages to make her way to the back pew and sit heavily on a cushion. Someone else turns off the main lights, and they all wait expectantly in the dim glow until the sister at the front speaks again.

"*Cristo, ten misericordia.*"

"*Cristo, ten misericordia,*" repeats the group.

Daniel glances down at the laminated blue card. The words in Spanish are there for him to follow along. Even if he doesn't understand the language, he knows "Lord have mercy. Christ have mercy" when he hears it.

"*Señor, ten misericordia.*"

"*Señor, ten misericordia.*"

The candles flicker on the front table with the ebb and flow of voices as they speak the prayer as typed on the blue card. The foreign words give an air of incantation to the blessing. Daniel searches the room, wondering where the priest is to lead the service, then gathers that the nuns take care of it all themselves. Another thing that has changed since he was growing up.

"*Orad por los peregrinos.*"

"What's does that mean?" Daniel asks Ginny under his breath.

"Pray for the pilgrims," she says, interrupting her own recitation. She has her eyes closed, repeating the Spanish words along with the rest of the women. She doesn't need the blue card.

"*Amén.*"

"*Que el Señor dirija vuestros pasos con su beneplácito.*"

"Please don't ask me to translate that," she says, still with her eyes closed.

"*Amén.*"

"Ginny."

A sound, he's heard it before.

"*Y que sea vuestro compañero inseparable a lo largo del camino.*"

"Ginny."

He hears it again. Just like that night, hoarse and throaty in the corn.

"Honestly, Daniel, use the translator on your phone."

"*Amén.*"

"Ginny, do you hear it?"

"What?" she says, finally opening her eyes and turning to him, annoyed.

"That," he whispers. And there it is again, that unmistakable rasp, a breath full of liquid and labour, with no life to it, a death rattle. He turns around to the back of the darkened room to see where it's coming from.

The woman is there beside the aged nun with the socks, holding on to her liver-spotted hand as if they are old friends. She wears the traditional nun's garb of his youth. Blood has seeped into the white of her starched headpiece and spread like an advancing disease. She strokes the fingers of the elderly nun with one hand and holds one finger of the other hand to her lips. He notices, even in the candlelight, that her knuckles are streaked with red dirt and ooze, her fingernails broken down to the quick.

"Ginny," he says quietly, reaching for her beside him, but she is already up and moving out of the pew.

"*Cristo, ten misericordia.*"

"*Cristo, ten misericordia.*"

"Ginny!" he yells after her.

She is dashing down the aisle, past the lead nun who stops her recitation and scolds Daniel with her eyes for the outburst before continuing on again.

"*Señor, ten misericordia.*"

"*Señor, ten misericordia.*"

He turns around again in his seat, hoping to see something different. The woman is no longer in the back pew.

He bends forward, elbows resting on his thighs, head down, trying to steady himself. That's when he feels the crawling sensation of slippery fingers on the back of his neck. He looks down and across to see mud-splattered hiking boots peeking out from beneath the tatters of a black robe, so close he can read the brand. Merrell, like Ginny wears. The woman's broken mouth spews the words directly into his ear as she leans in from beside him.

"*Orad por los peregrinos*, Daniel."

"Christ!"

The nuns stop their prayers, look up at him with fear and confusion. The woman whisks herself out of her seat and takes off up a side aisle and out the door that Ginny just ran through. Daniel stumbles out of the pew, following her, the trails left behind by her jagged wet fingertips still fresh upon his neck. He throws open the door and runs after both women into the night.

"Ginny!" Daniel shouts her name down the deserted street. His voice comes back to him off the limestone walls of the village. A cold sliver of moon draws out the shadows. His heart beats loudly in his chest, but it's not loud enough to drown out the chant of the nuns resuming their prayers behind the thick convent doors. He runs across the street and peers in the window of the local pub. Ginny's not there. Although, the local priest is, looking shocked as Daniel brings his wild face up to the window.

He turns and takes the stairs two at a time that lead back up to the plaza. Everything is quiet and undisturbed when he reaches the top. *Ginny couldn't have made it back to the albergue already*, he thinks. He checks just the same, panting as he demands from a stunned Dores whether she's seen her. She hasn't.

Outside again, he looks over the stone ledge onto the lower tier of the village. He can see most of the streets from this vantage point, and nowhere does he see Ginny. Or the other one. Everything about the village is drowsy and silent, asleep for the night, until he hears a match strike loudly to his right.

"Looking for someone, are ya?" Mark stands only a few feet away. His face lights up orange from the long wooden match.

Daniel can see his two friends behind him, holding each other up. The man with the straw boater hat pulls the drunken girl to the stone wall and forces her to bend precariously over the edge. She laughs when it hits her hard in the gut, doubling her over. Then she stands, wipes some spittle from her mouth and slips the guy the tongue.

The Englishman lights his cigarette, then holds the burning match in front of his eyes, watching as the flame makes its way down to his fingers. His gold and silver rings flicker in the light. "I think I know where she might be," he drawls once the fire starts to singe his skin.

Daniel forces himself to stay through the sickening odour of burnt flesh, to hear what Mark knows. Once he does, he runs back down the stairs to the main street. The harsh bray of the drunken girl's laugh follows him all the way out of town.

✳

Ginny's standing on the edge of a bridge looking over it when Daniel finds her. Much as she stood with him at the Salt River, except this time it is the dusky flow of the *rio Urbel* that captures her attention rather than the poisoned run of the *rio Salado*. The water level is low. Daniel can't see anything reflected in its murky surface, not even the gaunt moon. It is cooler outside the walls of the village and Ginny has tied up the hood of her jacket against the wind. As he gets closer, he stops. A heavy curtain of hair hangs out of the front of her hood and he thinks he can see something ripple unnaturally underneath. She turns and parts the hair to look at him, and the illusion disperses.

"Daniel." She runs off the bridge and into his arms, burying her face in his shoulder, holding him like he's rescued her from the depths of the dark river below. He enjoys for a moment the forgotten bliss of having a woman in his arms, murmurs reassurance and other inanities. He rubs her back. Mostly he just revels in the way her body relaxes into his, buoyed by his ability to comfort her with his presence and his touch. It makes him feel like a man again.

After some time, he speaks, breaking the spell. "Ginny, you saw her, didn't you?"

She starts to cry softly but manages to nod, still buried in his shoulder.

"Who is she, Ginny?"

She looks up at him, tears falling onto the strings of her hood, her mouth slightly open as if she is about to respond with a question of her own. He knows her secret now. She sees the woman just as he does. The horror of that image is what has perhaps bonded them all along.

When Ginny brings her full open lips up to his own, he is not as surprised as he might have been. That kiss had been coming ever since the first night they saw the dark figure hovering over the fields of Azqueta.

When she finally pulls away, he still has enough wits about him to ask again. "Who is she, Ginny?"

She bites down on her lower lip in the way she must know by now tortures him. Even with the fetid breath of that creature still clinging to his skin, he still feels a solid tug of longing for her. He keeps his gaze serious, hopes she can see in the dim moonlight that he is not going to be swayed from an answer, despite her inviting lips.

Ginny takes a step away, looks down at the ground. "It's my friend," she says. "The one who was supposed to walk the Camino with me."

Daniel moves toward her, takes her chin in his hand and lifts her face up to his. She turns her head and closes her eyes.

"That woman's dead, Ginny," he says.

She starts crying softly again, and he takes his hand away. For a while, they stand like this together, with the sound of the weak river trickling beneath the bridge and Ginny's soft hitching breaths above it. She turns to face him again, her mouth only inches away from his. Her eyes are wide and searching behind the tears. He swears he can see a moon sliver reflected in each one.

"I know, Daniel," she says, collapsing into him again. "I know she's dead."

CHAPTER 11
Rabé de las Calzadas
to Población de Campos

THE NEXT MORNING, GINNY asks to walk alone. She says she needs some space, a nonsensical excuse that Daniel knows is polite code for "bugger off." He agrees to her wishes, despite what happened the night before, and they decide on a meeting place for the following morning. It is easier to do this than argue with her; she is stubborn and her mind is made up. He doesn't want to scare her away again. He checks the empty plaza before he leaves, wary of the Englishman and his crew, but they appear to be sleeping in or already gone. None of them emerges from the doors of the rival *albergue*.

That day he walks mostly by himself, feeling out of place and sorts. The blister on the side of his foot finally gets the best of him, and he is forced to pull over and lace it with a needle and thread the way the Englishman had lectured. He chooses a bench beside a *bodega*, which he has learned is not a corner grocery store like back in Jersey, but a dome-shaped earth dwelling built into a hillside. The guidebook says these are only used to store wine. But a middle-aged matron in a house dress comes flying out of the hobbit-like front door in the ground and chases him away with a straw broom.

"My God, woman, they're just feet," he shouts as he hops away, his injured and bare foot trailing black thread. He is not usually a rude or angry man, but raw nerves are beginning to eat away at his self-control.

How can the woman be Ginny's overdosed friend? It's ridiculous. And yet, the terror of those fingers on the back of his neck, the beetle he saw crawl in and out of the slack mouth in the corn. Ginny's explanation is the first thing that has made sense, yet it's preposterous. He is an engineer, after all, a man of science. He doesn't believe in *Santa Compaña* or banshees or butter witches. He didn't even really believe in the woman who's following them, until Ginny admitted to seeing her, too. He tries to put it out of his mind and concentrate on the trail, but the landscape is uneventful with little shade or notable sights to distract. Endless fields that would be filled with bright poppies and other wildflowers in the spring and summer are tawny and depleted in the fall. Wind turbines, like those he'd seen at *Alto del Perdón,* turn perpetually in the distance.

The monotonous call of cuckoos distracts him, at first, then begins to irritate. If only with the frustration of trying to figure out where the bloody birds are nesting with so few trees around. He tries to find an answer in the guidebook and ends up spilling his water bottle out onto the pages. They wrinkle and he knows they will dry all stuck together. It is not a good day.

He arrives in Castrojeriz and signs in at an *albergue* with fifty people allotted to each room. They are not full, but close enough. He makes a point of staying indoors and among people. The woman, whoever she is, seems to avoid crowds. As Daniel lies awake in his bunk bed, he marks off the hours by the passing of gas and other bodily eruptions of dozens of strangers. At least he doesn't dream — the one benefit of insomnia.

The next day, he hits the road at dawn, weary and not expecting much. Ginny is waiting for him, as promised, at the crossroads just outside of town. They exchange brief greetings, then carry on in silence, a result of the untimely hour as much as their awkwardness. He wonders where she stayed the night before but doesn't ask. He wants her to start the conversation. She finally does when they are half-way up the steep slope of *Alto de Moselares*.

"I thought the *meseta* was supposed to be flat," she complains.

Daniel would normally feel the need to explain that a *meseta* is a geological plateau characterized by alternating high plains, but he has more pressing things on his mind.

"Are we going to talk about this, so?" He pauses halfway through the sentence, taking an extra breath to help with the climb.

"About what in particular?" she asks, stopping to free one of her hiking poles from the ground where it has gotten stuck between two rocks.

"About what happened back in Rabé de las Calzadas, Ginny," he says, surprising himself by remembering the name. He stops and braces himself standing sideways on the hill. He agreed to the earlier separation, but he's not letting her off the hook about this.

"The kiss?" she asks innocently, and he feels his face begin to colour.

He's not ready to talk about that. She had caught him off guard with her lips. His body had reacted enthusiastically, but the rest of him felt as guilty as hell. "The woman," he says, picking the less frightening of the two subjects. "Who is she, Ginny?"

"I told you," she says, then plants her hiking poles ahead of her and starts climbing again.

Daniel follows her. "That doesn't make sense, Ginny. Are you wanting me to believe there's a dead woman following us? One of these *Santa Compaña* or what have you?"

"She's following me, not you. And do you have a better explanation?"

"I have about a dozen better explanations." He draws up beside her. The backs of his calves are starting to cry out in protest. Why the hell couldn't they have had this conversation before they had to scale Kilimanjaro. "It could be anyone, dressed up to scare," he says. "Perhaps it's even that sister of yours. She sounded like a right piece of work." The words are out of his mouth before he has a chance to think about how unbelievably callous he's being.

"She doesn't even know where I am," Ginny says, unfazed by the sensitive subject. "Besides, last thing I heard she married some Silicon Valley software exec, probably popped out a couple of kids by now."

"Perhaps someone else you know, having you on, playing a prank."

"Some prank."

Daniel's breath comes in huffs now while Ginny keeps up the pace without getting winded. Must be the hiking poles. He decides to ask a question requiring a more detailed answer so she can do most of the talking for a while and he can save his breath.

"Right, then tell me, why are you thinking it's your friend?"

"Because it looks like her, or at least what I can see of her through the … you know."

Daniel knew.

"And that red Columbia sweater and the Merrell hiking boots that we bought together back in Berkeley, they're all hers."

"Sure, hundreds of people have that form of a sweater. And Merrells are as common as dirt."

"The last thing she said to me was that she would die before she'd let me go alone on this trip," Ginny says.

"Given that the woman did die, I reckon she made her choice." An inappropriate comment surely, but his sarcasm gives rise to an idea. "Do you think she might have faked it?" he suggests.

"Her death?" Ginny stops now and leans on a hiking pole, pulls her water tube from where it's clipped on her shoulder strap and takes a drink. "I don't think so, Daniel. I saw it, I mean, I saw her. Dead."

"Where?" Daniel asks.

She puts her hands on her hips, and the poles dangle on either side of her. "In a convertible Fiat, driving thirty over the speed limit on the I-80," she says. "For Christ's sake, Daniel. In a casket. At the funeral. Where else?"

"Could have been staged, like," he suggests, but only half-heartedly.

"Listen," she says, "this is all bullshit, I know. But all I can tell you is yes, I've seen what you see, and yes, she's scary as a Stephen King novel, but I'll tell you what else." She leans in to him so closely he can smell the creamy sweetness of the *café con leche* she had at breakfast. "I don't care." She pulls back quickly and starts walking again.

Daniel stands on the hill for a moment, stunned. Then strides up the rocky dirt path to catch up. He stands in front of her this time, blocking the way, forcing her to talk directly to him.

"You don't care? What do you mean you don't feckin' care?" he says with heaving breaths. He's at the end of his wits as well as his lung endurance. How can she not care that a dead woman is stalking her?

"I mean exactly what I said. I don't care. I just need to get to Santiago. To finish this. It's all about getting there, and I'm almost halfway now. She's not going to stand in my way." Ginny takes one of her hiking poles and raises the pointed end to his chest. "And neither, Irish, are you."

❋

The two of them come into Población de Campos in the late afternoon. By this point, Daniel is resigned to his predicament. They are being followed on the Camino by the rotting corpse of a woman who overdosed six thousand miles away in another country. Not to worry, though, the good-looking girl he made out with two nights ago doesn't care, so why should he? He'll have to update his sister on their next Skype call. She'll be bloody delighted for him, probably suggest a good coroner who specializes in the undead.

There is strength in numbers, though, even when it comes to madness, and just knowing that there is at least one other person who sees the woman makes him feel better. Although, he still wants to believe it is someone made up to play the part — someone who has it out for Ginny, perhaps, but she doesn't want to talk about it, too embarrassed or something similar. A person can do wonders with stage makeup. His sister had dressed as a cadaver one Halloween when she was in her first year of nursing. One of her drama-student friends had gotten that goo in a tube that dries like rubbery skin, and she'd created all sorts of gruesome counterfeit injuries for herself, even worn a toe tag for authenticity. The Dean had called her to the office the next day for borrowing a zippered black bag from the teaching-hospital morgue. She ended up having to pay for it on account of the leg holes she'd cut at one end so she could walk.

He cannot buy into the supernatural explanation that Ginny accepts, despite tales of the *Santa Compaña* haunting pilgrims along the trail or the Dutchman's talk of ghostly shipmates with messages. He wishes Rob were with them now so Daniel could bounce these latest developments off of him. He and Ginny haven't seen his familiar painter's hat in days now.

They follow a jumble of crooked streets that leads them to Población's only *albergue,* a long one-storey red brick building with a flat roof. The building had operated as a school in the sixties and seventies and sits on a pleasant patch of grass, the remnants of an old playground set rusting out the back. After settling their gear and washing up, the two run into the Spaniard Daniel met at the hotel restaurant in Torres del Rio. He has used the *albergue's* small kitchen to make pasta with the help of some others in his group. A picnic table has been set up in the schoolyard with a collection of mismatched plates and ridged plastic tumblers for wine.

"You are welcome to join us," he says, sealing the invite with a handshake.

"We'll be there," Daniel says, accepting with a firm grasp on behalf of both himself and Ginny. Perhaps a little too quickly.

"Do we have to go?" Ginny asks after the Spaniard is gone. She's rubbing her lower back with the heel of her hand. "It's been a long day."

"Ginny, if I am forced to eat another pilgrim menu dinner, I'll go mental. A man can only handle so much pork and chips."

"The ice-cream bars are good," Ginny says, and Daniel remembers the one they shared a few days ago. Ginny's neat little bites finishing off her half, licking what was left of the cream from her lips. But he will not be distracted. Right now, his fantasies centre around getting some good honest food with fresh ingredients. What he would give for a good curry from the Indian place back in Jersey. Homemade spaghetti will have to suffice.

"Sure, it will be good for us. To be around other people. C'mon now, Ginny." He actually bats his steel-blue eyes at her — his best feature, according to his mother. He's pulling out all the stops.

She rakes one hand through her hair, still wet from the shower, and looks out over the fallow fields that border the schoolyard, searching before she turns back to him and his eyes. "Okay, Daniel," she says with a sigh, "I'll go."

When they sit down to dinner, he takes a quick, nervous glance around for the French-Canadian girl, but she's not at the table. Two American women and a retired army officer from South Korea complete the guest list. The pasta has been made with ripe red tomatoes and green peppers purchased at the small *tienda* on the corner. It is basic, but filling. Daniel shovels it in with a force only a man in need of serious carbs can muster. When he offers to contribute some money toward the meal, none of the others will hear of it.

"That's not the way on the Camino, my friend," the Spaniard explains.

"Besides," the younger of the two American women says, "the wine was only a euro a bottle. I'll spend more on trips to the restroom than I will drinking it." She giggles into her clear plastic cup and the red wine froths. At the price, Daniel isn't expecting much, but is pleasantly surprised by his first glass of *vino tinto*, served chilled as is the custom here with fresh red wine. It's delicious.

Ginny, on the other hand, hasn't even bothered to serve herself any spaghetti. There is no meat in it, so that can't be the problem. He's about to ask her what's wrong when his Spanish friend interrupts.

"So, do you still plan to go to Finisterre, Daniel?" The Spaniard remembers his name, while Daniel has forgotten his.

Daniel finishes chewing his latest mouthful of pasta before he replies. The others wait patiently. "I do," he finally pronounces after a heavy swallow. He hadn't fully decided until just now, but yes, he will go there after Santiago. He doesn't see himself finding the right place to spread Petra's ashes before then.

"I am glad to hear it," the Spaniard says, his eyes lighting up. "This is the original destination of the Camino, after all."

"Not the shrine of Saint James in Santiago?" the bespectacled American woman asks. She is considerably older than the young woman. Daniel places her at a well-kept late fifties.

"The shrines in Finisterre came long before Saint James," the Spaniard tells her. "Like many things, Christianity has superimposed itself over other traditions. Pagans were walking the Camino a thousand years before Christ to worship the sun god at Finisterre."

Daniel has heard some of this before, at the restaurant back in Torres del Rio, but he is enjoying the deeper details. He doesn't know which he is more impressed by: the thought of the Camino predating Christianity; or the fact that the Spaniard knows an English word like "superimposed."

"Why there?" the South Korean asks. He eats his spaghetti with a concentrated precision that must be a carryover from his army career. This is one of the few times he's spoken.

"The pagan pilgrims believed the sun died at Finisterre. That the two worlds of the living and the dead came closer together there at the *Costa da Morte*."

"The Coast of Death," Daniel says, not particularly liking where this conversation is going but fascinated all the same.

"Yes. They made sacrifices there, at *Ara Solis*, the altar where they worshipped the dying sun god each evening to the west," the Spaniard says, glancing around the table for reaction.

"Were they human sacrifices?" The young American girl is completely drawn in now.

"Who knows?" the Spaniard says with a wink to Daniel.

Daniel doesn't wink back. He's beginning to wish they would talk about something safe, like politics or religion.

"Maybe that's what happened to that girl who went missing," the young woman says, spilling a few drops of *vino tinto* on the white tablecloth. She is making good use of the one-euro-a-bottle wine. "Maybe someone took her up to Finisterre and — you know." She makes a cutting motion, dragging one finger forcefully across the soft flesh of her neck.

"That's ridiculous, Caleigh," the older American woman chastises. Daniel realizes she must be the younger one's mother. Parental wrist-slapping is distinctive in tone. "Besides, I am tired of that subject." She turns to Daniel. "What part of Ireland are you from?" she says, smiling. "We have relatives in Derry."

"I'm from County Limerick, in the south." Daniel doesn't bother correcting her geography, so relieved is he that they have found a different subject. Derry is in Northern Ireland, a country with an all too violent past that his granny had quaintly referred to as "the Troubles." People often did not realize that this was a separate country from the Republic of Ireland, where Daniel is from. He gets tired of explaining that he didn't grow up with bombs in his mailbox or an uncle in the IRA. "I've been living in New Jersey for over ten years now. Sure, Ginny is from the States as well," he adds, hoping to pull her into the discussion.

The American woman follows his gaze to Ginny and nods.

Worrying she may misread the situation, he feels the need to explain further. "Oh, we're not a couple or anything," he stammers. "We came on the Camino separately, only met up on the path." He clears his throat. "What I mean to say is I came here alone. But not alone at the moment, obviously." He swallows what was meant to be a laugh but comes out sounding like a suppressed hiccup. "At any rate, we're only friends." Realizing he's sinking in the flood of his own babbling, he tries to divert the flow of conversation elsewhere. "Ginny's from California, of course. Where is it in California you're from again, Ginny?"

"Orange County," she replies, picking at her napkin where it flutters on the table in the breeze. "Originally."

Daniel waits for something more, but Ginny doesn't volunteer anything further. People start to look uncomfortable.

Despite the noise of Caleigh slurping a long strand of spaghetti up into her mouth, Daniel feels the need to fill the silence.

"That's right, Orange County. I was after forgetting. But sure, you live in the north of the state now. Near the prison. Tell them about where you work, Ginny. Now that's a lark." He smiles widely at her, his face cranking up a shade with the effort. Ginny just glares at him and says nothing. The American woman looks back and forth between the two and raises a finely tweezed brow to her daughter. Ginny casts her eyes down at the table, embarrassed. He has made a complete bollocks of this.

"This meal is wonderful, Roberto," the retired army officer finally chimes in. "Thank you so much for making it."

Roberto, that's his name. Daniel remembers now. Like the Dutchman. How could he forget?

The group resumes conversation, obviously not believing Daniel's account of Ginny and their relationship. This irks him. Even Roberto has caught Daniel stealing glimpses of his attractive walking partner across the wide-planked picnic table more than once tonight, so who does he think he's kidding.

After dinner they offer to help with the dishes, but Roberto tells him not to worry. The rest of them clear the plates and head back to the kitchen to wash up. He feels like he and Ginny have been dismissed. The Camino can be so damn cliquey. Or maybe they didn't want to get involved in what appeared to be a lover's spat. As the group walks away, the young American woman lets out a raucous laugh before being silenced by her mother. She trips up the front steps in her flip-flops and through the *albergue* screen door.

"Were you not after feeling well?" Daniel asks Ginny once the rest are out of earshot. He is wondering about the untouched spaghetti, her lack of interaction with the group.

"No," she says, walking back toward the picnic table. "I just don't like people knowing where I'm from."

"You didn't mind the Dutchman knowing."

"He's different."

Daniel is about to ask why when a disheveled old woman in oversized army boots catches them both off guard. She has walked in from the street to the schoolyard, wearing a long, stretched-out wool cardigan over a blue polyester night dress. Her hair is flat on one side as if slept on, and she doesn't appear to have all her teeth.

"Cigar-ette?" she says, as her upper lip pulls up in a nervous tic.

"Pardon?" Daniel asks, although he's heard her perfectly well.

"Cigar-ette, *por favor*." She brings her crooked fingers up to her face in pantomime. "*Me estoy muriendo.*"

"What does that mean?" Daniel asks Ginny.

"She says she's dying," Ginny tells him with a smirk.

"Is she?"

"For a smoke, it seems."

"That much I gathered."

"Cigar-ette?" The woman comes closer to them now, harmless but still demanding with her one English word. She coughs then spits out phlegm on the grass. Charming.

"I'm sorry," Daniel says. "I don't smoke." He shrugs his arms out from his sides in what he hopes is the cross-cultural sign for "Ain't got none."

Ginny gets a bar of chocolate out of her waist pack and offers it, but the woman seems put off by this and backs away, going out to the street again through the rear garden gate.

"Well, that was interesting."

"I hope the old girl didn't escape from somewhere," Daniel says. He watches the torn hem of her nightgown drag on the pavement as she disappears around a corner.

"I kind of hope she has," Ginny says, refilling their wine from what's left on the table.

She moves down the grass yard to the playground. Daniel follows. They each take a seat on one of the bleached wooden boards attached to rusty chains that pass for swings. Ginny leans back and pumps with her legs. Hinges squeak in protest as she goes higher and higher, still managing to hold onto her wine in the plastic glass. Daniel tries copying her and ends up watering the playground dirt with half of his *vino tinto*. After a few minutes, she slows down using the heels of her hiking boots as a brake. They make an uneven drumbeat on the ground.

"It seemed very important to you to explain we weren't together tonight," she says, as her swing arc diminishes.

He starts to slow down as well, but doesn't answer her.

"Are we, Daniel? Together?"

"Well, we're walking together, of course," he says.

"We are, but I think you know what I mean."

He does know what she means. He lets the swing come to a complete stop before responding. "I reckon I'm just not ready for that at the moment." He takes a sip of what's left of his wine with an arm curled around the swing chain.

"Just like you're not ready to move back to the farm in Ireland?" she asks, tilting her head, her swing now stationary as well.

"That's a whole different matter," he says. Damn it, why did he tell her about that. Now he'll have both her and Angela inquiring after his delaying tactics, bidets and all.

"Is it?" she asks, gazing out to the west, where the sun is starting to set. It glows orange between the tan adobe dwellings of the village.

"I have some things to take care of first. The house and my business," he says. "Ah, shite."

"What?"

"I was supposed to call my partner's wife." He'd totally forgotten about Cynthia and Gerald and their whole little drama. Well, the hell with it anyway. Even if Gerald wants him to sell, he's decided he's not going to. His partner will need to find some other way to pay his gambling debts. Serves him right after what he tried to get away with. "But the business isn't the only thing, I reckon."

"I gathered," Ginny says. She leans back in the swing again. "How long has it been since Petra died?"

"Over a year."

She looks over at him, but doesn't comment.

He crumples up the plastic tumbler and drops it on the ground for throwing out later. "You don't understand."

"Try me."

"I don't rightly know," he says. He toes the cup on the ground with his boot, pushing it around in the dirt. "I suppose, it never seemed entirely real to me." Despite the inevitable lead up to Petra's death, Daniel had a hard time with the everyday truth of it. "Back home, I'd often wake up expecting to see her in the bed," he says, recalling the sunlight falling through the bedroom window, his rolling over to wrap his arm around her and finding nothing but the cold side of the mattress. "It felt like a mistake, a trick." He kicks the plastic cup onto the grass. "As if she might leap up from under the bedsheets and yell 'Ta-da' at any moment."

"Like the dove pan," Ginny says, putting her wine down for a moment, twisting in the swing toward then away from him.

"Aye, like the dove pan." He takes his hands from the cold metal of the chains, rubs them together.

"I was thinking maybe since you hadn't been there when she …" Ginny hesitates. "Well, you didn't get to say good-bye and all. Maybe that makes things harder."

"Sure, there's that," Daniel says, keeping up the lie. He had been there when she died, in the most sinister of ways. But it was more than that — something he can barely admit to himself, let alone to Ginny. Instead he concentrates on things that might have a chance of being forgiven.

"I don't think I ever got around to imagining a life without her," he says, shoving his hands in his pockets. The sun has almost entirely set now, the temperature dropping with it. "That's why it's hard, the idea of you and me. It feels like I'm after cheating." He thinks of the heat of that kiss by the river and buries his fists deeper in his jacket. "It's as if she's still here."

"She is still here," Ginny says. "She's in a bag in your backpack."

"I reckon you know what I'm saying."

"I guess I do." She pauses, draining the last of the wine and dropping the cup. "But you know, Daniel, that she isn't really here, right?"

Daniel feels his pride bristle. "I know that, Ginny. I'm not daft."

"It's just you keeping her here."

"Says the woman with a dead addict after her."

"That's a cheap shot." She pulls her fleece sleeves down over her hands from underneath her jacket. "You're not the only one feeling guilty here."

Daniel remembers their discussion beneath Da Vinci's portrait of Mary Magdalene. "Sure, you're not talking about when you and your friend were kids? What harm, Ginny, but that wasn't your fault."

Ginny glares at him. "Have you ever known a person who is battling an addiction? Mental illness?"

Daniel had a cousin who suffered from an overwhelming desire to eat chalk, but he doesn't think that counts. "No," he says.

"Then you wouldn't know."

He lets that fair comment settle for a while. Eventually, she continues, less defensive.

"I wanted to help, but sometimes it could be so hard." She lowers her voice. "She could get really difficult."

Daniel nods. If her friend really was the one following them, then he knows how feckin' difficult she can be.

"I started to find reasons to avoid her," Ginny continues, her voice betraying a small tremble. "I told myself she needed to learn to stand on her own, you know, to get stronger. That's what the Al-Anon people tell you. No enabling. But the truth is, I guess, I wanted to distance myself for my own protection. I was doing the right thing for the wrong reason."

"Sometimes that's the best a person can do," Daniel says, looking away. For the second time this evening he feels the conversation take a turn down a road he doesn't want to travel.

"I just wonder if I could have done something, you know, to change things." Ginny digs a couple of fingers into her thigh, as if to remove something stuck to her hiking pants. The nails make a little shriek as they drag along the fabric.

"Her overdose is on her, Ginny."

"That's a bit cold."

"A person can't be laying their offences on anyone else's doorstep," Daniel says.

"How can you say that?" Ginny grabs tightly onto the chains, stops twisting in the seat to address him steadily. "Sometimes people can't help themselves. Sometimes things get out of hand."

"And you think that's why she's following you on the Camino? Because you were after causing her death?" Daniel doesn't appreciate any line of thinking that will make the dead woman any more real. "C'mon, Ginny," he says, discounting her. Never a good plan with women or anyone else.

"I didn't say that!" Ginny twists away from him, pinching her finger in the chain. Jumping up, she thrusts the sore digit into her mouth to suck on it. The swing bounces back and forth empty as if she were still in it.

"I was only after saying ..."

"You were only saying I should get over it. And in that, you'd be a hypocrite, Daniel Kennedy," she says, taking the finger from her mouth. She stoops over, picks up her discarded wine tumbler from the ground. "I'm not the only one who's followed on this Camino," she says to him before she turns to leave. "The only difference is I don't carry my ghost in my backpack."

She's up the yard and back in the *albergue*'s front door before he has a chance to call after her, probably a good thing. He's not sure what he'd say. After all, she's right. Nothing leaves a man more speechless than being faced with the truth about himself. But he won't go in after her. He has enough wounded ego for that. He knows he's been harsh, even sullen. He blames it on lack of sleep, the stress he's been under. Despite his talk earlier of culpability and doorsteps.

The young American woman's laughter drifts out the window of the *albergue,* followed by a loud bang and her mother hushing her. Ten to one the girl throws up in her bunk bed. He hopes Ginny called the top one.

After awhile he starts to feel childish sitting out on the swings all alone. He stands up to go inside. When he bends down to retrieve his plastic cup, he sees a pair of army boots planted in the grass off in a darkened corner of the yard. The old woman in the nightdress comes out of the shadows. She's got a cigarette now. By the cloying perfume of the smoke, he guesses it's Turkish.

"*Sé lo que hiciste, peregrino*," she snaps at him, her rheumatic eyes focused in accusation.

"Ah, Jaysus," he says, in no mood for this. "*No entiendo.*"

The woman moves with incredible agility for her age and is up in front of him before he has a chance to react. Then she speaks to him in perfect English, so close she gets old lady spittle on his jacket.

"I know what you did, pilgrim."

She steps back and takes another hit of the heavily scented cigarette. Behind her he sees another figure standing at the playground gate, like a mother waiting for a child who will never come. The old woman goes to join her, and their heads touch as they exchange whispers. Laughter breaks out between the two of them, one hacking and rattled, the other hollow and mewling, a sound made less than human by illusion or design.

He backs away to the porch of the old schoolhouse, never taking his eyes off either of the women that cackle into the night. He locks the old school door firmly behind him, hoping to God it will keep both of them out.

CHAPTER 12
Población de Campos to Calzadilla de la Cueza

THERE ARE TWO WAYS to Calzadilla de la Cueza on the Camino. One is by a shaded path that runs beside the soulless N-120 *autopista*; the other is along the two-thousand-year-old *Via Aquitania*, the Roman road.

"It's a ten-mile walk with no water or toilets," Daniel tells Ginny over lunch in Carrión de los Condes. There he has managed to find his favourite adopted-country cuisine, the American hamburger.

"If it was good enough for Caesar, it's good enough for me," Ginny says, picking across the table at the salad that came with his meal. They sit outside at a patio table in shorts. A blast of summer has returned for one last kick at the weather can before the tempered chill of northern Spain's winter starts to set in. Neither she nor Daniel has mentioned their argument on the swing set. The unresolved conflict draws a curtain between them that they hide behind with weak attempts at good humour.

"Arguably, Caesar had an entourage to carry him," Daniel says, holding the guidebook map open with his elbow as he grabs on to the greasy bun of the burger with both hands. "We won't be so lucky."

They had already travelled almost ten miles that morning, having made a brief stop to find and visit the church dedicated to Mary Magdalene in Población. It had been closed. The only trace of the Saint was a sad little battle-grey statue covered in bird droppings, propped high in an alcove above the doorway. *La Magdalena* held her raised hands together, as if pleading for release from her be-shitted pedestal prison. Ginny took a picture for her collection.

"I'm okay to go alone," she says as she polishes off the last limp leaf of the salad. "If you want to go the other way."

"Okay," Daniel says, still chewing on his burger.

They both know he's coming with her and that she'll let him, despite their exchange of words last night. Daniel would say he feels a sense of responsibility to their partnership, though, in truth, that sense swims through a strong current of all the other complicated feelings he has for her.

❋

If it hadn't been so hot, it might have been all right. If the weather had been more seasonable. If the afternoon sun hadn't started to cut them down like a sweltering lumberjack with an axe to grind. They might have warmed up to each other again with a cooler day. But it didn't turn out that way.

The top of Daniel's head roasts under his hat, and the shade is non-existent as they make their way on the raised gravel road, elevated by one hundred tons of rock substrata, thanks to Roman slaves. Daniel hasn't seen a tree since they passed some stunted broom bushes in the monastery ruins just outside town. Both their water bottles and the bladder in Ginny's backpack are empty. Ginny had forgotten to refill it at the restaurant. They had taken a break earlier and Daniel had rooted through his own pack, hoping for a forgotten apple or orange with juice that might help to slake his thirst, but all he found was a saliva-sucking honey granola bar. Ginny told him he was lucky to have that. He told her she should have refilled her water at the restaurant — where, it turns out, he has also left his sunglasses behind.

Deep in the distance, the cool shadow of mountains hovers on the borders of his sight, teasing with their snow-topped peaks. Other than those far-off frosty tips, the terrain is painfully flat and unblemished. This great interior plateau region of central Spain is called, simply, the *Meseta*, the largest plain of them all.

"It extends over eighty-one thousand miles," Daniel tells Ginny.

"Certainly feels like it."

"Of course, the Tibetan Plateau in Asia is far bigger."

"I see."

"Almost a million square miles. It contains the third largest store of ice in the world. The monsoons —"

"Give it a rest, Irish."

He does.

By late afternoon it is close to ninety Fahrenheit, a temperature swing of over twenty degrees from the day before. The *Meseta* can be like that. Its wide-open spaces are filled, unimpeded, by whatever wind blows in. Ginny's voice is starting to show cracks like the baked mud in the fields that surround them.

"How much farther do you think it is?"

"Two miles," Daniel says, his response measured with irritation as well as distance. He's been trying to calculate their position by the amount of time they've been walking, but because there are no landmarks to gauge their progress, he can't be sure. He's been convinced they are only two miles away from Calzadilla for at least the last two hours. During that time, Ginny has asked him four times how much farther it is.

"Maybe we should go back," she says.

"Are you serious?" Daniel asks, so forcefully it causes him to cough up a not-entirely-swallowed grain of granola.

"Or maybe turn off the Roman road," she says. "See if we can find the *autopista* again."

"Take a look at where we are now, Ginny." Daniel gestures to the expanse of nothingness on either side of them. "A man could sit on his porch and watch his dog run away for a week for Christ's sake."

"I'm just saying. You don't have to get so goddamn touchy."

"I'm not touchy," he says, kicking a piece of gravel with the defiant toe of his boot.

She ignores him, shields her eyes against the sun, and scans the trail up ahead as they follow a curve to the left. "Wait, what's that up there?" she says.

In a small depression in the landscape, a one-lane paved road bisects the Camino. The view is distorted by bent air that waves up from the hot tarmac. They can both just make it out, off to the side, a blot of colour and two or three rough leaning structures. As they walk, the hazy images sharpen into recognition.

"My God," Daniel says. "Are those …"

"Teepees," Ginny says, shading her eyes from the sun. It cannot entirely eclipse a sliver of her delight.

The proprietor of the roadside rest stop not only has teepees, but also hammocks and, frustratingly, a broken water pump. He stands shirtless behind a makeshift bar made from a surfboard and two orange crates, all draped beneath the roof of a large Indian rug. A neon sign with no electricity to light it is tied precariously to an imitation palm tree. It reads with dimmed but hopeful hospitality, "Welcome to the El Mocambo."

"Sorry, man, I'm usually only open in the summer," he says in perfect English when they inquire after cold beverages. "I came out today to take down the teepees." He turns around and starts rifling through an old-style stainless steel cooler behind him. When he bends over, his loosely tied loincloth forces Ginny to avert her eyes until he stands up again. "I've got this, though," he says, holding up an opaque black bottle with a white triangular label. Bold calligraphy spells out the brand: Hendrick's.

"Sorry, no tonic," he apologizes, as he pulls out two shot glasses and places them on the surfboard.

Ginny sighs. "Great. Only rest stop in miles, and it's run by a hippy exhibitionist selling moonshine."

Daniel steps away from her potshot and up to the bar. "I think I'll take some of that moonshine if you're pouring." The tension of last night and today have been simmering within him alongside the elements. He needs cooling off inside and out. A cold beer would suit better, but he'll take one of the best gins in the world instead, if that's what's on offer. He sits down on a crooked three-legged stool and drops his backpack to the dusty ground to fetch his wallet. "How much?"

"*Donativo*, my friend, only *donativo*." The hippy indicates a large Mason jar on the broad end of the surfboard as he serves. Daniel drops in a couple of euros. They join a business card and a large ball of tape.

"A man can't afford too many bottles of Hendrick's on *donativos*, I'm thinking," Daniel says as he throws back the gin all at once. It races down the parched horizon of his throat like liquid lightning.

"The Camino provides," the hippy says, tossing back his own shot. He wipes his mouth with the back of his hand, leaving a little bit of saliva behind in his beard. "And I must provide for the pilgrims," he says. "It's my duty."

"A frightful disability is duty," Daniel says with uncharacteristic cynicism as the hippy pours them both another shot. The hippy is like the woman volunteering in the *albergue* back in Grañón: once a pilgrim, now a penitent who serves others. "I gather you walked the Camino before, so."

"The first time was in 1974. Walked it five times since then. The Camino gave to me. Now I give to the Camino. It's payback."

Jesus, how old is this guy? Daniel thinks. Then looks a bit closer at the crow's feet around his eyes, the patches of grey sprouting in the unkempt garden of a beard. He puts back another shot of the premium liquor. It doesn't quench his thirst exactly, but it is starting to help him forget about it. "Sure, your English is very good," he says, fighting back a belch.

"I'm from Boston," the man tells him, going to pour a third, but Daniel holds his hand over top of his glass. "I met someone here during university. Never left." He puts the bottle of Hendrick's down without pouring himself another, lights up a hand-rolled cigarette instead. "You know how it is."

"I know," Daniel says, then turns around to see if Ginny is listening, but she's gone to check out one of the teepees. He watches her cautiously opening a flap of canvas to peer inside. The hippy barman follows his gaze as she bends over to get a better look. "Oh, we're not together," Daniel finds himself explaining for the second time in twenty-four hours. He cocks his head in Ginny's direction after turning back to the bar. "She's just a friend."

"She is?" asks the hippy, scratching his beard. An act that Daniel notices with relief removes the speck of saliva. It had been a visual distraction, much like the guy's loincloth. "A woman like that can be hard to stay friends with," he says with a smile. "And how long have you and your *friend* been walking together?" he asks, leaning on the bar.

"A week, maybe more." Daniel can't seem to remember how long it's been now. Time can be tricky on the Camino. Then again, he can't remember being poured a third drink either, but there it is in front of him. He picks it up and rolls the cool glass between his fingers without bringing it to his lips.

The man nods and uses a surprisingly clean rag tucked at his waist to wipe down the surfboard. "This is a tough part of the Way," he says. "The *Meseta*."

"They're all tough, surely?" Daniel says. As hard and hot as today's walk has been, Daniel knows the Pyrenees were no picnic either. Straight up for miles and then a femur-jarring descent on loose rocks after you finally made it over the pass. His shattered kneecaps felt like a box of cornflakes afterward. Some people didn't even make it over the mountain range. There had been deaths, heart attacks from the effort, or people who got caught out on the peaks after dark or in storms. Daniel was in decent enough shape, but it had still taken him eight hours to hike the pass.

"Each of the three stages is challenging in its own way," the hippy says, still polishing the bar.

The faded denim irises of his eyes are surprisingly clear as he lifts them up to Daniel. They mesmerize Daniel slightly.

"And what are the three stages?" Daniel asks, putting his glass back down unemptied. He is still unable to look away.

"Well, the first part of the Camino is for the body," the hippy says, dropping his gaze and the polishing rag to fetch the burning cigarette. It's been resting perilously until now, the lit end jutting from its perch on the board. "You either get strong or end up in the hospital in the first part."

Daniel remembers his cereal-box knees and nods in agreement.

"The second part is for the mind," the bartender continues, pulling the smoke of his hand-rolled deep into his lungs. Daniel can see the rib cage of his skinny, hairless chest expand. "The same *meseta* landscape for days," he tells Daniel. "Nothing to feed the brain but an endless pancake of open ground. A pilgrim's thoughts turn inward. You can start to lose your grip with the monotony in the second part."

Daniel nods again. This is the phase they are in now and, despite everything, he's glad to have someone with him. He doesn't know what his mind might do with that monotony if he had only himself and his darker thoughts to break up the scenery.

"What's the last part for?" he asks, lifting the drink to his lips. This time the gin tastes sour. He grimaces.

"The soul."

"Aye, Santiago," Daniel says. "The cathedral."

"Not just the cathedral, my friend. Everything that leads up to the cathedral. Everything you were hoping to find there."

"Like the bones of Saint James?" Daniel says, his cynicism returning.

"Is that why you're walking five hundred miles, for some two-thousand-year-old bones?"

"Surely the Catholic Church has more impressive skeletons in the closet," Daniel says, trying to lighten the conversation with a whiff of sacrilege.

The hippy lets it drift away before he goes on. "No matter what you think you'll find in Santiago, it all comes down to faith, my friend. Faith that there is something you are walking toward. Something that will alter you as a person." He leans his elbows on the surfboard bar and blows two smoke rings up and to the right, one inside the other. They float past the fake palm tree then disappear. "Not all have a life-changing experience when they finish the Camino," he says, turning his attention back to Daniel. "Oh, some say they do, but it is like the story of the Emperor and his new clothes. The naked truth is they walked all that way and found nothing at the end of it."

"So, you're saying I'll either find my faith or lose it by the time I get to Santiago?" Daniel asks.

"I'm saying you'll either find or lose your soul," the hippy says as he drops his cigarette butt into a rusty tomato can, "on the last part." He whisks away the two shot glasses and drops the Hendrick's back in the cooler. "But the Way is full of lost souls, my man, or haven't you noticed?"

"I thought you were the Irishman that didn't drink?"

Ginny is standing behind him now. Her sudden presentiment knocks him off his stool and out of the spell the bartender wove around him. And it is some sort of spell, he thinks, as he rights himself with one unsteady hand. How else could he explain having just consumed three shots of gin in quick succession without fully realizing it. Ginny's right, it's not like him.

"I ought to get going, I suppose," he says, straightening up. "We're wanting to get to the next village." Daniel starts to collect his things, drops a few more euros in the *dona-tivo* jar. The hippy comes out from behind the surfboard and puts a hand on his shoulder. Leather and cloth bracelets tied in knots on his wrist slide down the mahogany tanned forearm.

"Listen, man, why don't you come in the truck with me?" He gestures to a late-model open-bed pickup parked partially behind a wall of hay bales. "I got a buddy in Calzadilla with a nice little hotel. I can take you there, set you up. I think you've walked enough for the day." He looks up at Daniel, his bushy eyebrows drawing together.

The man barely comes up to Daniel's chest. Daniel hadn't realized how gnome-like the guy was, must have been standing on a crate behind the bar all this time.

Ginny leans in. "Let's go, Daniel."

"Sorry, bro, got to listen to the missus," Daniel says, chuckling and wrapping an arm around Ginny, a poorly thought-out manoeuvre.

She tenses and makes a face as though she would enjoy running him through with one of the teepee poles. His arm beats a hasty retreat. Somewhere in the recesses of his lit-up cerebellum, he realizes he has made a grave tactical error. He never should have gotten so heavily into the Hendrick's with the hypnotizing little leprechaun. Chastising himself, he pulls on his backpack, yanking on the strap of the hip belt with a vengeance. It bites into his gut where the gin and the granola bar have set up for a quarrel with one another.

"Thanks," he says, reaching over when he's done gearing up to shake the little man's hand. It turns into one of those overhand clasps like they did in the movie *Mod Squad*.

"Take care of yourself, my friend."

"I will," Daniel says, hurrying off after Ginny. She is already back on the trail, speeding up to go ahead of him. Definitely pissed, he assesses, even as he runs to catch up.

"I don't like that guy," she says. They cross to the other side of the one-lane road. The tarmac radiates heat and is buckling in places. Not one car has passed over it since they've been there.

"Why not?" Daniel asks her. "I thought he was grand."

"That's because he only had eyes for you," she says.

"Perhaps." Daniel had gotten a similar vibe, but didn't have a problem with it. Neither did Ginny, he was sure. After all, she was from California. "Jealous?" he teases her, feeling lightheaded and witty, a combined illusion gin is all too famous for.

She speeds up on the hot trail and doesn't answer him. She isn't in the mood, he reckons, for teasing.

✳

"I thought you said it was only two more miles." Ginny sucks on the tube to her backpack hydration bladder, trying to siphon out a few drops. It makes a sound like a straw at the bottom of a milkshake.

"I thought you said you were fine to go on."

Daniel had pointed out the hippy's offer not long after they got back on the trail. They could still walk back and take him up on a drive the last of the way, he'd said. She'd been adamant in her refusal. He's starting to wish he'd pushed the idea a little more.

"I am fine to go on. Are you?" she says sharply.

They've been bickering with each other for the last half hour. Tired, hot, dusty from the trail. Daniel can feel the fine grit in his mouth, grinding on his teeth. The vast *meseta* still surrounds them, as flat as ever, but the Roman road built through it has begun to swell and recede in a cascade of rises that test their patience as well as their endurance.

"Maybe we should take a break," Daniel says, looking out over the horizon at the Camino disappearing over the next small hill, and the next and the next.

"We just took a break."

"Well, maybe we should take another one." He pulls his pack off roughly and throws it down on the ground, and a grey dirt cloud flies up into his eyes. He turns away, rubbing them with both his fists. Once recovered, he opens the ties of his pack and pulls out the guidebook, flipping through it hastily. The pages make noisy protest in his hands. The pleasant calm of the Hendrick's in his body has long worn off and left him with an angry rot in his gut. He's not at his best.

"I don't know what you think you're going to find in there," Ginny says, throwing her own backpack down. "It's not like we could have missed Calzadilla. There's been nothing for miles."

Daniel ignores her, running his finger along the yellow dotted trail in his guidebook. He still can't figure out where they are. They've crossed a couple of muddy streams on their way, but nothing big enough to warrant an entry on the map. They've been walking for so bloody long. They really should be there by now. He narrows his eyes inspecting the map, the sweat dripping down the back of his neck, convinced something will make sense if he just looks long enough.

Ginny throws off her own backpack and sits down hard on the gravel path, her back to him. "I hate this part," she says under her breath.

Daniel looks up from the guidebook. "What do you mean, 'this part'?" He closes the book in his hands with a snap, raises his voice a bit. It would echo if there were anything for it to bounce off. "What do you mean, Ginny?"

"Nothing," she says, still not turning around to face him.

"You said you hated this part," he reminds her. "Like you're after doing it before."

She doesn't answer him. He throws the guidebook back in his pack, cinches it closed again.

He takes a step closer to her. "Have you?"

"Have I what?" she says, standing up, brushing the gravel residue off her hiking pants.

"Have you walked it before, so?" he says, grabbing his pack and slamming it on his back. The loose sternum straps slap him in the chest. "Like the Englishman said?" He's not sure how it really matters. Who cares if she walked it before. Although it seems strange that she would lie about it. The possible deception fuels his rising temper. The last week has taken its toll, just as the Roman road has.

"Are you going to believe what that asshole says?"

"Are you after giving me a straight answer?"

She sighs and then tries to reason with him. "Listen, Daniel, you're hot, we're both exhausted. It can't be that much farther. Let's just keep —"

"What's that?" He's looking past her, ahead on the trail. A shiny twist of silver winks at them from atop the next hill. "Is that a water pump?" he cries out. The metal spigots are usually marked on the map with a blue *F* for *Fuente*, fountain, but he hadn't seen any when he consulted the guidebook. The prospect of water for his swollen tongue diverts him from his interrogation of Ginny. He begins marching toward the twinkling flash. Ginny follows him at a distance.

As they approach, it becomes more and more apparent that this is not a *Fuente*, too low to the ground and the wrong shape. When they get close enough, they stop. Ginny warns him quietly.

"Don't touch it, Daniel."

"What the fuck is this, Ginny?" The shiny pan with the fitted top sits in the middle of the road like an untripped bomb.

"I don't know, Daniel."

"You don't, do you?" he says, spinning around to face her. He is seething with anger now. He would spit on the trail if he had any saliva left. "It's a dove pan, Ginny. What the hell do you think a dove pan is doing in the middle of the Camino?"

"I don't know, Daniel," she says again weakly.

"I'll tell you what. It's here because I told you about it. And either you're some sick bitch or ..."

"No, Daniel, no ... I didn't ..."

She's starting to cry now, but he can't bring himself to care. His rage lifts him up, carrying him away.

"Did someone put you up to it? Was it that gobshite, Gerald? Pay you to try and drive the pathetic grief-riddled Irishman mad, did he now?" It all makes sense. Gerald could have arranged for this whole little charade, the woman following them, Ginny. All just designed to drive Daniel off the edge so Gerald could take control of the business and sell it out from under him. He looks down at the covered pan and then turns to Ginny, challenging her with his eyes. She still cries with what he firmly believes to be crocodile tears.

"Don't do it, Daniel," she says, her voice pleading. What an actress. And he'd almost fallen for it. Such a fool he's been. He reaches down and lifts the lid of the pan, throwing it off the side of the raised road into the cracked earthen field below.

The charred white feathers of the still bird inside flutter as a coward of a breeze blows over the crest of the hill.

"The hell with you," Daniel says. "The hell with all of you." He steps around the glittering pan and carries on walking the trail, leaving Ginny and the dead dove behind.

✳

When Daniel finally makes it into Calzadilla de la Cueza, he walks right past the municipal *albergue* with its communal quarters and checks in at the local hotel. He tells the proprietor that the guy with the Hendrick's and the surfboard bar sent him and receives a hearty welcome he sadly has no stomach for. After drinking copious amounts of bottled water at supper, he moves on to the bar and spends so much time there he doesn't get up to walk the next morning. Instead, he lies in the bed of the boutique hotel and drifts in and out of a fitful sleep, thrashing on the expanse of white cotton sheets, boundaryless after the familiar containment of his sleeping bag. He awakes to a pounding headache sometime after lunch, its origin as likely from heatstroke as his trip to the hotel bar. Getting dressed and swallowing a few Aspirin, he takes the richly carpeted staircase down to a more modest lobby restaurant in search of coffee and Wi-Fi.

"You better watch it or you're going to become a stereotype, Daniel." Angela arches one disapproving eyebrow at him from the screen of his phone. "There is only one thing more cliché than a grieving Irishman, and that's a hungover one."

"Stop, Angela." Daniel downs half of a bottle of water he ordered with his *café con leche*. "I'm not needing this now."

"Fine. Whatever you say. Far be it from me to ever tell my brother when he's being a right pillock. But tell me, what does your friend Ginny have to say about this new alcoholic side of yourself?"

"She's history," he tells her.

"Why?"

Daniel tells her everything. About the first sighting of the woman in the corn, his encounter in the cemetery and the nunnery. Ginny's ridiculous explanation that the dead spirit of her friend was following them. He's grateful there's no one in the restaurant to listen.

"Jesus, Danny, you really were out in the sun too long," she says.

He doesn't tell her about the dove pan. It is too personal and too fresh. Instead, he tells her about his suspicions about Gerald. How it was all an elaborate con so he could take control of Daniel's portion of the firm then sell out to pay off his gambling debts.

"I think he hired that other one, *and* Ginny," he says, spitting out her name over the table. "I'm sure she's lied about all she had to say for herself. No doubt she's not even from California or even the feckin' West Coast." He takes a sip of coffee with steamed milk and feels the caffeine wash over key regions of his aching brain. When he takes his forehead in his hands and closes his eyes, he ends his tirade with a final admission less aggressive in tone but more damning for his spirit. "Sure, I just can't believe she played me like that, Angie."

"Daniel," he can hear Angela say, treading lightly with him. "I talked to Gerald."

His head jolts up from the table, knocking the smartphone over from where it was propped against the napkin canister. He picks it up quickly and shouts into the video feed, "You talked to Gerald?"

"I'd had enough of Cynthia's wailing, so I tracked him down myself. The wanker's in Atlantic City with some youngster with a soap opera name, works in your office."

"Kendra?" Daniel asks in disbelief. Their receptionist. She couldn't be more than twenty years old, straight out of community college. The kid was so young she probably still had placenta behind her ears.

"Aye, Kendra. Didn't she make a play for you once?" Angela asks.

She had, when Petra was in the hospital. A few women had at the time. There are few things more magnetic than the loneliness of a grieving widower before his wife has had a chance to die.

"He appears to have won back all the money he owed and then some," Angela continues. "Living it up like a king he is now, if you want to believe him. No wonder Cynthia was upset. I'd have him strung up by his clackers myself."

"Jesus."

"The thing is, Daniel, he told me the corporation pulled out. The one that was so hot and bothered for your outfit. They retracted their offer right after you left for the Camino. Bought out your man in Newark instead, Bara— something or other."

"Baracon," he says, with the inflection of a sponge. He knows Steve, the CEO. They used to play squash. He holds up his sister's Skype image, her contour and colouring so like his own. Her expression mirrors back a conclusion that he is only slowly coming to. "What are you saying, Angela?"

A disgruntled teenager comes into the empty restaurant and drops a bucket on the floor with a crash, starts to mop up. The acrid smell of disinfectant washes across the tiles of the restaurant and into Daniel's nostrils, making him wince.

His sister speaks to him from the palm of his hand and eight hundred miles away.

"I'm saying whatever reasons that girl may have to try to drive you mad, Daniel, they're her own."

CHAPTER 13
Calzadilla de la Cueza to Portomarín

DANIEL STEERS CLEAR OF the Roman road after that. The guidebook allows for more than one route out of Calzadilla and beyond. He chooses the dreary dirt path next to the *autopista* rather than chance the open *meseta* again. A new wind has blown in from the mountains, bringing with it more seasonable weather. He is back to needing a jacket in the morning more than a broad-brimmed hat.

Cars fly past him, rustling the barren shade trees planted at unnatural intervals. Beyond this, the vegetation struggles to cling to the flatlands, burnt up and pollution stunted. It is a drab box-top world sliced in two identical hemispheres by an asphalt ribbon. Only the occasional Formica-riddled road-side café breaks the pattern, or an abandoned *bodega* with a door locked tightly into its sparsely grassed dome. Fellow pilgrims are scarce although he does bump into the mother-daughter team from his shared dinner at the schoolhouse. The two offer polite but strained *Buen Caminos* followed by stilted small talk. He takes the hint and moves on. They must feel confirmed in their earlier assessment of a lover's quarrel, given Ginny's absence. This annoys him though he is grateful they didn't ask where she is. Mostly because he doesn't know.

The Camino eventually leads him to a nondescript municipal *albergue*, where he stays the night, keeping to himself. The room he shares with four others opens out onto the street, and he stands and watches the late-afternoon pilgrims trickle in as he hangs his wet clothes on the veranda. After a time, when he can no longer convince himself he isn't looking for someone, he turns away.

After a poor sleep, he gets up and does the same thing again. He is back in the rhythm he had when he first started walking the Camino, the daily physical hardship of hundreds of lonely steps, the cyclical search for shelter and a place to wash off the dirt from the road at the end of the day. He eats when he can and finds inconspicuous and inventive places to relieve himself when needed. This, despite seeing a sign at one of the crossroads that showed a defecating stick man with a line drawn through his crouched linear body. *The hell with them*, Daniel thinks, wringing out his wet wool socks that night. *If they don't want a man crapping on the Camino, then they ought to build some public lavatories.*

By the time he makes it to León, he is a walking automaton, unable to appreciate the charms of the capital of the province. Instead, he is needled by its seedier side. Comic-strip lions with addled faces point the way to Santiago instead of scallop shells and gilded arrows. Buskers on the sidewalk sell Saint James fridge magnets and Blessed Virgins that glow in the dark. One vendor has T-shirts fanned out on the pavement like cards, each emblazoned with a cartoon character in a blue pilgrim cape, walking staff in hand. A man stops dead in front of him to pull a beer-bellied Homer Simpson from the deck. Daniel moves to get around him and hits the oncoming flow of pedestrian traffic. People bump into him and knock his backpack about.

Crossing a pedestrian overpass surrounded by cloudy Plexiglas, he gazes out across the sprawling city as through smoke. He can see the parade for *San Froilán* snaking its way through the downtown core in honour of León's patron saint, a former hermit never seen without his familiar, a tamed wolf carrying saddlebags. Beyond his lupine sidekick, *San Froilán* is famous for epic journeys of faith that earned him a bishop's ring. *Too often*, Daniel thinks, *the biographies of saints read like a cross between Tolkien and a teen vampire novel.*

Even from this distance he can make out the bright crimson whirlpool that is the Flamenco dancer's spinning skirts, can feel the far-off beat of the music reverberate against the Plexiglas. It brings back memories of the Rioja festival, his dancing down the street with Ginny and the Big Heads. How stupid he must have looked, bumping and grinding like a *Saturday Night Fever* reject. He cringes thinking about it, walks on toward the older part of the city away from the celebrations.

He attends the cathedral in the main square, more by rote than by choice. The setting sun streams through all of the 125 magnificent stained-glass windows, but there is no warmth in it. Kneeling in a pew in the vast sanctuary, he tries to form a prayer in his mind but is distracted by the music that travels faintly through the thick stone walls — the sound of the festival nearing the medieval quarter. He knows the parade with its floats will not be allowed in. Vehicles of any kind are banned in this historic section of León, a collection of Gothic-style architecture built on Roman ruins, now a fashionable district of squares and narrow streets in which to see and be seen. Even at this time of year, stylish sophisticates spill out of the converted upscale restaurants and wine bars onto the quarter's paved stone plazas, seated around tables draped in red-and-white checkered linen cloth. When he had walked through earlier, each crowded plaza seemed to open out endlessly onto the next, like a cascade of mirrors reflecting cosmopolitan chic that he wasn't prepared for in his humble hiking gear. He had checked into a convent-run *albergue* next to a four-star hotel then walked over to the cathedral. A corporate-looking nun talking on her cellphone had taken enough time out from her conversation to give him directions. In the pew now, he clasps his hands together tighter, trying to concentrate as the priest mounts the steps to the altar. Head bowed, eyes closed, Daniel prepares to mouth the words he learned in childhood.

Lord have mercy.

Señor, ten misericordia.

Christ have mercy.

Cristo, ten misericordia.

The Spanish words bring back the night in the nunnery. He can see the woman in her blood-stained habit, feel the touch of her bent skeletal fingers on the back of his neck. How repulsed he'd been, even though he had later realized how much those hands resembled Petra's, after the cancer had taken most of her flesh to stoke its cellular bonfire. He looks up at one of the windowpanes depicting Christ at Calvary, a weeping Mary Magdalene clinging to the base of the cross. On the bridge that night, when Ginny had kissed him, she'd been so vulnerable, her tears falling to bead on the front of his nylon jacket. Could she really have faked it all?

Daniel leaves the cathedral before completing the Mass. The parade threatens outside the thick walls of the quarter, the music and drumbeats pulsing at its gates. He turns his back on the revelry and hurries on, passing through busy plazas one after the other, his backpack slung across one shoulder like a heavy afterthought. Laughter and lightness float around him as he moves through the crowds who drink and eat in honour of saints.

He walks into the *albergue* and lies down on a bunk in a room that sleeps one hundred and fifty.

Never has he felt so alone.

❋

Daniel continues on like this, by himself, one day blending into the next, a simple existence brought down to basic needs. He pushes his body to its limits, walking longer and longer distances. His muscles ache then harden. He uses physical punishment and the meditation of miles to keep his mind clear of more painful thoughts, swears off alcohol even though it might have helped him with that. He doesn't see the woman. He doesn't see Ginny. Even Petra remains at the bottom of his backpack untouched. His emotions have been dammed up with a barrier of will and obsession. Reaching Santiago is his only goal now. After that, he doesn't know anymore.

His opinion of cities has not changed when days later he reaches Astorga. The glorified river town is not as big or as trendy as León but still tries to compete, like an ugly stepsister tarting herself up. Daniel walks through the morning market on his way to the museum, the smell of overripe produce and sickly sweet churros assaulting his nose. Discarded lettuce leaves and sticky wrappers are strewn along the walkway. He picks his way around the trash so as not to soil his hiking boots. Later, a city worker will come and sweep it all away. The propensity to litter seems to be directly correlated with the knowledge that somebody else will clean it up.

In almost every shop window is a notice about the missing woman, Beatrice McConaughey, seeking information about her disappearance in both Spanish and English. *Her given name seems so pedantic for a young woman caught up in such extraordinary circumstances,* Daniel thinks. He is quite sure they had a Jersey cow named Beatrice on the farm when he was growing up — although, they rarely named the animals. His father hadn't wanted anyone to get attached.

There is no photo with the posters that he notices, just a short physical description — five feet, seven inches tall, long brown hair, medium build, a small tattoo of a bar of music on her inner forearm. The description is as mundane as the name although the music tattoo is a surprise. As he reads a poster glued to a cement lamppost, Daniel wonders what melody the missing woman chose and why she picked such a tender place for it. It must have hurt like hell.

He also wonders where Ginny is. The posters warn women not to walk alone on the next few stages of the Camino. There have been reports of assaults, even a failed abduction, as Mark, the rotten Englishman, had said. It makes Daniel angry to think that women have to worry about this kind of brutal bullshit on a pilgrimage. Or ever. But like most men who care about such things, he doesn't know what to do with his outrage. He pushes his anger as well as his fear for Ginny aside, shoves his hands in his pockets, and walks away toward the tall black iron gates of the *Museo de Catedral.* There, he pays over three euros to a fleshy-faced man reading a newspaper behind the front desk and pushes in through the turnstile.

His eyes need time to adjust to the gloom. The museum has no central lighting, only wall- or ceiling-mounted lamps that bend to illuminate each painting and sculpture. Daniel counts no fewer than a dozen likenesses of *la virgen con niño* as he walks down the narrow entrance hallway. The last one shows a blond, rouge-cheeked version of Mary holding a sprightly curly-haired Jesus. Too Hollywood for Daniel's taste. It is hard to take the mother of the Messiah seriously when she is depicted as a Disney princess.

The next section is dedicated to all brand of beast and malignant spirits, a favourite muse of European art of the Middle Ages — the Spanish being no exception. He takes a picture with his phone of one painting of a man and woman standing naked, holding hands in what appears to be hell. The artist has rendered long-toothed fiends and lascivious monsters where their genitals should be. He'll send the photo to Angela when he next finds some Wi-Fi. She'll appreciate the carnival madness of a pubic purgatory.

In the next room, he stops in front of another painting, but doesn't take a photo. It is Mary Magdalene in one of her *Playboy* poses, reclined on her side with evil-looking cherubs dancing around her. Or maybe they just seem evil to Daniel. He's had a distrust of angels from a young age, ever since his brother told him the devil used to be one.

"He drove seven demons out of her, Christ did." The voice booms from the cavernous shadows of the gallery.

Daniel starts and turns around. Mark leans on a wall at the opening of a murky passageway. He walks up to the painting and runs his thick fingers along the surface of the brush strokes, following the curves of Mary Magdalene's hip.

"You have to wonder where they went once he got rid of 'em," he says, turning his face to Daniel, his filthy hand still feeling up the saint. "Or maybe you know already, don't you, Danny boy."

The Englishman may be broader than Daniel, but he's older and not as quick. Before either of them realizes what is happening, Daniel has thrown Mark against the wall next to a bust of Pope Callixtus III. The Englishman's backpack cushions some of the blow. Daniel hopes there is something hard packed inside of it that is gouging him in the spine.

"Are you following me?" he demands, more to justify his reaction than due to any real suspicion. All his pent-up anger — over the loss of his wife, the tawdry street vendors, Ginny's deceit — is being channelled, and now further fueled by his disgust for this pervert.

"Now, why the hell would I be following you?" The Englishman doesn't move, even though Daniel has the front of his fleece grabbed in his fist. He holds Daniel's furious gaze, waiting for him to back off, which he eventually does. After Daniel releases his grip and steps away, the big man remains where he is, reclining against the wall with a smirk.

"You have to be more relaxed if you're going to make it to Santiago, boy."

"I'll be making it to Santiago just fine. Thanks," Daniel tells him.

"Not everyone does," Mark says, moving into the light. He makes sure to keep the bust of the pope between them. "Where's your little friend?"

"Ginny?" Daniel says, staring the bastard down.

"Yes," Mark says, brushing his fingers against the stone head of the long-dead pope. His fat rings make a scraping sound. "Ginny."

"I don't suppose I know," Daniel tells him and then adds, "As far away from you as she can manage, no doubt."

The Englishman smiles widely, a shit-eating grin that hints toward worse appetites. His teeth are small and perfect, like a child's. "You heard about our little misunderstanding."

"I heard you acted the maggot."

"Some girls just can't take a joke."

"I'm not after seeing anyone laughing."

The two men stand still for a moment, as if sizing each other up for another physical altercation, but the moment passes like a hot *meseta* breeze. Daniel shakes his head and goes to move past the Englishman toward the exit. He's had enough art appreciation for the day. His hand is on the bar of the heavy fire door when he stops and asks the question, looking down but not back.

"What did you mean when you said she had walked the Camino before?"

The Englishman is silent for so long, Daniel thinks he won't answer, but eventually he pipes up, unable to miss an opportunity to pontificate.

"Everyone here has walked the Camino before, mate."

Mark comes up close behind him. Daniel can smell the stale beer and sweat that clings to him, along with the faint aroma of sick.

"The real Camino is life, Danny boy. Or death, depending on how you look at it."

"Fuck you," Daniel says, just before he kicks open the door and walks out, squinting into the bright sunshine.

Mark's voice booms across the plaza, dispersing a flock of worried pearl-grey pigeons into the air. "You've walked this road before, Daniel," he calls after him. "You just don't know it yet."

Daniel stops and waits a moment before turning around. By then the heavy metal door is closed. The Englishman is gone.

✳

The next day Daniel mounts the path to *Monte Irago*, leaving the flat bowl of the *Meseta* behind him. Most people would have stopped at Rabanal overnight to rest for the steep ascent, but he keeps going, a destination in mind. He stands now in front of it, *La Cruz de Ferro*, the Iron Cross of the Camino. It sits atop a rough wooden pole rising twenty feet in the air, set on a towering mound completely covered in stones. This is not the highest point on the road to Santiago, but close, and a place of long-standing tradition. Pilgrims place a stone at the base of the cross to represent something they have left behind as part of their time on the Way — pride, greed, the usual vices. It's a similar practice to the small cairns of intentions Daniel has passed on the Camino from the beginning that so distressed him with their likeness to roadside tributes to the dead. This cairn is almost two stories high and bothers him less so. It is too large to mark just one accident. The magnitude of it is more in keeping with his own mistakes.

No one knows for sure about the origins of the *Cruz de Ferro*. Although it might have provided a beacon for pilgrims over the centuries to help find their way through the snowbound mountains. There is no snow here yet, but Daniel can look across to *Monte Teleno* in the southwest and see laced peaks of white. Other speculators believe the mound may have served as an altar to the Roman god Mercury, the patron god of travellers as well as luck, trickery, and thieves. *More Christianity superimposed*, Daniel thinks, like Roberto the Spaniard had said. Despite its possible pagan roots, Daniel crosses himself as he stands at the foot of the monument of rock and pebble. He has a stone in his hand he brought from his backyard in New Jersey. He had picked it quickly from beneath a favourite tree before he left, not considering carefully the size. It had weighed like a brick in his backpack. More than once he thought of ditching it before now. When he drops it on the mound with all the others, he knows that it doesn't really symbolize much of anything — except perhaps his need to unload.

No one is here to see him place his intention on the pile. Most will have found a bed by now, after visiting the shrine in the morning. He had planned it this way, having gotten used to the steady company of his own solitude. He hadn't wanted the intrusion of others while he contemplated the cross that moved so many. Or perhaps he was afraid someone might spot him not being moved at all. The sun has dropped enough to backlight the simple iron crucifix when he hears a familiar voice.

"Daniel from New Jersey!" The Dutchman calls out to him from the veranda of a small chapel on a rise overlooking the shrine. Daniel had explored it earlier and found the door locked.

"Rob!" He walks up the hill and goes to shake his friend's hand, but the tall man grabs him in a bear hug instead. Rob wears the burnished copper heart on the lapel of his jacket and Daniel can feel it press, strangely warm, against his cheek as they embrace.

"It has been a long time, Daniel," Rob says as he releases him. "Are you enjoying your Camino?"

"I suppose so," says Daniel. "I'm pleased to see the back of the *Meseta*, though." He glances at the Dutchman's sincere friendly face. "It's good to see you, Rob."

"It is good to see you, too," Rob replies. He gestures with his hand, and both men sit down on the edge of the small veranda. Together they look out over the ridge in silence for a few moments. A couple of wild horses chase each other in a meadow below, a pinto and a white stallion. Daniel hopes they don't cull them here for the meat, as they do the ones in the Pyrenees.

"Did you leave something at the cross, Daniel?" the Dutchman asks. The distant sound of the horses' hoofbeats drums up from below.

"Yes and no," Daniel responds. "Did you?"

"Not yet," Rob tells him. "First, I had to read my letter."

Only then does Daniel notice that Rob holds multiple pages of foolscap in his hands, lined, like the kind they'd used back in school. Each page is covered with careful blue-inked script, both sides, front and back.

"Looks like that might take a man awhile to get through."

The Dutchman smiles. "Not so long. I have read it many times." He gently folds the pages in his hands but doesn't put them away. "This is from my wife," he tells him. "She gave it to me before I left on the Camino but told me that I must not read it until I am here."

"At the Iron Cross?" Daniel asks.

"Yes," Rob says. "It was her wish that I read it in this special place. She would be happy to know I have done so." Rob gazes off into the distance as the horses disappear into a valley to the west.

"She must be after missing you," Daniel says, thinking of his own losses. Petra had not left him a letter. She had told him she wouldn't. Said she found the practice morbid. He had still searched for one, though, after she was gone, turning their home upside down in the process. If she did change her mind and write one, he never found it.

"She does miss me, and I am missing her, too. But this is the way it must be. Like the Dutch song, *Laat me*, do you know it?"

"Sorry, not familiar."

"A song of love and friendships that must be left behind," Rob says, closing his eyes as if to savour the music playing in his head. "The full title has a French word in it." He opens his eyes again, looks thoughtfully at Daniel. "You understand this word, *vivre?*"

"I do," Daniel says. "It means life, doesn't it?"

"It does. *Laat me, vivre.* Let me live. It is a sad song, but beautiful. Missing others is like this, don't you think, Daniel?"

Daniel nods but doesn't want to go where the Dutchman is leading. There is missing, and there is guilt, and when they are mixed together the beauty withers. Daniel's guilt weighs on him more heavily than the rock he'd brought from New Jersey.

"Sure, it won't be long now," he says, steering the conversation elsewhere. "Santiago is less than a hundred and fifty miles. You'll be seeing your wife by Sunday week."

The Dutchman sighs. "I will not, Daniel." The wind picks up, fluttering the pages he holds in his hand. "I will not be going home to the Netherlands."

"Why?" Daniel asks, thinking now there must have been more in the letter than Rob's letting on.

"Not for the same reasons you cannot go home," Rob says, even though Daniel cannot remember telling him about how his family was waiting for him on the farm.

"Ginny did not lie to you, Daniel. Not as you believe." The statement hangs between them, suspended in the air.

"I'm not following you," Daniel says, becoming wary.

Instead of answering, the Dutchman stands up, walks down the hillside to the Iron Cross. Daniel goes after him.

"I don't understand. What are you saying?"

When he catches up to Rob, he sees that he has rolled up the letter in his fist. He hikes up on the rocky ground of pilgrim intentions and places the scroll in between two larger stones at the foot of the cross, tucking it deeply in a crevice so that the mountain breezes won't have a chance to blow it away. Then he returns to stand beside Daniel.

"The ghost that follows you is real, Daniel. I have seen her."

Daniel takes a step back. "You're having me on, Rob," he says. How did Rob know about the woman? They'd discussed ghosts, but no specifics. Daniel doesn't even believe that what he's seen counts as a ghost. "Surely, you don't believe that," he finally says.

Rob takes his thumb and rubs the smooth metal of the heart on his lapel. "My wife gave me this because she wanted to protect me while I was on the Way," he tells Daniel. "But my real heart was no match for the Pyrenees." He turns to Daniel, puts a hand on his shoulder. "I never made it over the pass that first day."

"You're not after making sense, Rob." But the sense of what Rob is saying is starting to make Daniel's hands shake. He wants to reach out and grab the Dutchman in a bear hug again, feel the weight of his presence, the heat of his body, to confirm for himself.

Rob is running up the side of the stone monument again. Rocks left by the well-intended spill down the side and tumble past Daniel onto the grass. The Dutchman waves the letter from his wife from the top, even though Daniel never saw him retrieve it.

"Not all ghosts mean to harm you, Daniel," Rob shouts down from the tower of rocks. "But remember, they all carry messages." He disappears over the other side of the huge cairn, the sun lighting up his painter's cap from behind him like a halo.

When Daniel circles around the monument to find him, he is not there. Although, later he may admit to himself that he did not expect him to be. A small shiny piece of metal glints in the sun among the dusty stones. Daniel picks up the copper heart and holds it still in his open palm before fastening it to his own jacket. He stands for a moment, his head bowed. The horses' hooves beat the hard ground in the distance. He walks on.

✳

"What's the matter, Daniel?" His sister's concern is obvious even from the small screen of his phone. Her expression is pained. Her voice lowered. After giving out to him for not calling her in a week, she has finally calmed down enough to let him speak.

"I don't know," he tells her, sitting alone on a bench in the courtyard of the *albergue* in Portomarín. Everyone has gone inside to escape the evening's chill. White flagstones glow coldly in the dark.

"You don't seem yourself," Angela says.

Daniel feels the copper heart weighing down the material on the front of his jacket. It probably belongs more on his sleeve when he talks to his sister. Still, he keeps the story of the Dutchman to himself. Angela would not believe him if he did tell her.

"Are you after going to Finisterre?" she asks him. "To spread Petra's ashes, like you said."

"To be honest, Angie. I don't know where I'm going." He looks up at the rectangle of dark sky above the courtyard.

The moon has come up. It is a waxing crescent floating as a thin bowl. His sister gives him a little more time to explain then switches gears when he doesn't.

"I was reading in the papers about that woman, the one gone missing on the Camino," she says.

"Aye," Daniel says. "It doesn't look like they'll be finding her either. It's a feckin' shame."

"Sure, you never know. Maybe she's gone to the beach with a Spanish fancy man."

"Ginny was after saying the same thing," he says, thinking again about how much the two would have liked one another under different circumstances.

"Well, that makes sense. She's from the coast as well. They appreciate a good beach out there, so."

"As well?"

"The missing woman. Said in the article she's from California, like your Ginny."

Daniel leans into the phone, filling up his sister's screen. "Where in California, Angela?"

"Sure, I don't know, one of those surfer suburbs, sounds like a fruit."

"Orange County?" Ginny's hometown.

"Aye, that's the one. What the hell's going on, Danny, are you …?"

"I gotta go, Angela." He switches off the Skype feed and leans over, hugging himself on the bench, trying to slow the gallop of his heart. The crescent moon reflects off the blank screen of his phone like the open jaws of a trap. He doesn't know how long he's been aware of the woman standing in the far corner of the courtyard, but he knows she has been biding her time there. He can sense her moving out of the shadows now, her boots dragging along the flagstones of the courtyard. He screws his eyes shut tight, bent over, as if willful blindness might force her to disappear. He can hear a toned vibration begin to creep up from her damaged voice box, like a shriek shot with a mouthful of novocaine. It takes a moment for him to realize what it is. Singing.

"*Laat me, vivre.*" Let me live.

He wills himself to open his eyes, raising his head. She is standing close enough for him to see the blood-tinged saliva bubble up between the tragedy of her lips. Her tongue flicks in and out, almost half of it missing. *She must have bitten it off recently*, he thinks. The jagged meat of the stump still has a tooth embedded in it.

When she reaches out to him, her sleeves in tatters, he can see the criss-cross of weeping welts that slash through both forearms, defence wounds. One has sliced the blue treble clef of her delicately noted tattoo clear in half. The skin from it flaps over and hangs there, as though a musician has hastily turned the page.

"Let me live," she croons with her mutilated tongue. When she takes a step toward him, the front of her red Columbia sweater begins to undulate and ripple with something that slithers underneath.

He stumbles back to the entrance of the *albergue*, tripping over the cement doorstep. The phone slips from his hand and strikes the flagstones below, the screen cracking. When he picks up the phone, the moon reflects in pieces in the broken glass. Stumbling through the door to the warmth and strength of numbers, he tries to hold on to his sanity as well as his dinner.

He needs to find Ginny. He needs to find her now.

CHAPTER 14
San Paio (8 miles)

DANIEL WALKS ALONG THE forest path holding the collar of his jacket closed against the fierce wind. The imprint of the copper heart on his lapel presses through the thinness of his gloves. He wears a rough wool cap pulled down hard over his ears. He bought it in Portomarín when the weather began to turn. It is November now, after all. Or at least he thinks it is. Time, as he has observed before, can be tricky on the Way — particularly in this last part, where the wind can blow a man right off his course. The force of it bites into the land, rips what's left of the leaves from the trees. It shrieks between the gap of his backpack and jacket, chilling the little beads of sweat that run down his spine. Even with the protection of the forest on the path this morning, he can still feel the madness of that wind tormenting the edge of the eucalyptus, a breed of tree not native to Spain but nonetheless here, an interloper, much like himself. He'd like to tell Ginny about the origins of eucalyptus, but he still hasn't found her.

Beatrice stays with him, of course. The missing woman is always nearby. Today she tries to hide behind the twisted eucalyptus trees, but Daniel can still hear her sighs impossibly over the wind, as if she is getting bored with following him. He doesn't know when he became fully convinced it was her. Sometime after she reached out to him in the courtyard but before he saw her picture on the poster, a pixelated photocopy from before, smiling for the camera when she still had all her teeth. She pursues him all the more closely as he approaches Santiago, every day a little more brazen in her ways. She always makes certain that she is near enough for him to see the latest arrangement of her face. The one intact cloudy eye a little more sunken in than the day before. The skin flapping in the wind as it pulls ever farther away from the bone structure of her jaw. He tries not to let the sight of her get to him although the stench is hard to take, a cross between open sewage and an apple left in a bag too long. Today when he glances over his shoulder, she gives him a wry smile full of maggots, then lies down dramatically on the forest floor and lets the elements take her, becoming one with the black rotting leaves. Such a performer, she is. He watches as the sweet smell of decay sucks her under the ground like a filthy kiss.

Head down, he pushes his way through the wind. It is only eight miles, a day's journey, to the cathedral he has crossed an entire country to reach. But that no longer matters. He needs to find Ginny before Beatrice does. He knows she must be close now or the dead woman wouldn't plague him so. It is the thought of protecting Ginny, rather than the nearness of Santiago, that gives him the strength to resist sinking into the forest floor himself, to keep on walking even though he knows Beatrice is still there. The way he kept going to the hospital every day for Petra as death hung in the doorway but wouldn't quite come inside, the pain and the drugs so thick she didn't even know him half the time. Her drape of semi-consciousness was a blessing he hid behind like a traitor in those final days.

His boot treads are getting slick with the wet black eucalyptus leaves that carpet the path. They cling to the space between the heel and sole, interfering with his stride. He sits down on a large rock and begins to pry off the viscous clumps with a stick. They fall to the ground beside him in raw chunks. When he finishes, he scans the path and catches sight of Beatrice, about fifty feet away, slowly tracing his steps in her mud-caked Merrell hiking boots. Gore from her head wound has coagulated on the strands of her long brown hair, coating it into a nest of grey speckled ropes. The wind whips them around her head, obscuring her face. She looks like one of the Furies. Another blessing. For a moment, the two freeze and regard one another, like the worthy adversaries they have become. A truce called under the canopy of wind-swept trees. But then, the stiff arms slowly reach out in accusation, straining the sleeves of the red Columbia sweater, and Daniel can see the colourful beaded bracelet with the silver shells gleaming brightly on one blackened wrist, the twin for the one on Ginny's own. He bolts from the rock and gets back on the trail.

He has to find Ginny soon. He can't wait and look for her tonight when he reaches Santiago.

Santiago, he knows in his heart, will be too late.

✳

The eucalyptus forest gives way to industrial fields surrounding the airport, but Daniel never sees any planes in the air, just a high fence with barbed wire, grown over with exhaust-choked ferns. He walks for an hour alongside the empty *autopista*, never seeing a car, only a dead rabbit with its head caved in tossed carelessly toward the median. *Roadkill*, Daniel thinks. *We have that back home as well.* The thought makes him inappropriately nostalgic although he's not sure for which home.

He has rarely seen wildlife on the Camino — only the occasional small lizard skittering along a rock wall, but nothing

warm-blooded, like the rabbit. Of course, there are the domes-
ticated animals, placid farm livestock, or mangy dogs snarling
along property lines both chained and unchained. Even now,
a sleek dark cat crosses in front of him to stand in an icy pool
on the road. Daniel stops to watch it lap up the brains from
the dead rabbit's skull as if from a cup. Repulsion is just a
hair's breadth away from fascination, he realizes. Maybe that's
why his sister likes those forensic shows so much.

Thankfully, the rabbit is the only dead thing he's seen
since the forest. The approaching industry seems to have
caused Beatrice to fade, making her transparent, and then
finally, gone. Daniel begins to relax as he makes his way into
the outskirts of the village of San Paio. It feels good to be
free of her, even for a little while, alone with his footsteps
and the morning. Even the sun starts to shine, further light-
ening his mood.

That's probably why he got lost. He should have known
from past experience that you need to remain vigilant in the
built-up areas. The telltale bright yellow arrows that point the
direction to Santiago are often missing or vandalized in the
towns. At times, they are even replaced by counterfeit arrows
leading to local proprietors greedy for the lucrative trade of
foreigners in search of spiritual journeys, as well as coffee and
trinkets. Not so in this village, where all the merchants seem
closed for business, the deserted streets leading him only into
a state of limbo. There is no one to ask for directions, even
with his limited Spanish. The one sign of life so far has been
an unmarked delivery van that raced toward him when he first
entered the village on a narrow cobblestone street. He'd had
to flatten himself in a doorway to keep from being run over.
Daniel holds the useless guidebook open in gloved hands and
tries to find his way back to where he knew where he was going.

Beatrice returns to make the occasional appearance, still
keeping her distance. He can see her right now through
a window, sitting on the couch next to a young woman

watching TV. Before that she was lying on a bench, down a laneway, covered in newspapers like a vagrant. Another time she perched high up a church belfry in a stork's nest, the yolk of an egg dripping down her chin along with the remnants of a partially developed bird embryo. Beatrice is like a page in a pop-up book, animating Daniel's confusion, always just far enough removed to be avoidable but close enough to be a surprise, as though she is not sure of where she is going either.

Finally, Daniel rounds a bend that opens onto a good-sized plaza, the village centre. At the far end, past a disabled fountain, he sees a sign turned the right way around in a café window. *Abierto.* He strides across the square toward it, clutching his guidebook in one hand as he tries the door with the other. It opens.

"*No funciona! No funciona!*" The man at the bar is adamant as he shouts at him. The heat of the room is stifling after spending so many hours in the frigid outdoors. Daniel removes his wool cap and gloves before he responds.

"I know the coffee machine is broken, for feck's sake. I don't want a coffee." He lapses into English as a way of frustrated rhetorical commentary. He can see the coffee machine in pieces behind the bar, the nozzle for the steamed milk corroded with something burnt and bubbly. He is unilingual, not stupid.

"*No funciona!*" the bartender repeats, as if shouting loudly enough will make Daniel go away. It doesn't, but it could. The man is rotund in that threatening way, where the excess weight just means more power. Daniel wouldn't want to be on the receiving end of it.

He pushes the guidebook forward on the bar, open at the map page.

"*Dónde está el Camino?*" he asks. Where is the Camino?

"*En todas partes,*" the man replies, pushing the book back. Daniel's blank expression forces him to translate. "Everywhere," he says, spreading his beefy arms out for illustration. He turns and begrudgingly removes a bottle of lemonade from a dark fridge and hands it across the bar. It is warm to the touch. The electricity must be "*no funciona*" as well.

"Have you seen a woman with a ponytail come by here?" Daniel takes the chance that the man's English is better than he lets on. "She has a backpack the same as mine." He turns and shows the man his turquoise pack, the one that embarrassed him so much when he first started out that has now become a part of him.

"No." The man's answer is emphatic. Daniel is not sure whether he hasn't seen her or just doesn't understand what Daniel is saying. Either way he's out of luck.

"*Gracias,*" Daniel says, giving up. He retrieves the book and the lemonade and goes to sit at a round wooden table by the door.

The barman chases after him. "*Cerrado!*" he bellows. Closed. The Spanish are serious about their siesta. But surely it's too early for that.

Daniel looks down at his watch and finds it gone from his wrist. He must have left it at the last *albergue*. He'd departed rather abruptly when he found Beatrice waiting for him in the men's toilet floating above the stall.

The bartender ushers him roughly out the screen door and into the plaza as if he's stolen something. He'd be more embarrassed if there had been anyone around to see. The plaza is as empty and abandoned as it was earlier. Only a few painted cast-iron patio tables leftover from the summer dot the square. He sits down on the numbing metal of a chair and opens the lemonade with his Swiss Army knife. The wind stings his bare hands like a spray of sharp needles. He should put his gloves back on.

That's when he sees her, sitting at the edge of the plaza at a similar table. Too far away for Daniel to see her properly without squinting. Beatrice's face seems to swim and writhe in the distance, her hair pulled back in an unbalanced pony-tail. *I suppose it got in her eyes,* he thinks. She turns and looks away, dismissing him.

"Damn it!" He slams the bottle down on the table. "Damn it to hell!" He is tired of this. He is so fucking tired of this. The sour lemonade presses back up into his mouth like bile. Beatrice, unimpressed with his outburst, continues to look away.

"Why are you doing this to me?" he shouts across the plaza, made brave by the distance and his anger. His voice echoes through the empty square, bouncing off the stone walls of the vacant village. The guidebook lies open on the table as he grips the edges of its pages, white-knuckled and furious.

That's when things change, the way they sometimes do. Time and space can play games when you have been walking for days, alone in the screaming wind. Beatrice likes games. Because while she is still there at the table at the edge of the plaza, with sudden clarity Daniel knows she also stands behind him, peeking over his shoulder at the guidebook, her face bent down beside his own. The foul stink coming from her mouth is unmistakable, warm and gaseous as she brushes her lips against his hair. He refuses to turn around and look. Instead, his hands grip the pages of the guidebook as he stares straight ahead, unable to take his eyes off the apparition at the edge of the plaza, willing it to only be in one place, and not in this impossible duality both ahead and behind him.

The maggots start to drop on the page from over his shoulder, one by one, writhing on the paper streets and pathways of his map, like pale blind pilgrims who have lost their way.

The woman on the other side of the square gets up and starts running toward him, her ponytail bouncing behind her, along with the turquoise backpack just like his own. Ginny calls out his name as she runs. It fills the plaza like a scream.

CHAPTER 15
Lavacolla (6 miles)

"GODDAMN IT!" Ginny winces as Daniel passes the cold metal sewing needle through the bottom of her foot.

"You'll be wanting to stay still for this," Daniel says, pulling the piece of black thread through one of her blisters. He hopes it will help it to drain although he is concerned it may be too late for that. A dark red line is starting to move up her leg from the ankle. Blood poisoning. "You should be seeing a doctor, Ginny."

Ginny takes a deep breath in as he ties the thread in a tight knot. "Are you kidding me? We're only six miles from Santiago. We'll be there by this afternoon. I'll go to the clinic when we get there."

Daniel wasn't sure how far away they were at this point. He's lost his guidebook, having dropped it back in the plaza in San Paio. Though he supposes with Beatrice's maggots on it, he really didn't want it anymore. They've been walking through open parkland since finding their way out of the town and back onto the Camino, the trail now well-marked with the faithful yellow arrows. Their progress has been steady. Which is good, since he has seen storm clouds gathering in the hills off in the distance.

They'd had a light rain earlier even though the sun still shone.

"A smile and a tear," he had remarked to Ginny at the time. That's what his mother always called it when the weather contradicted itself in this way.

"A smile and a tear," Ginny had repeated though she never took her gaze off the road ahead.

He was surprised when she made the rare request for a rest stop. When she had taken off her boots and socks he had seen why. Two blisters, one on each foot, sat bloated between her toes like pus-filled bubbles of misery. They'd hiked down a grassy knoll at the side of the trail toward the sound of water and found a small stream beside a chapel ruin to rest and tend to them. Large white rocks dot the surface and make for shallow rapids. The sound of the water rushing over them is soothing, even in their predicament. It would be a good place to rest if not for the huge black crows that stand on the rounded rocks like sentinels. Daniel doesn't know what unsettles him most with the birds: when they stand there silently and stare at them, or when they pierce the quiet with a random squawk.

He cups his hand around a pocket lighter so he can sterilize the needle in the flame before tending to her other foot, but the wind keeps blowing it out. He finally gives up, rinsing the needle in the icy stream and then plunging it into the second blister. Ginny gasps and closes her eyes, the hot puss mixed with blood runs down her instep like sweet relief.

"There now, Ginny, you're doing just grand." Daniel can feel heat radiating from her foot and into his hands. He pulls the second piece of thread through and ties it, trying hard not to add to the hurt. "Looks like you've been at this before," he says, seeing the remnants of an earlier attempt, the dirty black thread embedded between her toes where the skin has closed over it. He digs through the Band-Aids and Aspirin in his first-aid kit and pulls out a pair of twee-zers, but she protests.

"Forget it," she says. "I can't take anymore."

"Ah, Ginny, we can't be leaving it like that."

"What are you worried about? That it'll work its way through my bloodstream and kill me, like they used to tell us splinters would as kids?"

"I'm more worried about the infection getting worse than it is now," Daniel tells her although he can't help pic-turing the threads travelling through her body as they speak, like nasty black pinworms aimed at her heart. He reluctantly puts the tweezers away in his kit.

She takes off the pink baseball hat to fix her ponytail. When she pulls the elastic out, a fair bit of hair comes away with it in a dry fuzzy ball. She throws it to one side and it blows away like a tumbleweed. A lot of women have this problem on the Camino. The stress on the body of miles of walking extracts this toll from them.

"It's like I have that disease where you start to lose all your hair," she says. "Like that British model. What's her name. Gail Borden."

"Gail Porter," Daniel says. She's actually Scottish. They projected nude photos of her on the House of Parliament. You don't forget a woman like that easily.

"Okay, whatever," Ginny says, preparing to stand.

"Gail Borden invented condensed milk," he says, offer-ing his hand to steady her.

"You really can't control yourself, can you?"

He doesn't suppose he can. Daniel helps her over to the stream where she thrusts both feet into the biting cold water, and the shock of it makes her gasp again. The crows squawk angrily at them but stay on the dry domes of the rocks.

"Do you know her, Ginny?"

"No," she says quietly. They each know who they're talking about. By now, they've both seen the posters with

Beatrice's picture and know the missing woman is the one that follows them.

"She's from Orange County, like you are," Daniel says. Ginny stiffens beside him. The blood from her feet flows in little rivulets down the stream.

"Do you have any idea of the population of Orange County, Daniel?" she says. "I live four hundred miles north of there now. I haven't been back in sixteen years. Not since ..."

She can't finish, but Daniel knows since when. Since she ran away from home and the dangling hair dryer, her sister calmly talking on the phone as Ginny cowered in a frigid tub.

"So, you don't know her," he says, more gently.

"No, I don't know her."

"And your friend, the one who died of the overdose? What harm, but you were thinking it was her at first. If they look similar, maybe they're related." He's grasping at all the straws now.

"No."

"Maybe she ..."

"No, Daniel." She is shutting the conversation down, as she has since they reunited in San Paio. She doesn't like to talk about Beatrice.

"We could contact the police, I suppose," he says, wondering why he hasn't thought of this before.

"And tell them what, exactly? That we've found the missing woman and she's gone all *Santa Compaña*, stalking us on the Camino for our souls? That would go over well."

"We could leave," he says. After all, they are not without options. He has a cellphone. Even with a busted-up screen it still works. They are not in the wilderness. He could ring for a taxi to pick them up and take them to the airport. Although, he realizes, reception has been spotty for a long time now. He can't even remember the last time he talked to his sister.

"I'm not leaving," Ginny says emphatically. "We're almost at the cathedral." She pulls her feet out of the water, flexes her toes once or twice to bring the feeling back into them. "Besides, I've tried," she adds like an afterthought.

"You've tried?"

"A few times. Each time, I just end up back where I started when I wake up the next day."

"What are you saying, Ginny? We can't leave?"

"We just have to make it to Santiago," she says, taking his hand. She may be running a fever from the infection, but her fingers are cold as ice through her gloves. "Once we get there, we'll be free of her," she says.

"How do you know that, Ginny?"

"Yes, how do you know that?"

Both Ginny and Daniel wince at the sound of the booming voice. The Englishman stands at the top of the knoll surveying them before he marches down the hillside and drops his huge backpack on the grass. He pulls out a cigarette from behind his ear and lights up on the first try despite the wind. The birds flap their polished ebony wings anxiously.

"Seems to me," Mark says as he exhales his smoke aggressively into the air, "that you'll never be losing that bitch."

"What are you after?" Daniel says as he stands up, trying not to betray how much Mark has startled him. *At least he's not Beatrice*, he thinks. They haven't seen her since the plaza. Maybe she's downstream somewhere, bathing her own wounds.

"I'm not after anything more than you, mate. Just a place to rest." He sits down on the ground, stretches out his legs, and leans back on his hands. "In fact, this is where the pilgrims used to rest and purify themselves, right here at Lavacolla," he says, removing his hat and placing it on the grass.

"Purify?" Ginny asks.

"That's right, love. Purify."

He moves a little closer to where she sits on the grass. Daniel steps in protectively to block his way. The Englishman continues with his impromptu lecture regardless.

"The medieval pilgrims would stop here to wash themselves before entering the sacred city of Santiago, probably stank to high heaven, fucking peasants." He spits onto the ground, as if the stinking peasants are still there. "That's where the name Lavacolla comes from," he says, "the Spanish word for 'wash.' I thought that's what you were doing here. Didn't you read the guidebook?"

"We lost it," Daniel says evenly, standing his ground.

Ginny looks down at her wet feet still hovering over the stream, and Daniel hands her a micro-towel to dry them off. He has no intention of sharing a rest spot with Mark. At least not for long. Catching his drift, Ginny reaches for her damp socks and pulls them on, not even taking the time to search for a fresh pair. As if sensing their discomfort, Mark gets up and goes to stand downstream, seemingly content to contemplate the smooth rocks and the birds for a moment before he speaks again.

"There are worse things, you know, than that woman," he finally says.

"Like yourself?" Daniel says.

This earns a chuckle from the Englishman. Ginny starts to lace up her hiking boots.

"Worse than that," Mark says as he unzips his fly. "But you'll find that out soon enough."

Daniel cannot believe the crass dirtbag is going to relieve himself right here in front of them. What a lout. Then he sees a long tentative talon creep out through the man's pant zipper, a forked tongue between pointed teeth follows it, flicking, as if tasting the air. The nightmare artwork of the museum in Astorga is coming to life right in front of them. The black crows begin to squawk in earnest.

"I tried to purify myself here," Mark tells them. "After the accident." He ignores the abomination between his legs as he steps into the water. Rapids rush over the top of his walking shoes, soaking them.

The birds take flight but don't go far. They wait in nearby trees to see what will happen next. Both Daniel and Ginny wait as well, paralyzed by the sight.

"It *was* an accident, you know," he says angrily, turning around in the stream to address them, the icy water splashing up onto the bank. "Though she had it coming, that girl. I was just being friendly. I warned her." The Englishman has started to sink into the water as if his long body is on an elevator, or disappearing into quicksand. They watch as the water turns dark red and starts to bubble.

"But she wouldn't listen. She was a tease, just like you, and that other one." His eyes narrow in on Ginny.

She grabs for her backpack, fumbling with the straps as she pulls it on. Daniel reaches for his own pack and throws it over one shoulder. Still, he can't take his eyes off the big man, sinking into the stream bed, the demon's face now fully visible and leering at the front of his hiking pants.

"How she whined and complained. 'No, please stop.'" He says the words with a mocking falsetto voice. "She kept it up even after I put her in the backyard! No matter how deep I buried her, I could still hear her bitching and pleading. Pissing and moaning every night, she did, until I had to dig her up and cut her into pieces for the bin man!" Mark is nothing but a head now above the stream, his eyes madly twitching. Spit flies from his mouth.

Daniel moves forward to help Ginny, but a crow swoops down in front of her and she loses her footing on the soft earth at the water's edge. Her right boot smashes squarely into one of the round smooth rocks.

Only it is not a rock anymore. None of them are. They are all heads like the Englishman, screaming in the boiling current of blood. Daniel pulls Ginny from the ground where she stumbled and drags her up the hillside. The head Ginny has kicked with her boot bellows after them, "You fucking bastards! Haven't I suffered enough?!"

A crack of thunder sounds from far away, and all the crows come down from the trees, chattering and calling to one another. They dive and swoop around the bodiless heads, snapping and pecking without mercy. As Daniel takes a last look around he can see one working an eye out of the Englishman's face, flying away with it like a prize.

Daniel and Ginny run down the road toward Santiago, Ginny trying not to trip on her boot laces. She hadn't had time to lace them all the way. One pant leg is wet from her fall at the water's edge and terror flows in tears down her face. Daniel holds her up so she won't fall, and the two hobble together toward the dark clouds forming on the horizon. The heads continue to shout abuse after them, Mark still snarling about the relentless voice of the woman he murdered. The sun moves as if to protect itself behind the approaching clouds.

Maybe the Englishman is right, Daniel thinks. *Perhaps there are worse things than Beatrice.*

※

Daniel had been warned about the last part of the Camino, of course. That it would be disheartening with its commercialism. He and Ginny slog up the steep paved path approaching the western side of *Monte del Gozo* in the driving rain, careful not to slip on the wet cement as they tiptoe around the garbage left by day pilgrims. Some like to walk just the last few miles into Santiago to show their piousness or solidarity or just for something to do on a Sunday afternoon. Day pilgrims' backs are conspicuously without packs, their hands full of souvenirs bought at the dozens of shops and stalls that line the pathway during the season. None venture out in this weather. The ancient walls of the approaching city are covered in loud graffiti; the gutters stink of garbage. Someone has spray-painted "Abandin all hope, ye who enter here" on the entranceway of the under-pass they move through. *Funny*, Daniel thinks, *how a person could know Dante but not know how to spell "abandon."*

The stalls are empty now and the stores closed, shut-tered firmly against the two lone pilgrims in the driving rain. This is owing to both the time of year as well as the time of day. It is afternoon siesta, or at least Daniel thinks it is — he still can't find his watch. It always seems to be siesta lately.

Fat beaded drops slide down their raincoats. Despite their treated nylon protection, much of their clothing has soaked up the rain and hangs heavy on their bodies, drag-ging them down. November is usually a dry month, but sometimes it rains. With the wind, it doesn't come down, but on an angle, finding its way into every crevice of their clothing and equipment. The temperature has dropped to a point where Daniel knows at any moment rain could turn to snow.

Their boots are supposed to be waterproof, but there is only so much any kind of material can take. *Only so much any of us can take*, Daniel thinks, chuckling, starting to find it all amusing. Like walking across Spain with a beautiful woman and monsters on his tail is some kind of a lark. Maybe he's getting delirious. Although, he worries more about Ginny for this. He'd felt her forehead earlier and her fever had risen. He listens as her socks squish as she walks, making a sucking noise in her boot — no doubt feeding fresh blisters. His own boots are making the same noise. He has blisters of his own to worry about now.

"Why did you come?" Ginny asks through the rain on her lips. Of course, she has asked him this before.

"Sure, you know why I came," he says, pulling his jacket sleeves down over his hands. Too late, unfortunately. His wool gloves are already saturated.

"To spread Petra's ashes?"

"Aye."

"Seems to me you could have done that anywhere."

He thinks about that for a while before responding. "I reckon I needed something to prepare me for it. Something hard and rough to burn the grief out of me first." The hardship of the Camino was a punishment, he realizes, to clear himself of his guilt as well as his sorrow.

"Has it worked?" Ginny asks him.

"I don't know," he says honestly. "I suppose I thought that the Camino, a pilgrimage, would be more than this."

"More than what?"

"More than just a long walk."

"I guess that's where the spiritual part comes in."

Daniel nods. But the truth is despite all the awe-inspiring cathedrals and enshrined chapels he's entered on this trip, he hasn't managed to pray once. Even in the face of what follows them.

"And what about yourself?" he asks. "Is this what you imagined? What you were after coming for?" He shoves his frigid hands in his pockets and glances over at her. She's shivering and visibly limping now.

"It's different for me," she says, wiping the wet snot from her nose with the sleeve of her jacket. "I have to be here."

"Why?"

"For you, Daniel," she says, looking across at him, but not stopping. There are raindrops caught in her eyelashes.

They keep on walking through the chilling rain without saying anything more.

✳

As they come around a sharp bend in road, they see a man standing behind a fruit stand. A crooked roof of old shingles and plywood keeps the weather off him and his wares.

"*Peregrina*, why no you smile?" he calls out to Ginny. The man's eyes crinkle up in good humour.

Daniel thinks he must be daft to wonder why a frozen wet pilgrim wouldn't be smiling.

"*Quieres una naranja?*" he asks, holding out an orange, so bright and luscious in the bitter grey rain.

"Oh, yes, please," Ginny says, forgetting her Spanish. "*Cuánto?*" How much? She goes for her wallet.

"*Donativo*," the man says, pointing at the coffee can with the slit cut in the lid for donations. He is another penitent, a former pilgrim providing charity and assistance. Like the hippy back on the Roman road. Although, Daniel doesn't see any Hendrick's behind his cart.

Ginny slips a euro into the coffee can and takes an orange. She removes her gloves, but her fingers are so numb she can't peel it. The man reaches out and takes the orange from her. Using a sharp silver knife, he deftly cuts away the rind before handing it back.

"*Gracias,*" Ginny says gratefully.

Daniel waits patiently, but he knows they can't stay under the shelter of the little fruit stand for long. Ginny's infection is getting worse. He has seen her stagger once or twice and even slur her words. It is also getting later, the window for arriving in Santiago before nightfall is getting shorter and shorter. He'd force her to take a taxi at this point if he could. But she is adamant that she wants to finish the pilgrimage to the Holy City her own way. He couldn't call a cab if he wanted to now anyway. His phone hasn't had even one bar of reception since they started climbing the mountain.

He is getting ready to suggest that they move on when he notices the fruit man has taken his knife out again. His eyes crinkle up, even as he puts the blade into his mouth and splits his face up the middle with it. It gets stuck on the cartilage of his nose for a moment and then races straight up to his heavily lined forehead where the skin peels off neatly on either side. He pulls the top of his skull off like a lid and a black crow flaps out and flies off into the dusky sky.

"Ta-da," says Beatrice from beside him, with a magician's flourish of her hand. When she takes a deep bow, one of her ears falls off onto the wet pavement.

A deafening flash of light on thunder strikes above them, and the birds start to shriek. Daniel hears the crack of the heavy branch too late. It collides with the back of his head and knocks him down flat on the asphalt. Before he loses consciousness, he looks over to see the fruit man's skull with the perfectly peeled skin lying open on each side.

Just like the orange, he thinks, before the rain and Beatrice's torn ear lying beside him fade to the deep black of a crow.

CHAPTER 16
Monte del Gozo (2 miles)

WHEN DANIEL COMES TO, the storm is raging in a night-time sky. A huge branch the size of a tree lies across the trail in front of him, naked and slick, blocking the path up the mountain. Luckily, he'd only been hit by one of its smaller offshoots. The painful lump at the back of his head sprouts throbbing tentacles that reach down into his neck. Lying on the ground with his cheek wet and raw in a filthy puddle, he wills himself to get up. The most he can manage is to lift his head a few inches off the ground to take a glimpse around. Water gushes through the gutters on either side of the path. Beatrice is gone, as is the fruit vendor. After a minute, he is able to force himself into a seated position. That's when he realizes Ginny is gone, too.

Shaking, he stands then climbs over the huge branch. He starts making his way up the greasy incline, slipping and falling, his head still woozy from the blow, his feet burning from blisters that are probably infected now. He is part robot, part beast, mounting *Monte del Gozo* in the dark. The frightful image of Ginny alone and hurt somewhere grates like brittle glass in his fractured mind. He must get to her. He may have not been able to save Petra, but maybe he can save her.

Beatrice is not far behind, gliding, not walking, up the mountain. The toes of her hiking boots hover above the path. She is gaining on him, her hair plastered down with the rain. Forest-green ooze runs freely from the crater in her skull where her abductors bashed it in with a shovel when they were done with her — the same shovel that dug her grave in one of the farmers' fields that border the Camino. Daniel doesn't know how he knows this, but he does. Perhaps she whispered it to him as he lay prone on the ground. The thought of what else she might have done to him while he lay unconscious makes his insides wither.

He hikes down a gully to get past another tree that has fallen. This one is too big to climb over. Not in this storm. Not in his state. He slides in the wet muck, catching his ankle forcefully between two rocks, unable to remove it. The pain bursts, sharp and immediate. Yanking on the leg of his hiking pants, he pulls madly to free himself, but his boot won't come free. He drops his backpack and pulls harder. He's desperate now, crying out as the thunder claps over-head. He can't hear the birds anymore over the rain. He can't hear anything but the roar in this head — until a faint melody reaches him, drifting up the hill. Beatrice has started to sing again. Her song shapes and shifts and finally coils around Daniel's ear like a serpent, calling to him with sickly sweet seduction, daring him to turn around. To walk not toward Santiago, but back to her, where she will envelop him in her stiff decomposing arms, smothering him deep within the folds of the red Columbia sweater.

"Daniel ..." The voice is small and weak, but oh so familiar. He feels the gentleness of a light hand placed on his back. The rain starts to let up. Then a warmth pours over him as she wraps her arms around him from behind. The waves of her unfettered hair flow down over his shoulder and onto his chest, covering the metal heart the Dutchman gave him. The familiar sound of her speech is like a salve that heals every part of him. Even Beatrice's song disappears into the ether, like storm clouds that have come and passed.

"Petra." He weeps openly now, pulls her hand to his face, fully fleshed and healthy. He kisses each finger, one at a time. He doesn't need to turn around to know it's her. A man knows his mate. "I thought I'd lost you."

"Shh," she coos. "It'll be okay, Daniel."

He takes both her hands in his, pulls her more tightly around him. He can feel the swell of her breasts pressing into his back. But her chest is still, just like the last time he saw her.

"Where have you been, my love?" he asks.

"Not far," she says.

He lowers his chin to his chest, closes his eyes against the tears. "Oh, dear God, Petra, I'm so sorry."

She pulls him toward her and cradles his head in her lap like a child. "No, Daniel, I'm sorry. For asking you to help me. It was too much." It had been too much. It had almost broken him.

"I was weak though, Petra," he protests. "I was after letting you suffer for so long." He lifts his head, turns around to bring his fingers up to her face, her beautiful, intact, untouched-by-disease face. "And then ..." He can't finish, thinking about that day, the feel of the crisp, white pillowcase on his hands as he pushed down over her mouth and nose, crushing the weak spasm of breath left in her.

"You only did what I asked you, Daniel."

It is true — she had asked, begged him even. And part of him had hated her for it, that final request. But not as much as he hated himself. It wasn't what he did that he can't accept. It is why he did it. Doing the right thing for the wrong reasons. It can plague a man worse than the evilest deed. But it is time to tell the whole truth, no more dealing in halves.

"It was you I was supposed to be doing it for, Petra. I loved you so much. Love you so much," he corrects himself.

"But in the end, at the end ..." He stops, pulls her to him, buries himself in her neck. She smells like the freshly laundered dress he buried her in.

"At the end, you wanted me gone."

He lets out a deep moan she absorbs with her body. She has voiced what he cannot. He had done it not for her. But for himself. His own selfish weak-man self. The endless trips to the hospital. The bedside vigils next to the skeleton that was no longer his wife. The tubes and the needles and the swish of the nurses in and out with looks of efficient pity. The eternity of waiting and watching as her life drained out, so painfully, so slowly. The strength he'd needed to do what she'd asked came not out of his love for her, but because he just couldn't stand it any longer. He had acted not to lessen her suffering, but in a desperate bid to end his own. Letting her die thanking him for a kindness he never proffered.

His arms pull tight around her like the drowning man he has become since she left him. She takes in his sorrow, allows it to run its course. *It's not enough*, he thinks. He is cursed. He can never be released from his own culpability. It imprisons him, locks him in limbo, as surely as doomed sailors on a ghost ship.

"I should have been a better man. A stronger man," he says, loosening his grip on her. He puts his wet forehead on hers. "I could be that man to you now, Petra, I could." And at that moment he believes he can. He will follow her wherever she's gone, and he will be the man he should have been, the man she deserved all along.

"You have to let me go, Daniel," she tells him, tracing a tear on his cheek. "I'm not meant to be here." She kisses him softly. Her lips are as icy as the rain. "You are the only one keeping me here now."

"It's been you?" he asks, looking up, unbelieving. "You, Petra, following us all along?"

"No, Daniel, that is another." She pushes back his curly wet locks where they've fallen into his eyes, just as she had done when she was alive. "And it's Ginny keeping her here, not you."

"Why?" he stammers. "How?"

"I'll tell you." Her long pale arms reach down and move the rock that had trapped him as if it weighs nothing. "But then, Daniel, you have to promise."

"Promise what?"

"To let me go."

✳

When Daniel reaches the road at the summit, the storm has peaked again. Thunder and lightning overflow the night sky. Through the rain, he can see the haze of city lights shining far below. Stinging cold water runs down his cheeks as he pictures the people inside their lit houses, watching TV, making love, talking with their families over a meal.

"You know what they say about the Camino, don't you, mate?" The Englishman stands on the sidewalk. He is a towering menace with a drenched black backpack.

The fruit vendor stands beside him, his scalp still hanging open like two glistening petals exposing his sleek, pulsing brain.

"It's everywhere," Mark tells him, as the barman who chased Daniel out of his little coffee shop in San Paio comes to stand beside the big man. Glinting in his hands is a round-point steel shovel. He lifts it high above his head. It is streaked with the rain and smears of Beatrice's brain matter.

She stands behind him, fingering the shell bracelet on her wrist, her one dead eye bright with anticipation. She and Ginny had bought the bracelets before they left for the Camino. Beatrice had them made specially to match. Friendship bracelets. Daniel knows this now because Petra has told him all about Beatrice, Sheena's twitchy little sister. Beatrice, Tris, Trish. The old friend Ginny had to leave behind.

"Go fuck yourself!" Daniel says as he rushes into the street.

The chapel is the right place to go. The only place to go. It stands on the north side of the empty roadway on the edge of the mountain, perched and private. The small wooden sign above the entrance reads *Capilla de San Marcos*. Daniel can just make it out by the pale red light that glows from inside. He makes a run for it despite his injured ankle. Blood from the gash the rock left behind fills his right boot, but at least the ankle isn't broken. A heavy iron ring hangs from the wide-planked front door like that from a bull's nose. His fingers almost freeze to the metal as he pulls on it. After a few desperate tries it opens. Stooping under the low doorway, he slams the door shut behind him, locking it with the metal cylinder of the deadbolt. A blast of thunder goes off outside like a gun salute.

Inside it is warm and dry, not like the other churches and chapels he has visited on the Camino that were chilled, drafty places. He sees Ginny sitting in a pew up front, shivering and rocking herself, the water dripping from her clothes and hair. When he confronts her, he can see she has left a puddle on the grey stone floor.

"You left her behind," he says, but not the way she told him. "The first time you walked the Camino." His own clothes drip onto the sanctuary floor as he stands to accuse her. A crucifix looms above them showcasing pierced bloody feet and hands. The eyes of the Saviour are white and veined, rolling up into his head. The crown of thorns drips blood as their clothes drip rain water. Ginny lets out a wail, the agony of Christ somehow mixing with her own.

"You don't understand," she says.

"You knew those men were after taking her, and still you left her behind."

"It wasn't like that."

"Your friend didn't overdose before the trip," Daniel says, his voice and breath measured. "She came with you." Petra had shown it all to him. All he had to do was close his eyes as she spoke, and it was as if he had been there.

He had watched as the tension between the two women blossomed from their first day in the Pyrenees and worsened from there. Beatrice was weak both physically and mentally, often fretful and complaining. Ginny had become resentful over time.

"You argued in Mazarife," he says. "You went on ahead. She followed, begging you to slow down."

"Stop it, stop it!"

He'd watched it all unfold. Ginny had reached the next crest of hill after the ravine with the dirt road running through it. She would have still been able to hear Beatrice below, where she struggled desperately to keep up. To hear her cry out with a voice that was different than the pleading that had come before. Not angry or plaintive, but clipped, like a bird fallen abruptly from the nest.

"Did you hear the van," Daniel asks, "before they took her away?"

"I looked down," Ginny whimpers, covers her face with her hands and starts rocking herself again. "And I thought I saw her." But really, he knew what she had seen. Two men speeding away in a beat-up Renault.

"You ran away. You were well able to run for help, but you didn't. You could have gone somewhere. Told someone."

But Ginny hadn't told. She'd just kept on running, convincing herself that Beatrice was okay. That she had just decided to go back to the *albergue* — her friend who had become like an albatross around her neck with her methadone and her moaning. She ran long and hard from the threat in the ravine, the way she had run from her sister and the deadly bathwater sixteen years before.

"I didn't know!" she cries into her hands.

"You did know!" He is being cruel, letting out all his fury on her. His anger at her deceit, certainly. But it is more than that. He wants to punish her, just as he sought to punish himself and, he realizes now, Petra as well. "Why did you run?" he demands. His rage echoes off the walls of the tiny chapel.

"Because," Beatrice says quietly from a pew at the back. "She didn't see me when she looked behind her."

Daniel turns to observe the dead woman. Knows what she says is true. Petra had shown him. He had seen what Ginny saw when she looked back into the ravine that day.

A strip of red fabric abandoned in the dirt, the collar torn roughly from the red Columbia sweater. Just like the scream from Beatrice's lips when they took her away.

✳

Beatrice swoops across the sanctuary like a bird of prey. Daniel is forced flat to the floor, where he knocks his wounded ankle hard against the base of the baptismal font. Pain explodes up his leg. Ginny screams and runs for the side door of the chapel behind the sacristy, Beatrice close in pursuit. When Daniel recovers from the shock of the pain, he limps behind the two of them, dragging a streak of his blood across the chapel floor.

"Ginny!" He calls out to her in the storm from the arch of the doorway.

The gutters are flooded, the water coursing down the steep roadway. Ginny runs into the street, slips, and falls in the water. Daniel takes off into the rain, dragging his leg behind him, even as he sees the headlights come speeding around the corner. Even as she struggles to her feet. He no longer seeks to punish her with his words. He knows about running — from life, from guilt, from the scene of a crime — about hiding from the truth. But the car gets to them first, sending Ginny sailing into the air. She hits the pavement with a sickening thud of bone and cartilage. Only clipped by the sleek chrome bumper, Daniel is knocked down at the curb, where he tries to crawl to her across the wet pavement, one leg bent the wrong way behind him.

"Ginny, I understand. I do."

She is too far away for him to touch, for her to hear. He uses what strength he has left to lift his head. The car is gone. A hit and run. He sees a man with a white collar run out from behind the chapel.

"Help her," Daniel pleads. "Please." His voice is a mangled croak. The cold rain runs down his face, mixes with hot tears. He can't lose her. He can't let another woman's death be on his hands.

The priest is beside him now, sounding far away as he speaks in a language Daniel doesn't understand. Lowering his cheek onto the muddy asphalt, Daniel can see Ginny's body lying prone a few yards away. He doesn't know what happened. He had been right behind her, reaching forward to push her out of the car's path, but something had held onto him, grabbed him by the collar of his jacket, and pulled him out of harm's way at the last second. He looks up, past the priest, expecting to see one dead woman, but instead finds another.

Beatrice brings one finger to her lips before she walks away to lie down beside Ginny, her arm protectively wrapping around her old friend. But not before she opens her palm to show him the copper heart that came off in her hand when she pulled him from in front of the deadly wheels of the speeding car.

He sees the hairy black roots of eucalyptus grow up through the roadway, snaking their oily branches around the two intertwined friends. The largest morphs into a purple-green arm with a colourful shell bracelet gleaming at the wrist. It forces its fist into the screaming mouth of one of the heads from the stream bed that have sprouted up like sickly spring buds on the other limbs. Daniel watches the face contort as it chokes on the bright round beads mixed with shells. Beasts like those he saw in the paintings at Astorga claw with yellow talons from below the ground, gnashing their sharpened teeth. He hears the priest beside him, talking on a cellphone in Spanish. His voice fades in and out with the roar of the rain. As Daniel loses consciousness, he watches the roots of the eucalyptus pull both women down below the street and the rain and the storm, to a place where artwork comes to life in a thousand nightmares.

✳

Daniel lies in the impersonal hospital bed not wanting to hear what the priest has to say. Outside his window, he can see the two towers of the cathedral that dominate the Santiago cityscape. The North Tower is intact, but the Tower of the Bells on the opposite side of the Baroque facade is imprisoned behind a cage of grisly metal scaffolding.

"I'm so sorry," Father Bruno tells him, sounding like a doctor who must deliver bad news. Daniel's had enough of doctor's messages. They tell him the same thing as the priest. He suffered a severe concussion. Needed stitches for his ankle and a cast for his leg. The car had fractured his left femur where it clipped him. No one else had been injured at the scene of the accident. No woman named Ginny found. Just him, alone on the side of the road where Father Bruno found him.

"I'm not crazy," Daniel tells the priest, whose English, like so many here in Santiago, is surprisingly good. He feels bad for being so rude to him after he was kind enough to visit. Daniel is told he should be able to go home tomorrow. *Home where?* he wonders. He still hasn't booked a flight.

"No, son, you are not crazy." Father Bruno plays nervously with his fedora, turning it round and round in his hands by the brim. Daniel can hear a hushed whisper behind the hospital curtains, a moan for more meds.

"You were there, *padre*," Daniel says. "You must have seen her."

The priest nods. He has straight dark hair growing at the sides of his head but not at the top, like Friar Tuck. Daniel can see why he wears the hat. "I was there," he says simply. "But I did not see her. Only you, in the road."

Daniel shuts down. Closes his eyes and lies back on the pillow. He is tired of hearing this version of events.

The priest waits patiently then leans in across the hospital bed. "But I have seen her," he says quietly. "Before."

Daniel opens his eyes, turns to the priest. "You mean you've seen Ginny?"

"In the pews," he tells him, looking around to see who might be listening. "Sometimes in the confessional just before vespers. I see her. The woman who was hit by the car."

"But they told me there was no one else, only myself brought in." Daniel tries to pull himself up from the bed, his head pounding with the concussion and confusion.

Father Bruno places a hand on his upper arm, guides him gently back onto the mattress. A nurse appears from around the curtain, but the priest dismisses him with a shake of the head.

"I brought her to the hospital that night," he says. "Like you." He puts his fedora down on the bedside table next to Daniel's uneaten supper. "But it was too late."

"What night?" Daniel rubs one of his aching temples. "I don't understand, Father."

"Poor soul, she had almost made it to the cathedral when it happened. I gave her the last rites although I do not know if she was a Catholic." He puts one hand on the side of Daniel's bed. "She was killed two months ago."

Two months ago.

"I am sorry, Daniel. May I call you, Daniel?"

This is wrong. It is all wrong. He sits up in the bed on his elbows, despite the pain that blurs his vision. He grabs the crisp bedsheets, one in each fist. "She was alive. I walked with her," he says. "I was after walking the whole damn Camino with her."

But even as he says it, he remembers the strange looks, the way others tended to ignore Ginny. Only the Englishman and the Dutchman seemed to interact with her. Maybe part of him had always known and Mark had been right: he had walked this road before. At the side of a woman straddling the divide between life and what comes after. A dead woman walking.

The priest glances at his hat, as if it holds the answer to Daniel's questions. "She had a burden that night, when I found her on the road. But I was not able to take it from her." He looks back at Daniel with true regret. "This thing she could not bring herself to speak of, even as she lay dying."

"She had a friend —" Daniel begins but can't go on. He lies back down in the bed and closes his eyes again. The idea of Ginny gone before he ever started the Camino, from that first day at *Alto del Perdón*. And then Beatrice. "I saw something else, Father," he admits, behind closed lids. "Sure, I thought it came from hell, but then ..." He hesitates, no longer sure what he saw anymore. His senses have done nothing but betray him this entire trip.

The priest accepts a pitcher of water from the nurse who has returned from behind the curtain. "Sometimes the devil is not as black as he is painted," he says, placing the pitcher on the swing-arm table next to Daniel's bed. The nurse beats a hasty retreat.

"You're after quoting Dante to me, Father?" Daniel says, turning to look at the priest. He remembers the quote from *The Divine Comedy*, a book he had to study as part of his one English credit requirement in engineering school.

"Dante was always a favourite of mine," Father Bruno says. He stands to pour a glass of water and offers it to Daniel. When Daniel refuses, he takes a sip himself then sets the glass and pitcher down again.

"Tell me, Daniel. Why did you come to *Santiago de Compostela?*" The priest uses the full name for the Camino's destination. Some say *Compostela* means *star*, a Latin translation paying homage to the celestial guidance of the pilgrimage that roughly follows the Milky Way.

"I came because my wife died," Daniel says, staring up at the tiled white ceiling. Though he knows it was for much more than that. "I fear I wasn't after being a good husband to her, Father." His voice cracks a little, a ripple of a deeper break.

The priest nods without judgment, sits back down in the visitor's chair. "Guilt is a hell we make for ourselves, my son. Chaining ourselves to the past, as if by staying there, we can change what has already come and gone." He takes another sip of water from the glass then continues. "Better to admit our transgressions as well as their finality, I think. Only then can we forgive ourselves, and the past can stay where it belongs." He runs one hand through what little hair he has. It stands up and then obediently falls down on one side. "What is it the Persian poet said? It is so haunting in English."

"'And the moving finger having writ, moves on.'" Daniel says automatically, quoting from the small gilded pocketbook his granny kept under her pillow. He'd found it there after her funeral, hidden from the rest of the family. She probably didn't think it was Catholic enough.

"Yes, Omar Khayyám," says the priest. "Another favourite." Father Bruno smiles.

Daniel notices he has one gold cap on an upper tooth. Clergy dental plans in Spain must be generous.

"I have been around life and death a great deal in my work," he says, returning to the earlier subject. "I have seen many things that cannot be explained. This woman comes to me because I was there when she passed over. If she comes to you also, I believe it must be for another reason."

You have to let me go, Daniel.

Daniel can hear Petra's voice, soothing and whole, as she held him in her arms during the storm on *Monte del Gozo*. He knows now the message Beatrice sought to give him. The one Ginny cannot hear as she holds her guilty secret in close, where forgiveness can't get in.

He sits up in the bed and leans heavily into the priest, his head down, eyes closed against the tears that force themselves out the corners. He makes the sign of the cross as they fall pure and honest onto the front of his hospital gown. He is ready to accept that what he did will never change, but he still can.

"Bless me, Father," he begins, "for I have sinned."

CHAPTER 17
Carn N'Athair

LOW-LYING GREY CLOUDS cling to the horizon as Daniel stands in the small clearing of a mountain forest he knows better than he knows himself. Hedges sew together the green squares of farmland below him, including the one in a lush forest glade that his family has cultivated for centuries. He holds a zip-lock bag in his hands.

He'd never gone to Finisterre after Santiago. Only left the hospital and returned to New Jersey, where he sold his half of the business to Gerald and the house to a nice young couple, before coming home to Carn N'Athair. He had thought of travelling to California to visit the grave and lay flowers. To see her full name, Virginia, inscribed beneath the name of her mother, who had died three years earlier. But he decided against it. He knew this was not where she rested anyway. Nor did she rest at all. Although, he wishes that someday she may.

His father was waiting for him in the doorway when he pulled up in a rental car.

"Sure, you've been a long time coming."

He'd never unpacked from the Camino. With the exception of the burlap bag, the turquoise backpack is mostly as it was when he collected it from the hospital staff in Santiago. He had intended to visit the cathedral after his discharge, despite the crutches, but didn't in the end. He was not prepared to wait in line with the other pilgrims to embrace the statue of Saint James. To fight the tourists as they held their cellphones in the air filming the swing of the ancient *Botafumeiro* spewing incense over the crowd. He believes he has had enough of cathedrals for a while. Though, he did go as far as the entranceway before he left Santiago, to place his hand on the pillar of the *Portico de la Gloria*. Centuries of pilgrims before him had worn a deep impression in the stone. The smooth indentation had felt cool and reassuring beneath his fingers.

At the airport, he had made an anonymous call to the local *guardia* telling them where they could find Beatrice's body, buried in a farmer's field just outside Mazarife. Later his sister will tell him she saw on the news that they'd made arrests. He hopes it brings the people who may have known and loved her some closure.

Standing on a peak high above his father's farm, his sister tries to wait patiently until he is ready. Her new girlfriend, Lisa, a pathologist, is down at the house getting the third degree from his well-meaning mother. Just as she grilled him about the sap on his boxer shorts so many years ago, after Petra and he had their tryst in the woods on the hill.

"Why did you choose this place, so?" Angela asks him, after he has let the ashes fall away into the wind. They move on a current of air and into a stand of Scotch pine where the sap always runs just a little too sticky.

"No reason," he says, smiling to himself. He puts the bag carefully into his zippered pocket, next to the copper heart he no longer needs to protect him. He'd found it on his backpack when he got home, attached to the outside flap.

A soft rain starts to fall even as the sun begins to rise over the other side of the hill.

"A smile and a tear," Angela says.

"Aye."

As they turn and walk back down to the farm, Daniel can feel the sun shine warm onto his back. It lifts the grey of the horizon from his shoulders, like so many burdens.

EPILOGUE
Villar de Mazarife to Infinity

THE MATTRESS IS SLIGHTLY uncomfortable but dry as Ginny starts to awaken. She feels down her torso to her legs and feet and finds herself miraculously healed. No blood, no festering blisters, no pain in her side where the car struck her so hard she thought she'd been cut in half. She stretches her legs and flexes her toes in her warm wool socks. The priest must have brought her to the hospital, she thinks gratefully. The accident mustn't have been that bad.

"I made it," she says out loud, the tears beginning to well up. "I made it to Santiago." And to assure herself, she sits up in bed and opens her hopeful eyes. As her sight adjusts to the darkness, she can see the shadow she casts in the moonlight across the open courtyard of the *albergue* in Mazarife.

Beatrice sits up beside her, wrapped up in her own sleeping bag, her face sloughed off now in strips. Blow flies busy themselves in her empty eye socket, seething like an ant farm Ginny saw on a field trip as a kid. When Beatrice reaches her arms up in a V to stretch, her red Columbia sweater hikes up and Ginny can see the tiny brown mushrooms that have sprouted up in her abdomen. When her childhood friend squirms out of the bedroll, what's left of her tongue quietly falls off and into the scallop shell hanging from her backpack.

Ginny remembers now, her choice to sleep outside to try to escape her difficult walking mate. And Trish dragging out a mattress to join her in the courtyard just the same, crying and complaining the entire night. Ginny gazes up at the pre-dawn sky as the woman the posters called Beatrice digs for something in her pack. Ginny, too, has come to think of her as Beatrice. The shortened version of her name that she used in life seems too trivial for what she has become. Ginny looks up. A full moon the size of a cymbal shines above them.

"Want to walk together today?" Beatrice asks with her tongueless mouth, unintelligible to anyone but Ginny. Beatrice pulls the bracelet from the bottom of her backpack and draws it over her skeletal fingers and onto her wrist, snapping off her pinky in the process.

"Look, we're twins," she says, holding up her wrist, pulling Ginny's arm toward her so that the two beaded bracelets meet, the matching silver shells dangling in the light of the moon, one set shiny, the other dirt caked and dull.

Beatrice starts to hum a happy tune as she rolls up her sleeping bag. She knows Ginny cannot say no. Cannot deny her request. It is always the same. Only a matter of time. And there is so much of it, here on the Way, for those who are lost in the torment of an endless loop of misgiving, with secrets they cannot forgive themselves for, nor ever run or walk far enough away from. Souls caught between heaven and hell, playing out their roles for eternity in the irony of their own *Divine Comedy*.

"Sure," says Ginny, trying not to scream. Trying not to let on. Promising herself that this time she will walk with Beatrice the whole way. This time she will not run. This time she will not leave her behind.

But somehow, she always does.

ACKNOWLEDGEMENTS

SO MANY PEOPLE TO thank, so little space.

I would like to thank the staff at Dundurn, both past and present, who read my book and believed in it. You make dreams come true.

I would like to thank John McFetridge for always treating me like a real writer, Denise Boyd for being my faithful beta reader, and my friends and family for putting up with me. Also, Eduardo for his Spanish translations, my own command of the language being restricted to asking for fruit.

Without the benefit of John Brierly and his awesome guidebook I would never have found my way to Santiago or this book. Thanks for showing me the Way.

And finally, thank you to all the people who have walked with me, on the trail, and through life. All paths lead to here, and two does indeed "shorten the road."

Book Credits
Project Editor: Jenny McWha
Editor: Kate Unrau
Proofreader: Shari Rutherford

Cover Designer: Sarah Beaudin
Interior Designer: Sophie Paas-Lang

Publicist: Saba Eitizaz

🌐 dundurn.com   📷 dundurnpress
🐦 @dundurnpress   📌 dundurnpress
f dundurnpress   ✉ info@dundurn.com

FIND US ON NETGALLEY & GOODREADS TOO!

🏛 DUNDURN